Kir LUKOVKIN

The URANUS Code

Good Luck on your journey!

Yours, Kir Lukovkin

Citadel World
Book One

Magic Dome Books

The URANUS Code
Citadel World, Book One
Copyright © Kir Lukovkin 2017
Cover Art © Vladimir Manyukhin 2017
English Translation Copyright ©
Petr Burov 2017
Published by Magic Dome Books, 2017
All Rights Reserved
ISBN: 978-80-88231-41-7

1

THE RUNNER to the right fell down and Rick barely managed to move out of the way. The thick tip of a cracking whip flashed before his eyes, scratching his cheek. Rick did not stop. The man that fell was sure to die and had to be forgotten like last night's dreams. An ivy would drag him into its lair and calmly digest him, as if he was a huge, sleeping fly.

Rick and the five other young men continued the Spring Run. Ten had been there at the start. Ten challengers, but only the strongest and most experienced would win in the end. The others would be lucky to complete the Circle alive.

They had entered the Blind Zone only a minute ago—a part of the corridor which was not illuminated with daylight lamps or emergency lighting. A zone of total darkness. Rick put on his ultraviolet filter goggles. He did it in the nick of time—an ancient and desiccated skeleton covered in rags appeared right under his feet. Its teeth shone in a baleful rictus grin. A huge centipede was writhing in one of its eye sockets. Rick easily vaulted over the obstacle.

The Run continued. Its name was an

ancestral tradition, from the times when it really was race through the corridors, trying to get the best time. It was an old form of entertainment, born when people could walk around any of the corridors free from danger. However, those times were long gone.

The challengers moved at a brisk pace. Everyone had the right to complete the route in any way they wanted, at any speed. The Run had but one primary rule—stopping was forbidden. The challengers kept close to each other for now, as the danger all around them was too great. However, the real competition was about to start when the Blind Zone would end and when they would manage to overcome the Gallery.

Rick deliberately let his opponents overtake him to save his breath. Going at a medium pace, he greedily took in the surrounding Expanse. He would never have got to see what was hidden by the thick protective barriers of the sector in his everyday life. The Commune only took up about a quarter of the habitable world.

The tall, thin runner on the left crashed into some sort of springy substance with full force. It was as if the air itself had turned into a transparent jelly that stretched out and pushed the man back. The youth let out a piercing scream—his hands and feet got entangled in dully glittering silver strands. Rick said a mental

2

farewell to his former compatriot. He did not feel sorry for the man at all, but understood the full extent of the terror that he was feeling now. When the sound of steps recedes, he will be left to hang in that trap all alone, many-legged monsters descending from the depths of the ventilation shafts, looking so vile they would make even the bravest faint.

Only five runners remained.

The first had fallen into a gaping chasm while trying to avoid the carrion bats at the very start.

Another decided to take a shortcut through one of the disused tunnels. A fool.

The third could not take it and turned back. A coward. The Commune will make him pay for this.

The fourth was dragged off by a poison ivy right in front of Rick.

And now the fifth was gone...

Rick could have been any one of them.

They continued the Spring Run. It was almost the end of the Blind Zone. Bone-chilling wind blew at them from somewhere above, carrying the cloying smell of decomposition to their nostrils. No one wanted to imagine the source of this thick and vile odor. Rick was starting to find it hard to breathe, his heartbeat heavy in his chest, his legs feeling as heavy as if he was wearing lead-lined boots... Ah, of course! Another unfortunate fell down to the floor behind him.

Shaky from the effects of the sleep gas, Rick held his breath and ran as fast as he could to pass the dangerous zone.

And then, there was light.

The four runners sprung out of the Blind Zone into the pale light of ceiling lamps. Rick could not control himself and stumbled. For an instant, his mind lost its mastery over his body. Rick prayed to all the gods of the Expanse to protect him from some beast grabbing him from above or below. He fell to one knee and watched the three leading runners disappear around a corner, the sound of their steps echoing off the grilled flooring.

Every second counted. This was not just because the distance between the runners was becoming greater. Well, that was not the only reason. The things which surrounded a man from the Commune beyond the walls of the sector were far more terrifying. The denizens of the hostile Expanse outside. Rick heard a noise right by his ear, which sounded like the fluttering of a moth's wings and then a quiet hissing redolent of a distant sigh. It was as if the sound was stealing towards him, crawling up to gently touch the skin of his neck, to caress him and then...

The elders said that this was the way that awareness was put to sleep.

"Machine God, preserve me!" Rick muttered and launched himself into action.

Rick's heart hammered in his chest. He was overcome by primordial terror, the feeling a mouse has when it is pierced by the sting of a she-spider that lives in the ventilation shafts beyond the habitable sector. Not daring to look back, he ran with the last of his strength, hoping to get away, to hide and escape from the mortal danger. The corridor gradually turned to the right, following the Great Circle of Life. The back of the last of the three runners appeared ahead. Rick caught a second wind. But it was too early to celebrate yet.

The Gallery would begin soon.

That is what the denizens of the Commune called the part of the Expanse where what was visible was not limited by the walls and ceilings that humans were accustomed to. The corridor suddenly came to an end, with the path seeming to continue into an empty void. Of course, this was a false impression—the runners had actually arrived in a vast enclosure which did have walls and a ceiling, but they were at such an unbelievable height and distance that they could be barely seen far off in the distance. It seemed like some incomprehensible and merciless force was about to grab the runners from the narrow path and drag you into the eternal primordial darkness.

As soon as Rick jumped out of the corridor into the Gallery, some ancient instinct forced him to fall to his knee and grab the edge of the walkway stretching out ahead. Rick looked at the shape of the Gallery surrounding him with a mixture of fear and awe. A gust of wind blew into his face and all went dark before his eyes because it seemed that he was falling downwards. But no, he was still holding on to the edge, trying to get used to this new position.

Now Rick understood what the greatest challenge of the Spring Run was.

He had heard of it many times, but no words could compare to that which was before him now. The world turned upside down—it was as if Rick entered a gigantic hall, with an endless expanse of floor and the ceiling for a sky, climbing up a stalk like a cockroach. But this impression was deceptive. The two endless flat surfaces were only walls that extended upwards and downwards. Rick tried to make himself understand this, but the image constantly shifted into something opposite in his head. He stared at the view before him for a long while, unable to tear himself away from the geometric perfection of the sheer and smooth walls.

The three opponents ahead of him also slowed down. One of them fell to his knees just like Rick, unable to handle his vertigo and fear of heights, another managed to keep to his feet but could not move and the third stubbornly pushed on, his head bowed as if he was walking into a strong headwind.

Rick seemed to hear the ghostly breathing and whispering again, so close that it raised the hair at the back of his neck. Overcoming his fear, he crawled forward on his hands and knees. He did not care about finishing first. All he wanted was to go through the Great Circle of the Expanse, complete the Spring Run and advance to the next level of his life.

The walkway stretched out over the bottomless chasm that seemed to go down to the netherworld itself. They said that if a man was to fall off, they would fall without end until they would be driven insane. The definition of hell.

Rick closed his eyes, feeling nauseous.

It was best not to look down. He made himself look ahead, confidently closing the in on his opponent. The other two had already reached the end of the Gallery. When Rick reached the runner who was still stuck on the beam, the man exclaimed,

"Wait!"

Rick kept going. He knew what the result of

talking to the man would be. Last year, one of the runners decided help another and they both went on a date with eternity. A hand grabbed Rick by the ankle. He tried to pull away but the grip was firm.

"Let me go!"

"No! Get me out of here! Please! We won't tell anyone!"

Rick became angry. He kicked out and hit something soft. He heard a scream of pain and surprise, but his foot was still trapped.

"No!"

Even though the walkway through the Gallery had handrails, the other runner lost his footing and stumbled to teeter close to the edge. If this went on for longer, he would drag Rick down with him. The eyes of the runner were full of terror. Rick gathered his strength, straightened himself out and punched his opponent in the jaw with full force. He fell as if struck by lightning, crying and muttering profanities. Rick hurried on ahead, followed by the man's plaintive curses. Because of the encounter or perhaps as a result of his own staying power Rick no longer felt the same fear of the void surrounding him and managed to get up off his knees, stooping and moving forward in a crouch. He never let go of the handrails even for a second, even though he had the feeling that nothing would happen to him if he did. Once he had almost reached the entrance to the corridor on the opposite side, Rick stopped for a moment to look back and remember the Gallery and the Expanse surrounding it.

It was absolutely stunning!

Rick dove into the mouth of the corridor.

Next came the final stretch of the route, which was called the Pipe. The Pipe had to be run through at top speed without ever looking around. Those who did otherwise would die. This was the talk of those who loved to spread rumors. Rick was clever enough not to take such talk too seriously, but also sensible enough not to ignore the rumors entirely. Following a quick break before the final push, he started to run. Rick heard the distant sound of voices ahead—the Commune was welcoming the winner.

The surface of the Pipe was springy under his feet. A strong wind blew in Rick's face, instantly drying the sweat upon his brow. The Pipe was divided by rings into sections over the whole segment of the track that was leading home. Rick ran, watching the steel rings approach and disappear behind him. Someone said that you could not look to the sides. So he would look up. Nothing special. Normal lights. And what happens if you look under your feet? A grilled floor, with a cavity full of a network of complicated wires, emergency boxes and lights, a pale face and the partitions between the segments underneath.

A face?

Rick came to a complete halt. An icy dagger of terror pierced his heart. He had to keep running! Home was close, but the Expanse was treacherous and full of traps! Rick glanced over his shoulder. The Pipe was silent, with no sound coming from ahead or from behind. He would not have hesitated to keep running, had it been the face of a dead man or the maw of a monstrous beast like a night crawler. But he saw a living person down below.

Rick slowly returned to the previous section of the Pipe and looked down again. A young woman was lying under the grilled floor in an unnatural pose. When she saw him, she opened her mouth as if to scream, but kept silent. She desperately jerked around but she could not escape. Her arm was stuck between the power distribution boxes. Without quite understanding why he was doing it, Rick jumped off the walkways, crawled under the supports and came face to face with the girl.

There was no Commune sigil on her neck.

An outsider!

The Warden had spoken about the barbaric tribes living outside the sector. However, she looked too smart for a barbarian—a gray, body-hugging suit, white skin, copper colored hair, a well-proportioned face without any abnormalities and thoughtful eyes which were full of pain. Rick stretched out towards her hand, which was stuck in a clamp up to the elbow. The girl recoiled, covering her face with her free hand. Something glinted in her ear, but there was no time to see what it was.

Rick felt her delicate wrist and found that the bone was intact. Only the spring of a single clamp had to be forced apart to free the barbarian girl. He braced his leg against the wall and pulled the clamp towards himself, to release it a little. The barbarian immediately pulled her hand out and darted behind a supporting strut, backing away towards the wall. There were doors all along the walls of the Pipe.

"Thank you."

The mystery girl disappeared behind a door before he could reply. Rick looked at the closed door, cursing himself for his indecisiveness. He snapped out of his reverie, feeling a pair of eyes upon him. He turned around and saw the runner that almost fell off the walkway in the Gallery. His name was Yeshua, or something like that. Before the start of the Run, he boasted louder than all that he would complete the route. The runner glanced at Rick down below and then ran along the Pipe towards home. Rick climbed back onto the walkway and followed him.

Rick finished the Spring Run last.

Four runners had finished this time.

2

EVERYONE feared and respected Warden Croesus. They feared him for his cunning and cruelty. They respected him for knowing how to read. An ugly scar slashed downwards, cutting diagonally across the face of the leader of the Commune from his forehead to his chin. It was said that this was a mark from the Machine God which Croesus earned when he was still a young and fiery warrior, back in the times when the Commune made war against the barbarians beyond the barrier.

Back in those good old bountiful days.

Now a respected patriarch, Croesus stood on a platform, holding on to the railing and looking down upon the people of the Commune. Rick stood there too, together with the other youths who had completed the Spring Run. The trials went on for exactly one month. Thirty days of trials, which included the Stand Above the Chasm, the Walk Upon the Walls, the Pit Fight and the Hunt for Carrion Bats as well as the

Spring Run. All of this was called the Spring Dance, a thirty-day dance of life and death. Those who survived reached the next level. Those who died became a sacrifice to the Machine God.

The Spring Dance had finished the day before. The sacrifice was great this year. Nearly a third of the young people that reached the age of twenty had died, disappeared into the chasm or went missing in the labyrinths of the Expanse.

Croesus did not hide his satisfaction.

"People of the Commune!" he called to the crowd, "The Machine God is pleased with us!"

Whispers. The upturned faces looked like wax masks, with pieces of glass replacing the eyes in their sockets.

"The God has heard our prayers and accepted our offerings! At last, he has been merciful to us, the pious people of the Omicron Commune! Winter is over. The hoarfrost on the condensers has thinned by a finger's breadth! This means that the cold is retreating!"

The crowd voiced its excitement.

"The Great Circle of Life turns! All hail!"

Croesus raised his fist in a victory salute. The crowd happily replied. But Rick saw that this was the joy of starving men—even though their mouths were smiling, their faces bore the harsh mark of hunger and loss. The Commune suffered from the frosts for many a year, while the food supplies dwindled and the rations kept being cut. Even though there was a farm and there were regular expeditions beyond the barrier, there was never enough food to feed the people.

"And now, let us greet those that passed the trials," Croesus pointed at the group of young people that stood apart from the main body of the crowd, "These young men and women have successfully reached a new level in their lives!"

The gathering started to applaud and shout their approval.

"This new generation has proven that it is worthy of taking its place in the society of the Omicron Commune. Each one of them will have their own task that will benefit the Commune. They will work at the factory, at the farm and in the corridors of the sector as your equals. They are now our brothers and sisters."

The crowd voiced their approval again.

"As always, I would like to pay special attention to those who were courageous enough to brave the Spring Run and who ran through the Great Circle of Life. Here come the brave!"

Croesus stepped back, gesturing for Rick and the others to come closer to the railing and hear the applause, which was genuine, happy and boisterous as there was always someone's father or mother, brother or sister, grandfather or uncle in the crowd, all of whom had prayed to the

Machine God for their relatives to return alive. Of course, not all the prayers were heard, but this was God's will and no mortal could oppose it. Even though he could not see her, Rick knew that his little sister Aurora was standing somewhere here too.

"These young men and women have shown themselves to be true warriors," continued Croesus, "which means that they are worthy of carrying out the most honorable and responsible of task—defending the peace of the Commune and protecting it from outside foes and saboteurs. I am honored to present the new warriors of the Patrol to you! Gus, the winner of the run, is appointed senior on this level!"

The happiness of those present knew no bounds. Rick trembled with joy. He had worked towards this moment for twenty years and it had finally come. The faces of the people seemed to meld together and everything around him seemed to descend into a fog. Rick felt so dizzy that he had to grab the railing. He did it! He would be re-homed on a higher floor, into a larger, warmer and brighter room and with a bigger ration, which meant that...

Someone roughly shoved him in the ribs. Rick turned around. It was Yeshua.

"Let the Warden pass!" he growled.

Croesus stepped forward once again. The

crowd went quiet. After waiting for the noise to subside, the Warden began to speak, this time with a note of steel in his voice.

"Our great Commune has now existed for a thousand years, since the creation of the Expanse by the Machine God. We are the chosen people, the truly righteous. But the great God always sends us trials to test our resilience and the belief of the people of Omicron in the order of things. Our ancestors were attacked by hordes of monsters from the Expanse outside, people suffered hardship and hunger and died from terrible diseases, but they stood firm in the face of these terrible trials, proving their greatness! If it wasn't for their strength, we would not be here today! Hardship makes a man stronger, and the harder it is the stronger we become."

Croesus paused. The crowd listened on in absolute silence.

"Our trials are not yet over. This is a good sign. The God wants proof of our loyalty. He wants to be sure that our strength has not left us. We withstood the piercing cold with honor. A new harvest will be ready soon and we won't have to conserve food. But our troubles are not over! The Omicron Commune faces a new danger!"

Croesus passed his gaze over the crowd and Rick was shocked to see an animalistic pleasure which bordered on madness in his eyes.

16

"The day before yesterday, the northern Patrol apprehended three infiltrators from the outer Expanse! These foul barbarians wanted to find out everything about us so they could attack the Commune. Their army is out there, outside, and it is ready to break in here to rob, burn and kill!"

The crowd gasped.

"They shall kill the men, they will take the women as slaves and do such things to the children and the elders that I cannot bear to utter them! But we will be ready. We have interrogated these vermin and discovered the plans of the enemy. They will not catch us unawares! This will never happen! The Omicron Commune will withstand any outside threat. We want peace, but we are prepared for war. We released one of the spies so that he would warn his leaders that they must not enter our territory. The second one killed himself before we could save him. Now, I present the third one for your judgment, People of the Commune. Here he is!"

Croesus made a sign and a convoy accompanying a bound captive marched into the middle of the square. The captive was a man with a pronounced limp who was supported under his elbows. His head hung down powerlessly to his chest. The prisoner was taken into the circle that spread among the crowd in complete silence. The guards stepped back. Almost immediately, he fell to his knees.

The crowd greedily looked over the outsider. Rick also had a look and was surprised that the man was dressed in a rather filthy silvery suit, but Rick was still sure that he had seen a suit of that kind somewhere!

"Here he is!" exclaimed Croesus, "Your enemy!"

The crowd started get noisy. They were pointing their fingers at the prisoner. The people looked at him with hatred, as if he was dangerous predator.

"Hey, you!" shouted Croesus. "Why did you come here? Answer me!"

One of the guards poked the man with an electric baton, making him moan. Croesus repeated his question, but the prisoner could only mumble incoherently. His face was a battered ruin and his eyes darted like the eyes of a caged animal. He tried to make a dash for it, but immediately stumbled and fell onto his back. The crowd recoiled. The women screamed.

"They can't even speak! They growl like animals!"

One man stepped out of the crowd and spat in the face of the prisoner. Another bounded up to kick him in the gut.

"Enough!" Croesus exclaimed. "Let's not act

like these animals. People of the Commune, brothers and sisters, hear me! I am giving this barbarian for you to judge, and I ask you, what should I do with him? I will do what you say. But I won't hide the fact that this beast seriously wounded one of our patrolmen. So, then, let me hear your verdict!"

The crowd stayed quiet. People were fidgeting, the human sea was getting rough, the waves were rising and hungry eyes looked at the body huddled in the middle of the square with absolute hatred. And then, someone shouted,

"Death to the barbarians!"

Another voice joined in from the other end of the square. Like an echo, the shout started to reflect off the walls and multiply to engulf all of those present. The crowd soon began chanting,

"Death to the barbarians! Death! Death!"

Croesus silenced everyone with a movement of his hand.

"Have I understood the sentence correctly?"

"Yes!" a thousand voices replied.

"In the name of the Omicron Commune! As Chief Judge and instrument of the will of the people, I sentence you to death, barbarian."

The prisoner barely lifted his head into the light, croaking weakly.

"We shall be merciful, and rid you of your pathetic life without undue suffering."

The crowd made approving noises.

"Let the sentence be carried out!"

Two guards approached the condemned man. One forcefully wrenched him to his feet, while the other took out his baton and switched the weapon to maximum power. The prisoner shuddered, spat out a bloody gob of phlegm and shouted, before the deadly lightning strike could turn his brain to mush,

"No! You must turn off the gen..."

An instant later, he was dead. Croesus addressed those present:

"Brothers and sisters! Considering the situation we are in, I ask for your permission to continue to do justice in the name of the Commune as I see fit, lawfully and fairly."

The people voiced their approval. The crowd began to slowly dissipate. Impressed and dazed, Rick stepped to the side without looking and bumped into someone. He looked up and saw that it was Croesus himself. Their eyes met.

"Congratulations!"

The leader of the Commune clasped Rick's hand and then departed, flanked by his guards.

Rick turned towards the square where the execution happened. They were already tearing the clothing off the body of the barbarian. In half an hour it will be missing, dragged off by the denizens of the lower levels. The ones whose rations were particularly poor.

3

"YOU'RE BACK!" Aurora exclaimed when Rick stepped into the room.

He patted his sister's curly head, noticing how she was now almost at a height with his chest, while she had only recently just reached his waist. She was growing.

There was someone else in the room. Rick immediately felt the presence of someone who was not part of the family. It turned out to be old Kyoto.

"Hello, Rick," he heard from a dark corner.

"Hello."

"I helped Aurora clear up a here a little," Kyoto smiled, leaning in towards the light and showing off his strong and even teeth. Something that could not be said about his wrinkled face— nothing can be done about age.

"Thanks, but to what do I owe this pleasure?" Rick warily asked.

He had got really tired over the last week. He had to go on patrol every day. The tension never left him even when he slept.

"Let's have some lunch!" Aurora said.

"Good idea," everyone agreed.

Rick never hurried when he ate, so that he could better digest his ration. Especially since it was bigger now—a piece of meat had been added to the potatoes, bread and beans. Meat! While his restless sister was looking for the spoon she dropped under the table, he secretly put a little piece on her plate. Kyoto nodded approvingly. Rick pushed his own plate away and took a gulp of homebrew, made of the fermented barley that did not grow on the farm properly and which would have been thrown away or filched by someone like Rick. He looked at the clock on the wall and asked,

"So it's not your shift today?"

"Nope," Kyoto was putting bread in his mouth piece by piece.

Rick nodded.

"Congratulations, Rick. A new and important stage in your life has come."

"Yes, thanks. Everyone says that."

"You're probably tired of hearing it."

"You always get to the root of things, as they say."

"You're an educated boy. You have a great future."

"Let's get closer to business."

Rick disliked drawn out conversations.

He wanted to clean his new uniform before

he went to sleep—a dark blue suit made of thick fabric that he was issued when he moved upwards. The uniform was beautiful. The hieroglyphic sigil of the Commune was on its chest, symbolizing the Circle of Life, an O. Omicron. He would now wear this uniform for the next ten years until he reached thirty years of age to again go through the trials mandated by the Committee and decide his fate. The same as all the people in the sector. As it was, so it shall be.

"Yes, you're right," Kyoto stroked Aurora's curls, "Go and play, little one."

Aurora stuck her tongue out at the old man and disappeared. Everyone in the Commune treated the aged with a certain degree of contempt, as the circle of their life was definitely coming to its end.

"That execution..." the old man began.

"Was necessary."

"Yes. But..." Kyoto hesitated.

Rick started to clear the dishes from the table. He put everything into the sink and sat in Aurora's seat.

"What do you want to say? Talk straight."

"All right. What Croesus said about the army of barbarians and infiltrators is a lie. Now you can give me to the Patrol. It's your direct responsibility."

"I'll have time for that later."

Kyoto swallowed. He did not look his best, just like everyone else from the lower levels. The old man stank. Down below they saved on everything, from lighting to water. The ice-cold logic of survival—the aged have one foot in the grave already, so why spend resources on them? Even though travel through the whole sector was allowed, the Patrol carefully monitored that each generation lived on their own level.

"All right. Do you know how old I am?"

"I don't understand what you're getting at."

"Answer the damn question."

Really, how old was he? Rick thought about that for the first time. Kyoto was an old man when Rick was born and his mother was still alive and working on the farm. He remained an old man when Aurora appeared and Rick became a man, without any change from those times. An old man is an old man, what's the difference?

"I don't know."

"Well, that's the thing. I'm seventy-five full years of age, and I have spent a third of my life below, digging around in the pipes. I was sent down before you were born and before your mother was taken as a slave from the neighboring sector."

"What?"

"Did you think that she was born and lived all her life here? No, my friend. She was a slave, like many other women that were taken here when the local girls were struck by mass infertility. The great Commune must live."

"You're lying!"

Kyoto smiled sadly.

"But how... That's impossible... Beyond the barrier..."

"...there are wild tribes of barbarians. The Expanse outside is full of monsters and no normal person could last a day there. Yes, that's what the Committee says."

"So? Are you saying this isn't true?"

Kyoto looked at Rick, sizing him up.

"Do you understand that this is heresy?"

"That doesn't matter now, son. We started with my age, so let's keep going in that order."

"What's the point of me listening to this nonsense?" Rick snorted. "You have completely lost your minds down below."

"That could be," Kyoto nodded. "But then, why did you stay in the square when that barbarian was executed?"

Rick did not reply. The old man continued.

"I have been watching you for a long time. You are much more intelligent than your peers, Rick. This gives us a chance. I would never have started this conversation if I wasn't sure of success. This is why I am asking you to listen to me first and then do as you see fit. Deal?"

"All right," Rick grimly replied.

Kyoto breathed a sigh of relief.

"Well then. We, the people of the Commune, were created in the depths of the Expanse by the great Machine God, who gave us intelligence and allowed us to settle the Omicron sector. The Expanse is endless and it spreads all around us, upwards and downwards, to the left and to the right."

Kyoto repeated the words from the Machine Treatise that were taught to every child from birth. He spoke of the way that the first generations of humans had lived in a golden age when they wanted for nothing—they had plentiful supplies of delicious food, their homes were warm and they never knew sickness or warfare, so they lived long and happy lives. However, the silver age then came to replace the golden age, and that was when man became mortal and the seeds of discord were sown. After that came the iron age, when lifespans decreased. And finally came the dark age after the iron, one in which the people of the Commune still live right now, a grim time of cold, hardship and struggling for survival.

"Why are you telling me all this?" Rick could not restrain himself, "Every child is taught this at the beginning of the Circle of Life."

"Be patient!" Kyoto cut him short, "We have almost got to the point. Throughout our history, our Commune has always been headed by a Warden, a man who could speak to the Machine God through the priests."

"That's right."

"The Warden leads the Committee, the members of which are those that are close to him. Each of them controls their own level of the sector. Only the members of the Committee can read the secret signs and glyphs left by the Machine God as guidance for the people. It is forbidden for anyone else."

"Such is the law."

"Yes. Only the Warden and his priests are allowed to enter the holy sanctum of Technology and speak to the great God."

"That's right."

"But what if I told you that I also know how to read these signs?"

"I don't believe you," Rick laughed.

"Of course you don't believe me. That's why I'm going to show you something."

Rick looked at Kyoto warily.

"Don't be afraid," said the old man, "it's just a drawing."

He took a piece of paper from his inside pocket which had been folded many times over, so old and shabby that there were visible holes worn through the folds. Kyoto carefully laid it out on the table. The edge of the paper looked like it had been unevenly chewed on one side, as if a rat had tried to eat it, so only part of the picture was visible. Rick stared at the interlocking lines covered with tiny glyphs and signs.

"What is this?"

"Our sector."

They both bent down over the picture, trying to make out the details. The light of the lamp grew dimmer, which meant that evening was approaching. The lighting would be switched off soon. Rick lit the ghostlight by cranking the handle of the generator. They kept looking at the picture, until Rick finally whispered:

"I don't understand anything."

"I couldn't for many years either," the old man admitted, "until I started to understand the glyphs."

"Where did you get this?"

"It was part of the spoils of the great war with the barbarians which was won by the Commune thirty years ago. I was a Committee member back then."

Rick stared at Kyoto, who smiled again and cackled dryly.

"I was the advisor of the Warden of that time. A senior advisor at the highest level. Croesus was just a snot-nosed kid back then, there was enough food for every level and there were no problems with light or heating. The

Commune went to war against a tribe of barbarians that lived near the Gallery. This all happened because the daughter of the chief of food production ran away to join a young man there. The Commune went on a campaign and won the war, gaining plenty of supplies, weapons and valuables, including packs of bound paper with glyphs and drawings. The Warden ordered for them to be burnt. There were many drawings in these packages, very many, and all of them looked like this one, as well as tables of glyphs and other signs which are called numbers. The Warden personally supervised their destruction, saying that the papers bore the mark of evil and that these were foul satanic spells that were an offense against god and a heresy. And that's when I committed a crime."

"You hid one page," Rick guessed.

"Yes. And you know why? Look," the old man pointed at a familiar glyph at the very edge of the torn side.

"The Circle of Life!" exclaimed Rick.

"The Omicron symbol."

When Rick looked at the drawing something suddenly changed in his perception of it and familiar shapes started to appear in the network of lines. He cranked the generator on the fading lamp and leaned closer to the drawing. A long minute passed.

"Here," he pointed his finger and drew a line from the left to the right, "this looks like the main thoroughfare."

"That's exactly what it is."

"Here is the Edge of the World... That means that the Chorda, the spine of the Expanse, must be there."

"Good thinking," Kyoto said approvingly.

"That means that this is a map," Rick continued, unconsciously lowering his voice to a whisper. "But everything is drawn here as if the sector only had one level. But it has fifty. This is a view from above."

They looked at one another.

"It took me several years to understand that," said Kyoto. "And it only took you a few minutes. You see? I knew that you had special abilities."

Flattered, Rick kept looking at the ancient world map that was taken from the depths of the Expanse, far better made than the drawings of the priests, and many questions started to occur to him in his head.

"It must be taken to Croesus," he muttered uncertainly. "Maybe he will be able to make sense of it?"

"You know yourself what would happen then."

Yes, he knew. Croesus will get agitated, take

the map away, interrogate Rick and apprehend Kyoto. No one was even permitted to look at the glyphs of the Machine God without special permission, let alone hold any writings in their hands. This was a serious crime, bordering on heresy for which the lightest punishment was exile beyond the barrier.

Kyoto looked at the clock.

"We don't have much time and we might not get a second chance. Croesus already suspects something. The patrols on the levels have become more frequent. It's time I went. Take another look at this map and remember it well."

"But it is so detailed..."

"Memorize it," hissed Kyoto, and kept hurriedly whispering while Rick was intently examining the map. "I studied this map for hours after work instead of sleeping, remembering every symbol and every turn. This is why I can draw an exact copy if it gets destroyed. I thought about it, trying to understand what is on this paper and correlate it with what the Wardens told us throughout our lives. You do know how they become Wardens, don't you?"

"Following the fifth life trial, the old Warden chooses a successor and leaves the Commune."

"Yes. The new Warden gives an oath of fealty to God in the temple of Technology. All my life, I carefully listened to the speeches of the Wardens and the sermons of the priests. And I saw that they were lying. I thought about their words and observed the world around me. For instance, they insist that there is no air beyond the Expanse and that we are surrounded by the darkness of primordial chaos, with the only things protecting our world from destruction being the external barrier of the Expanse and the internal barrier of the sector. The Expanse is shaped like a doughnut, and we are in the middle, while monsters and barbarians live around us, beyond the barrier. There is nothing beyond the external borders of the Expanse. There's nothing above or below either."

"What does that mean?"

"You know that I live on the lowest level, among the sick and the very old. I have been suffering from insomnia for the last few years. As I lie there at night in the darkness I hear strange sounds. They sound like a distant rumble. And once, I heard... voices. Shouting. A man was shouting. I put my ear as close to the floor as I could and kept listening and listening. No one believes old men, and I would have been laughed at had I come to the Warden with this."

"You kept silent and waited."

"I thought this time would never come. Now, pay attention to these symbols and arrows at the edges of the drawing."

Rick obediently took a closer look. The number 14 was written on the paper where the arrow pointed forwards as well as two strange and unfamiliar symbols of some sort. Where the arrow pointed backwards, the number 16 could be made out as well as two other different symbols.

"What does this mean?"

"I don't know for sure. But I think that this indicates other habitable worlds. Can you imagine it? What if there is someone out there beyond the edges of the Expanse as well?"

Rick forgot to crank up the generator on the lamp and the room fell into darkness. When he got the light to work again, the map was no longer on the table.

"I will walk with you," he said. "Or the Patrol might bother you."

They walked through the axial corridor of the level, holding their clothing tight against the cold. It became even colder at night, which is why no one went outside without need. The level was almost asleep. Occasionally, the residents moved between the rooms. Rick and Kyoto walked silently, warming their hands with their breaths. A Patrol marched by and Rick nodded at those he knew, continuing to descend to the children's level where Aurora lived using the central stairs.

"You don't have to accompany me any

further," said Kyoto when they approached the stairway.

There was an uncomfortable pause. Rick wanted to finish with this strange meeting as soon as possible, but something attracted him to the old man.

"Do you still keep the talisman?"

Rick touched something on his chest.

"It is always with me."

"Take good care of it."

Kyoto descended a pair of steps.

"By the way, do you remember the way that barbarian shouted before the execution? I know what he wanted to say."

Rick pretended that he was not interested.

"You must turn on the gen-er-at-or," Kyoto smiled. "Good night."

Rick walked along the corridor to Aurora's room and made sure that everything was all right. The light still dimly flickered here, an indulgence of childhood. The girl was lying on the bed and she opened her eyes.

"You're not asleep? Go to sleep, right now."

"Tell me a fairy tale!" she demanded.

Rick sighed, sitting down on the edge of the bed.

"The one about Rob the Seeker again?"

"Yes!" Aurora scrunched up her face with pleasure, pulling the edge of the blanket over her nose.

"All right. Once upon a time, a man called Rob lived in the Commune. Then one day, children started to go missing from the Commune..."

For the hundredth time, Rick told his little sister of the adventures of the amazing Rob, who was brave enough to go into the Expanse, wander around the Labyrinth, find all the missing children and defeat the monsters. Of course, he also walked along the edge of the chasm. He managed all this because he thought of tying one end of a ball of string to himself and the other to the entrance of the Labyrinth. This was a tale told to him by his mother and Rick had no idea where she had got it from. Rick also did not know who his father was or who Aurora's father was. All that was left to him was the talisman that his father asked to be given to his son before Expanse swallowed him up forever. After making sure that his sister was fast asleep, Rick closed her room and returned home. He lay there in the dark and thought about Kyoto's words, feeling his father's talisman under his clothing—a cross-shaped piece of extremely hard black material.

If insomnia was infectious, he had definitely caught the disease.

4

THE SQUAD walked through one of the side corridors. Five warriors. Five strong, strapping men. Rick was part of the rearguard, together with the patrolman walking behind him. He had been personally chosen by the grim and broad shouldered Ivon, who was completing the third circle of his life. Ivon now led the squad, carefully peering into the gloom ahead.

This was the first time that Rick had gone on an external patrol. Going beyond the barrier was considered to be the most dangerous duty because the people of the Commune were absolutely terrified of the Expanse outside. However, he needed an improved, larger ration because of Aurora. There had been a hunger riot recently, the first one for this year. The winter supplies were running out, so Croesus ordered for workers' rations to be cut by yet another quarter. One of the workers took something from another while the rations were being distributed. A fight started, which soon turned into a battle. By the time that the Patrol squads arrived, the level was as noisy as a hundred power conduits. Rick had never seen such anger on people's faces. The men were beating each other with fists, legs, chairs and anything they could find.

The women were tearing each other's hair out, hissing, biting and trying to scratch out the eyes of those they fought. Even the teenagers were rolling around the floor in a jumble of mindless violence. Everyone had forgotten about the food— the anger that built up over the long winter had finally boiled over. The smarter ones grabbed the pieces of bread that had fallen on the floor, eating them right under the feet of the combatants. One man got his throat slashed, another had his arm broken.

The patrolmen threw themselves into the fray, lashing out with their batons. Lightning started to crackle and the crowd turned to run. Rick was in the front row of the punishment squad. He mercilessly used his electric baton on anyone that got in his way, without caring if they were fully grown men or elders, male or female. Everything had gone blank, he was doing his job. The only things he could hear were the screams, moans and curses.

"Bastard!" A gob of phlegm flew in his face.

"Vermin! Stuffing your bellies on the upper levels!"

"Chasm take you!"

"Give us bread! Give it to us!"

The patrolmen pushed the combatants back towards the walls. By this time, the unrest had settled down.

"Halt!" Ivon commanded.

Rick shuddered, trying to push the memory from his mind.

The squad stood still. The five warriors listened to the fragile silence of the Expanse. Time passed. Nothing happened. The Expanse spoke with the sound of quiet creaking, with the distant drip of water and the howl of the wind. This corridor was well explored and mapped, but the Expanse was treacherous and always ready to catch the unwary. Night crawlers had attacked a similar patrol right by the barrier. They were vile, humanoid creatures that could somehow climb sheer walls and squeeze through the smallest openings with their scrawny bodies. Rick had only seen a crawler once, but it was already dead. A disgusting sight.

"Everything looks quiet. Let's move out," Ivon stepped out ahead. The patrol followed him.

They walked through a radial corridor which ran parallel to the barrier of the Commune sector. Markings left by previous patrolmen could be seen along the wall. There also many glyphs and signs applied to every surface by forces unknown to man in ancient times. Even though no one knew how to read, Rick took care to memorize each symbol, count the number of times it would repeat and the frequency that is combined with other symbols, trying to find a logical order to them. He tried to hide his interest from the other patrolmen.

Like every other worker, Rick used to think that the Commune took the shape of a sphere inside the Expanse, but that turned out to be untrue. The sector that the Commune was in was more like a piece of cake, with a thick edge on one side and a narrow one on the other. The Sector encompassed fifty levels which were connected by stairways and vertical shafts. The main corridor, which they called the Highway, was on level thirty. That was also the location of the central square, which occupied a large space that was five levels high and served as a location for the discussion of the most important issues in the life of the Commune. A curved corridor crossed the Highway behind the square, forming part of the great path of the Circle of Life, entering the Expanse at one end of the sector and coming back in on the other side. This was the path the people of the Commune used for the Spring Run.

Another small circular corridor cut across the sector before the square. There were not one, but five highways and corridors of this kind, each covering ten levels of the sector, like ribs extending from the spine. As a result, the five circular corridors had ten exits at both ends. If the exits from the smaller circular corridors were counted, this number could be multiplied by two to reach a total of twenty exits. Another five central exits from the radial corridors were added to this. However, four of them were sealed long ago. But all of this was nothing compared to the great number of side corridors, auxiliary corridors and other passages that filled the levels of the sector, especially at the edge of the Circle of Life and by the Chorda.

Even though most of these openings were sealed tight, guarding the ones that were still open took a lot of effort. The corridors by the barrier also had to be watched to prepare for sudden attacks or disasters. All of this was the responsibility of the external Patrol.

The squad reached a crossroads between the corridor and another, smaller pathway.

"Break."

They quickly changed formation, putting their commander at the center, as the warriors circled him to form a perimeter, facing in each of the directions on the compass. Then, everyone lowered themselves to the floor. Their shift lasted for half a day, which was why the warriors took bread and water with them. While one would eat, the other four would carefully watch the Expanse.

Ivon finished his meal and exchanged places with one of his subordinates. While he ate, the patrol started a quiet conversation.

"Things are bad," Ivon said, "The Committee has ordered the gathering of rats."

"Rats are real tough and stringy."

"When you're hungry enough, you'll eat anything."

"They're still tough. It's not meat, it's like chewing a rope."

"My father-in-law got a really big slug from the ceiling. He decided to fry it. He says it was all right."

"That's something you can still do. But mushrooms, you can't eat mushrooms, especially the green ones. It doesn't matter how big and beautiful they look. Machine God save us, they truly are full of filth and unclean energies. My grandfather told me how his friend cut down some of those mushrooms from the wall beyond the barrier and then fried and ate them. He went all black and swelled like a balloon the day after. He had a pet cockroach that lived in his pocket, and this cockroach simply exploded as soon as it came near him."

"Hey, newbie, was the ivy on the hunt in the Circle of Life this year?"

"Someone got dragged away by one right in front of my eyes," Rick answered.

"That means spring is bound to come. They're lazy in winter."

While the patrolmen had their lunch, they continued conversing quietly. People were very timid beyond the boundary of the sector as they were guests here. Ivon finally ordered the patrol to move out. They were walking towards the Chorda. Lamps glimmered with dull orange light under the ceiling.

"Maybe we'll get lucky?" asked one of the warriors, hopefully.

A week ago, he found a well-preserved jumpsuit made of warm and shiny cloth hidden away in a niche and he now slept in it to protect himself from the cold. Now, he wanted to find another one for his fiance.

They often walked past entrances to side corridors that led into the depths of the Expanse and Rick stared into their darkness with trepidation in his heart, expecting to see cold, shining and inhuman eyes every time.

But time marched on and nothing happened. They spent half of their shift patrolling the side corridors from the south. All five, apart from the upper corridor. They started with the large circular, turned into a parallel corridor, moved towards the Chorda and turned towards the smaller circular. They reached the guarded barrier and turned back to follow the same route. When they returned to their point of origin, they used a stairway to descend to the next corridor.

At first, Rick did not even realize that they had gone beyond the barrier, as the shape of the corridor mirrored that of the one they had left. However, when long curtains of mold appeared to fur the walls and he saw the thick layer of dust upon the floor, he worked out the patrol's current location.

"How far out have you been?" he asked Ivon at a convenient moment.

"What, newbie, can't wait to run off?"

After he finished laughing with the others, the commander answered condescendingly.

"As far as the next radial corridor, in both directions."

"Why didn't you go any further?"

Ivon's smile faded. There was the glint of a threat in his eyes.

"You come across as rather smart, don't you Rick? Well, then, don't disappoint me. You will freeze to death before you go hungry out there. Don't you understand that the Expanse is full of beasts that you couldn't imagine in your worst nightmare? What you saw during the Spring Run was but a tiny part of all that Mother Darkness can throw at us."

Rick wanted to argue, but Ivon growled at him.

"Eyes forward, private!"

Five pairs of eyes darted in that direction—

some sort of shapeless and dark mass lay upon the floor. Rick carefully edged forward, holding out his baton and torch in from of him. The mass did not move. A step, then another—the mass turned out to only be a dead rat.

"Commander?"

"Do you need a personal invitation, or something? Be quick and grab the carrion and bag it!"

"Yes, commander," Rick bent down over the rat.

The body was the size of a human baby. Visibly disgusted, he put the dead thing in his bag and looked over his shoulder to report that he had followed the order.

"Commander? Kurt?"

Silence. The cold air howled through the pipes. The patrolmen seemed to have vanished. Rick returned where he came from, to the crossroads between the radial corridor and a small circular pathway. He called out again. A short echo bounced through the corridors and died away in the gloom.

"Very funny," Rick clapped his hands, "Great joke. Wanted a laugh?"

No one answered. Rick decided to wait—they were bound to get tired and bored.

"Come on," he exclaimed, "Haven't you had enough?"

"Enoooough", a vile and gurgling sound whined right by his ear.

Rick shouted and blindly shot out with his baton. The recoil threw him to the ground. Something made a pattering sound under the ceiling, quickly fading away into the distance. A sharp and disgusting smell reached his nostrils. The baton kept discharging, sending lighting sparkling across the ceiling. Rick was struggling on the floor, trying to switch off the jammed weapon. A strong arm suddenly grabbed the baton away from him and switched off the power. Rick was dragged onto his feet.

"What d'you think you're doing?"

"I... You... There was..."

"Shut up!" hissed Ivon, "You will tell me later. Let's go. I will show you something interesting, I'm sure you've never seen anything like it."

Ivon dove into the gloom. Rick swallowed. He did not want to be alone in the corridor anymore. He followed the commander. He turned a few times, following the dark shape ahead of him and found himself in a small oval hall where the rest of the patrol was standing. Everyone stared at the center of the hall. Rick looked in that direction and was suddenly transfixed. At first, due to the blue flashes reflected off the walls, it seemed that there was an aquarium in front of him—like those that the workers used for breeding carp on the fifteenth level. But the pale light glowed evenly and moved in an uncanny way, much unlike light reflected from the surface of the water. A structure made of thick glass occupied the center of the hall, filled with some fluid that was thick, but clear enough to see the dark shapes inside.

The shapes were human bodies. Connected to twisting pipes, they were suspended as if they were half hanging, half lying down, separated from each other into sections. Rick was mesmerized by the half-naked woman nearest to him, who was wrapped in tapes and complex pipes with mysterious devices at the end. His eyes moved to her neighbor, an elderly man, and then onto the section which contained something slimy and covered in hair, a terrible, amorphous mass the sight of which turned Rick's stomach.

Once he finished retching, Rick asked in an unsteady whisper.

"What is that?"

Ivon signed for the patrol to leave, and only answered when they had come back out.

"We don't know. Franz from the third shift noticed that the door wasn't locked. Now we have yet another Interesting Place."

"What are you trying to say?"

Ivon winked.

"There's all sorts of stuff around here. People think that the Expanse is a cold, dark desert, and that there is nothing here apart from monsters and barbarians. That is wrong. I have been up and down these corridors for the last eight years, but that means nothing. Look at all of these doors down the sides of the corridor. They are locked, and no mortal man can unlock them. But they do open sometimes."

Rick looked at the rows of dark doors extending into the distance, labeled with incomprehensible symbols and glyphs. Meanwhile, Kurt marked the wall by the entrance and the squad continued on their way.

"There are empty bedrooms behind some of these doors, just like in our sector," Ivon continued as he walked, "some of the rooms have shelves and cabinets full of all kinds of things along the walls. Others are completely empty. Just walls, floors and ceilings. There are rooms which are alive, rooms full of traps and gigantic rooms that are the size of our square or even bigger. But there are also rooms like that one," he motioned behind his back towards the hall of aquaria filled with human bodies, "where you can't understand anything. Why are the bodies in the aquariums? Are those people alive?"

"Commander, tell him about the ghost," asked patrolman Sid.

"There's an empty room in one of the corridors below," Ivon readily continued, "It has a red circle in the center. As soon as you enter that room and look at the circle, the ghost of a man appears in it. Yuri, a man under my command that fell into the chasm a year ago, entered the room first. Yuri used to have black hair, but it went gray. The ghost spoke to him."

"So what did it say?"

"It kept on repeating, "Give me the code, give me the code". It seemed to be an incantation. No one goes in there anymore—the room has been marked as dangerous. I've got a whole list of them—the rooms that were forbidden by the Committee and those where our warriors perished," Ivon looked around, getting his bearings, "Now then. We've covered the whole of this wing. All quiet. So, we're going to turn towards the Chorda and you will get to see the chasm. I will show you the Stairway."

However, before they had the chance to take even a few steps, the Ether Voice on the shoulder of the commander came to life.

"All external Patrol squads! Red alert! Urgently attend level thirty-seven, north wing, minor circular corridor! I repeat..."

"Squad!" commanded Ivon, "Adopt battle formation. Follow me!"

There was no time for fear. Rick got himself

48

together and ran, looking at the back of the warrior ahead of him. The squad quickly reached the end of the corridor and turned towards the stairway. A rapid ascent of almost thirty levels was required. The stairs sapped strength, while fighters needed to keep it when going into battle. The warriors swiftly jumped over several stairs a time. Rick saw their flashing heels ahead and counted the levels under his breath. At last, they ran out into a corridor.

"After me!" shouted the commander. "Don't fall behind!"

They did not run around the perimeter of the sector but cut across using a small radial corridor, pushing the Commune members passing through aside. Breathing heavily, the squad reached the barrier and rushed into the Expanse from the north. A corridor, a left turn, another corridor, another left turn, a section stairway, then down three floors... They almost careened into the other patrolmen that started their patrol from this wing. Rick saw the reason for all the trouble.

Three barbarians were on their knees before the patrolmen with their hands behind their heads. Two men and a woman. Their skin was much darker than that of the people of the Commune, their bodies looked quite athletic and they stared straight ahead. Their silvery clothing looked new and hugged tight around their bodies. The men were bearded and wore headwear on their heads. Confiscated items lay in front of the barbarians. Some of these looked like they may have been weapons—smooth tubes with holes at one end and handles on the other.

Manuel, commander of the northern Patrol, greeted Ivon with a ritual salute signifying the Circle of Life. The other patrolmen followed their lead.

"You're right on time," exclaimed Manuel, "These barbarians decided that they can test our mettle, and this is what they got."

He nodded at the dead body of a man lying off to the side. The body lay on its back and it was being searched by patrolmen.

"Listen…" said the larger of the barbarians.

"Shut up!" Manuel shouted, barely hiding his fear, "It is forbidden to speak to barbarians! All eyes on the floor!"

The barbarian shrugged, but followed the order.

"Where did you catch them?" asked Ivon.

"They were trying to get in using the outside terrace and climb down using this equipment," Manuel kicked the pile of ropes and hooks with the toe of his boot, "We thought that it was rats, but Yeshua persuaded me to check. That's how they got caught, the bastards! They were crawling down one after another like cockroaches. Well done, Yeshua!"

While the commander of the northern squad described how his warriors captured and tied up the barbarians, Rick's eyes met those of the woman. He recognized her. This was the girl he saw on the route of the Circle of Life. That girl. Rick looked away indifferently.

"I see," Ivon got his breath back, "We're at your service."

"Thanks. We need to take them to the Warden. Let him sort them out. All rise!"

The barbarians obeyed. One stumbled, and another caught him. Manuel's warriors picked up their possessions and put them into bags.

"Forward! Over there!" Manuel waved the large barbarian towards the stairs. The other patrolman poked him in the ribs with a deactivated baton.

"Understood," the barbarian calmly replied.

This enraged Manuel.

"Get on with it, you swine!"

The barbarian glanced sharply at the commander, and Rick could swear that in another situation, if the commander did not have a weapon, he would be in for a hard time. The procession moved along the corridor. The men of the north patrol walked in front and those of the south patrol at the back. The escort group went up the section stairway and entered the radial corridor. The barbarians walked with their heads down, seemingly resigned to their fate. When they all started towards the smaller curving corridor, the girl smoothly moved to the side. Most of the patrolmen did not immediately understand what was going on—only Rick managed to grab her by the shoulder in time. The mysterious girl made another smooth turn and hit Rick in the stomach hard enough for him to double over. Then, the girl was running, running in the direction of the Chorda.

"Get her!" Ivon shouted.

"I'm on it!" Yeshua screamed, vaulting over Rick.

"I'll help!" barked Rick.

They gave chase—a slight barbarian girl that seemed to glide along the corridor, wiry Yeshua, and Rick, who had not yet recovered from her precise and painful punch. The chase lasted no longer than five minutes, but everything had to be decided in those moments. The chain of ceiling lights led to something that emitted a strong, deathly pale light. The corridor suddenly came to an end, and the three sprung into an open space that looked like a balcony. The girl ran to the very edge of the platform where the chasm began. Yeshua slowed his pace. Rick did too. He saw the Chorda for the first time.

A gigantic vertical pillar of incalculable breadth extended from below, piercing the Expanse. Rick did not know what he could compare its immense size to. The pillar of the Chorda was right in the middle of an even greater well, with the platform at the end of the corridor extending from one of its sides. A wide spiral stairway twisted upwards from the very edge, piercing the floors and ceiling of the level. This was the spine of the world, the backbone of the universe in which Rick was born and raised.

The barbarian girl was standing on the edge, quickly extending a thin wire from a circular spool with three hooks on the end. Yeshua slowly approached the escapee, like a predator about to pounce. The Expanse was suffocating him, but he was stubborn and would not retreat from his target. It seemed that the barbarian girl did not notice the appearance of the patrolmen—she kept unwinding the metallic wire, preparing to either descend or climb. Yeshua extended his baton and aimed.

"No!" shouted Rick.

It was too late. The bolt of lightning hit the runaway, making her shudder. Rick suddenly understood Yeshua's true intent. He leaped over and knocked the baton from the hands of the patrolman. Yeshua growled. The girl fell like a motionless doll at the very edge of the platform.

Yeshua and Rick fought, giving each other a taste of fists and elbows.

"Scum! You again!" Yeshua hissed, "I will throw you into the chasm!"

They rolled to the edge of the platform. The wind blew there, with the rising streams of air tearing at their clothes and hair. Rick felt the icy breath of the abyss. Just one more step, and it would be all over. Yeshua managed to twist and smash a fist into Rick's face, making his eyes go dark. Rick lost his spatial orientation for a moment and tried to grab his opponent, blindly feeling ahead of him with his hands and standing on his knees...

"There they are!" he heard from afar, "What happened here?"

"Quick! Grab the girl!" the voices approached.

"She's out cold!"

"Hey, what's wrong with Rick?"

"I don't know... I think she tried to push him off!" Rick recognized Yeshua's voice, "I managed to knock her out just in time!"

"Well done! She really did him in! Come on, get the guy up."

A strong pair of hands grabbed Rick and put him on his unsteady feet. With great difficulty, he opened his sticky left eye, while the right would not open—it looked like it was badly swollen. His head was throbbing. The patrolmen carried the unconscious barbarian girl to the side of the corridor entrance, while Yeshua picked up his baton off the floor.

"Everything's all right, man," Ivon said approvingly.

Rick had a somewhat different opinion on the matter. Before he lost consciousness and fell back, he saw the vague shining outline human figure far above, at a height where the darkness of chaos began. The mysterious stranger seemed to balance on the edge of reality, waving at Rick with his hand.

5

THE HALLS of the Committee were clean and well-kept spaces with high ceilings, well suited for thosc who were in power. Starting from level forty upwards, the heating operated at full capacity and it was possible to walk around without an insulated uniform. This is why Rick suffered from the heat as he sat in the reception. The light was also far brighter here on the upper levels, which is why everything seemed to be unbearably luminous and the colors were incredibly full. He was sitting on a soft sofa—a criminally soft sofa, and a platter of cookies stood on the table in front of him. The cookies smelled delicious—Rick was trying to guess how many minutes it would take him to eat them all. Five? No, he was sure he would manage to in three.

A girl wearing the golden tunic worn by all of the Highers emerged.

"Warden Croesus is ready to receive Brother Rick of the Commune. Please follow me."

Feeling relaxed and tired from the heat, Rick only managed to get up on his second attempt and shakily followed the girl. At first, he did not understand where he was—the corridor seemed unending. Then he realized that this was an extremely long room and that the Warden was sitting at a desk at the end. Croesus rose and came to greet him, arms wide open in an embrace, kissed him on the cheek and proffered his hand. Rick clumsily shook his hand, feeling confused.

"Hah!" Croesus exclaimed, "I had no doubt."

"Excuse me?"

"I wanted to give my personal thanks and shake the hand of the patrolman that showed such bravery and prevented the escape of the infiltrators. I kept thinking who could it be, and I thought of you."

"Oh, it was just a coincidence."

"I doubt it," Croesus shook his head. "In my

experience, there are no coincidences in our line of work. People like you are the bulwark of the Commune."

"Well, I am sure you see best," Rick agreed.

"The seniors of each level tell me about every brother and sister in the Commune. It is my direct responsibility to know everything about the people so that I can protect and look after them. This is what all Wardens did before me. This may be why the Commune has such a glorious and long history... So, this is why I always pay special attention to the new generation, because the young are the future. I noticed you a long while ago, and I sometimes showed an interest in your life. Physical training, contest results, knowledge of the Catechism and industrial production levels—everything you did always came to you easily, straightforwardly and without any particular issues. And then, it came to the current Spring Dance. You could have chosen the Pit Fight or the Stand Above the Chasm. Actually, no, you are terrified of heights. Basically, you could have chosen any of the trials, but signed up for the most dangerous one. Your actions speak for themselves. However, your bravery does have a negative side to it."

Croesus looked at Rick's bruise, which had taken on a noble purple hue with great sympathy.

"Those barbarians are strong as hell!"

"Honored Warden, it's not quite like that..."

"It doesn't matter," Croesus cut him short. "Have a seat."

They lowered themselves into comfortable armchairs. The secretary girl poured them a glass of a crimson drink each. Croesus immediately downed half of his. Rick carefully tasted it. The drink was tasty and spicy, burning his tongue a little.

"Don't be shy," the Warden encouraged. "Listen, Rick. Apart from expressing my gratitude, there's something I wanted to discuss with you..."

Rick carefully placed the glass back on the table. He was afraid to look Croesus in the eye. It seemed to him that the Warden would immediately find out the truth of what happened. If their eyes met, there would be no getting away from it. What if he knew already?

"It is about our great Commune," Croesus put on a concerned expression. "The issue is rather serious, which is why only a few should know of it. Only two or three young people know about this, the ones who are the best and the most worthy. You showed yourself well, and I think you also have the right to know."

Rick listened respectfully.

"But you must promise that our

conversation shall not go beyond these walls."

"Yes, of course."

"The Commune is fading away. The fire that was lit by the Machine God in the Temple of Technology in ancient times has nearly burnt out. Our priests piously pray to our God every day so that he might blow upon the flame and make it burn harder, but he is still deaf to our prayers. This is why we are forced to limit the use of heat and only use the sacred fire for the most necessary things—for the farm, because our harvest depends on it and for illumination, because we would be blind without light. That is the state of things. Do you understand?"

Rick nodded.

"Good. The barbarians you caught in the north wing yesterday are not sneaking around here for nothing. Those beasts are planning something. So far, I can't beat anything useful out of them, apart from the fact that they were crawling downwards for some reason. I don't understand it!"

Croesus spread his hands in dismay.

"But they will talk sooner or later. I think I have discovered their weaknesses..."

It seemed that the Warden had forgotten about Rick, lost in his own thoughts and moving his lips, with his eyes straining in their sockets. This lasted for about a minute. Then, Croesus came to and continued, seemingly unperturbed.

"Basically, they have some extremely important information. It might be that they have part of the holy fire, or they know where this fire is. That is the key to saving the Commune. It will help us to keep going. It's very important!"

"This is why I have decided to organize an expedition to the outer limits of the Expanse. Only the strongest and the bravest will be part of the expeditionary force. We don't just need experienced adult warriors, we also need those like you, who are young, energetic, and capable of swift action. The task of the force will be searching for the holy fire, or at least for the fuel it needs. Everything that we will need and everything that will be good for the Commune. Do you agree to join the expedition?"

The question stunned Rick.

"I don't know... I need to think about it."

"We don't have much time to think. The altar of the Machine God displayed a new symbol yesterday. This is a worrying sign."

Rick had seen that symbol. It looked like a "4" with a "%" symbol on the right. Before that, it looked like a "5" followed by the same symbol. Croesus narrowed his eyes. It seemed that he understood Rick's hesitation in his own way.

"You have a sister, don't you? How old is she, eight? That means that she is on level eight.

I bet it's not so good with light and heating there. Probably the food isn't that good either. I think that her situation could be changed somehow."

"Warden, you shouldn't... We are completely satisfied."

"All right," Croesus said. "Think, but don't take too long, as we really don't have much time. I am only selecting the best people for the expedition, those who have proven their ability to handle physical trials and the strength of their spirit. Those that can resist heresy."

He glanced at Rick when he said these words.

"Heresy roams through the Commune. It crawls around like a worm. That's understandable. The weak cannot take it, because their faith is untrue and they only care about filling their bellies. This is why they make up all sorts of stories when they're hungry and cause unrest among the people. They corrupt the youth. I remember, there was one that ambled around the bottom level and shouted that we are inside the gut of some beast and that this beast swims around in a gigantic chalice of water, and that this chalice is the universe. He was going around and saying that it's time to get out. Can you imagine it? Inconceivable stupidity!"

Croesus laughed. Rick smiled politely.

"And what of these barbarians? It's obvious

that they are pagans. They are dark lost souls that live in the darkness of the Expanse. But if you accept even part of their ramblings as truth, you could go insane. If you join the expedition, it's possible that you will come across tribes of this kind. Do you understand what I'm trying to say?"

"Of course, honored Warden."

"You must be strong of body and mind. You should not allow heresy to take you from the true path. There is the Machine God, the Commune and the Expanse. Such is the order of things. And our conversation is no accident, as I'm sure you understand. Only the best get to be here."

Croesus rose from his armchair and Rick hurriedly got up after him.

"In time," added the Warden, "once you show yourself well, I will reveal certain secrets to you."

"What sorts of secrets?"

Croesus answered with a vague wave of his hand.

"You shall see. Well, then, we're done. Thank you for your time. I will be waiting for your decision here at the same time tomorrow."

"Yes, Warden."

Croesus looked over Rick.

"You are just like your father. Just as serious, and always in concentration. Are you surprised? I knew him, he was an excellent brother of the Commune. However, he went to meet the Machine God way too soon, just like many others. By the way, he would have accepted my offer. Well, then, see you tomorrow!"

Rick felt as if he was walking through a thick fog as he left the Warden's office. He couldn't breathe. It seemed that all the air had suddenly been pumped out of the space surrounding him. The secretary girl smiled vacantly at him and left the room. Rick stood around for a while, trying to get his thoughts together, but they kept coming apart and it was impossible to concentrate on anything. His eyes fell on the plate of cookies again. This time, he was no longer shy about it—he stuffed them into his pockets and even gathered up the crumbs in his hand. For Aurora.

6

THE CEREMONIAL execution took place without the Warden this time around. His role was filled by one of the priests, a fat, doughy faced man who was escorted by several patrolmen to the Porch exit, followed by a gaggle of onlookers that was mostly composed of children and the disabled, those who could not work. The Porch was what they called the corridor that circled the perimeter of the sector. Part of its roof had once been transparent, but was now covered with filth and mold. If it was not for the dirt, the opposite wall of an empty sector of the Expanse could be seen, which was separated from the Commune by a chasm. The uninhabited sector was only connected to the Commune by passageways that were crisscrossed by minor and major circular corridors.

Part of the Porch had collapsed. The walls of the corridor had been breached and bent inwards with some terrible force. A dozen men could walk abreast through the resulting hole if they held hands. The opposite wall of the Expanse could be easily seen from there, covered with dark spots and stains. The escort stopped by the gap. The priest stepped forward and cleared his throat, coughing loudly. Then, he took the Holy Writ and a censer made out of a large gear tied to a rope out of his robes. While he was busy with his preparations, the patrolmen lined up the condemned men along the wall. The prisoners looked pathetic—beaten, disheveled and barely able to stand.

The priest nodded at the patrolmen. They stood still.

"In the name of the great Machine God!" the

priest began. He paused, casting an intense gaze over those present, and then continued.

"We have gathered here today to perform an act of justice. The sentence shall be read. The Commission has sentenced these criminals to the supreme penalty for a particularly serious crime—heresy against the teachings of the Commune. They committed this grave sin deliberately, congnizantly and with evil intent. They fully understood the dangers of their profane views, but these heretics still continued to sow discord amongst the people of the Commune and try to sow division among good brothers and sisters! An atrocious transgression! A vile sin!"

The priest gathered more air into his lungs.

"The Commission has carefully examined each of the crimes committed. All the mitigating and aggravating circumstances were taken into account and the worth of every fact has been carefully considered. The Commission based its findings only on truth, fairness and the laws of God. Even though the crimes were severe, we have tried to be as merciful as possible. Condemned Brother Peter!"

The guards grabbed a graying man by the arms and dragged him up to the priest.

"A night shift worker of the thirty-second level, accused of the organization and preparation of a rebellion, which means he is a heretic against the god-given power of the Warden. Using his position at work, this man prepared weapons and made a plan to bring down the Committee. He conspired with six workers and planned to capture the patrolmen of the level so that he could establish control over the whole level using the batons he took from them. He insolently and impudently stated that the Committee holds back food, heating and light from the brothers and sisters. He blasphemed against the great Machine God, personally insulted Warden Croesus and cursed the Commune. This man was apprehended thanks to the vigilant report of Brother August. Having studied the case materials and interrogated the witnesses and co-conspirators, the Committee has found Brother Peter guilty of the crime that he committed and considers him to be a heretic and a rebel, sentenced to oblivion in the Chasm. Once read, the sentence is to be carried out immediately!"

The priest stepped back with a surprising nimbleness. The guards dragged the condemned man to the edge of the Porch.

The one legged, crippled man standing next to Rick whispered to the man next to him, "He's going to squeal now! They always squeal like that, it's hilarious!"

When the patrolmen brought the condemned

man to the very edge of the precipice, he seemed to snap out of a nightmare and awaken, making futile attempts to break free and shouting, "I'm begging you! I have a wife and children! They will cut their rations! Please!"

The priest nodded at the guards and they pushed the condemned man hard in the back. He lost his footing, slipped and made one last hopeless attempt to grab at a protruding piece of metal. A patrolman struck his hand, and the man fell with into the chasm with a desperate scream. The howling of the wind quickly carried away the retreating sound of his cries.

"In the name of the Machine God," intoned the priest and made a ritual pass with the censer. "Next, Sister Edith."

The patrol brought a woman with an angular face and large dark eyes to him.

"A worker of the cereal warehouse of the twenty-ninth level, accused of the theft of valuable cereals which she secretly carried through the check-point, stored in her living quarters and consumed in addition to the lawfully permitted ration. She stole over two bags of grain and half a bag of rye, by which she committed an act insulting the Commune, took away from her brothers and sisters and thus profaned the name of the Machine God. The Committee has studied the case of this sister, and considers her to be guilty of the crime she committed. Taking her heartfelt confession and contrition into account, the Committee has decided to be merciful and sentences Edith to a year of penal fertilizer processing labor on half rations. Be on your way, and sin no more."

The patrolmen untied the woman's hands and let her go. The priest pompously swung his censer and looked at the three remaining barbarians who had been recently caught by the northern Patrol.

"The next criminals are not people of the Commune. They were caught at the scene of their crime and caught red-handed as harmful enemy infiltrators. They had weapons, cunning devices and rolls of demonic writings that profane the Machine God upon them. They ardently and firmly believe in the greatest heresy, that denies the existence of god and twist the face of creation. Moreover, they tried to malevolently corrupt the Patrol and the priests into their foul ways, including myself. They do not consider their heresy a sin and they do not repent before the face of the law and the Holy Writ..."

"Enough!" exclaimed the hulking barbarian that Rick already knew. "How long can you keep talking..."

One of the guards immediately stung him under his ribs with a bolt of electricity. The barbarian growled some unfamiliar curse.

The priest stared at him wildly, gulped, and hurriedly continued.

"The Committee has studied the case of these three barbarians from the outer Expanse, listened to their statements and based on the facts in their possession considers them to be heretics and schismatics that profane the glorious name of the Machine God by their very existence. Considering the malicious character and the danger posed by their heresy, as well as their conviction in their diabolical views, the court finds no reason to reduce their punishment and sentences the barbarians to oblivion in the chasm. The sentence is to be carried out in stages. The first heretic will be executed today, the second one tomorrow and the third the day after. This decision was made to bolster the understanding and cognizance of their fate by the criminals. Carry out the sentence!"

"He," the priest pointed at the large barbarian, "will be the first."

Five patrolmen immediately grabbed the prisoner, hindering each other more than helping. There was a tangle of bodies. Rick carefully watched the other barbarians—this was the reason he was posted here. The imprisoned barbarian girl looked at him in desperation. Her lips silently mouthed some word. Rick answered with a barely perceptible shake of his head.

"Throw him in there!" the one-legged cripple exclaimed happily, as he stood among the onlookers shaking his crutch.

The barbarian was strong—he was a whole head higher than the others, had broader and stronger shoulders and he resisted desperately. However, even though he tried to fight he was still dragged to the edge of the Porch.

"Stop!" shouted the second barbarian, a bearded man. "Behave like humans and stop this madness!"

The guard immediately rewarded him with a backhand across the mouth. Tears started to stream down the cheeks of the female prisoner. But Rick understood that those were tears of hopelessness, not of pity, and that she was ready to throw herself into the fight at any moment.

The priest signaled the guards and asked the two barbarians, "Are you going to talk, or not?"

"We have nothing more to say! We don't know anything!"

The priest made a disappointed grimace and nodded to the executioners. The barbarian howled like the blare of the horn that Rick heard when there was a fire in their sector. In a final, desperate attempt to escape, the barbarian tore through his bonds and knocked down one of the patrolmen with a punch, but the other four pushed him back towards the edge, as the barbarian continued to howl loudly. There was no hint of fear in his screams—only rage. He balanced on the edge for a seemingly endless moment and then grabbed the nearest patrolman and pulled him towards himself. They both collapsed into the chasm. The guard screeched like a dying animal. The patrolmen leaped towards the edge, trying to make out the details, but Mother Darkness had already consumed its prey.

"Scum!" the barbarian man shouted. "Disgusting pagan savages! Why?"

He kept shouting, and the girl kept crying all along the way to the prison level, while Rick escorted them together with the other patrolmen and did not dare to steal a glance into the eyes of the prisoners, feeling as bad as he had not felt since his mother's death from stomach fever.

He approached Ivon.

"I'm feeling sick. I'm no warrior today. Put me on a guard post somewhere."

Ivon understood everything.

"Go to the lesser circular. I'll tell the man on duty."

"Thank you."

"Hey," Ivon waited until there was no one nearby and quietly said, "You know what I like most about the external Patrol? That you don't see the sort of shit that we saw today."

"I think I agree with you, commander."

"Oh, I also just remembered something. We were once walking along the Porch towards the Chorda. We stood around there, and we were about to turn back, when a man flew down from above. He was there for the blink of an eye and then fell further down. Funny, isn't it?"

Ivon laughed.

Rick felt completely empty. He decided to visit his quarters to get a warm jacket and some other things. Kyoto and Aurora were standing in front of his door. Both the old man and the girl looked worried.

"What happened?"

"There are interruptions in the heating of the children's levels. They switched it off for half the day today, and it immediately got cold. I gave your little sister some of my rags. They're clean. I hope you've nothing against that?"

"Of course not. And how are you doing?"

"It's still all right," Kyoto smiled. It is a couple of degrees lower. Some of our people died, but they wouldn't have lasted much longer anyway. I warm myself up with moonshine. There are rumors that they are preparing to downsize, so they can save on energy. The Commune will contract from fifty levels to forty. How much more..."

"Listen, I need to go on duty, so make yourselves comfortable, get warm, and all that. We'll can chat later."

"No problem. You know me, friend Rick."

"Don't leave, Rick..." Aurora suddenly started to cry.

"Why?" he bent down towards her. The girl clung to him, hiding under the open flaps of his jacket and hugged him.

"I don't know. I'm scared."

Rick stroked her hair.

"Don't be silly. Everything will be fine. I will come back from patrol soon, and uncle Kyoto will stay with you for now. He will feed you and play with you. Won't you?"

"Of course."

Rick exchanged glances with the old man. Kyoto shooed the girl into the room and came out into the corridor.

"Something is going on in the sector," Kyoto muttered. "Something bad. A child has gone missing. A girl. No one has seen her, and they can't find her anyway. It's a child, so it's understandable. She can't fight back. Old people like me aren't that strong either. Neither are the women... Be careful, Rick. I saw how a patrolman was walking through a production facility and told off a worker for something, so the worker spat on his boots. And then, the patrolman did nothing, because everyone immediately stopped working. They were looking at him. The idiot had gone into the production facility all alone."

Rick nodded.

"Here, take this. No one is going to search you," Kyoto shoved a rolled up piece of paper at him.

"What for?"

"I'm telling you, take it."

Rick put the piece of paper in his pocket and left without saying goodbye. His heart was heavy. He could feel the eyes of the old man upon his back.

After joining the guard detail, Rick stood by the south entrance to the lesser circular for his allotted time. Lost in thought, he watched the empty and dark space ahead of him. While the features of the corridor could still be made out nearby, total darkness began further ahead. Darkness and cold. The darkness surrounded them on all sides, crawling towards the sector and biting into everyone that lived there with its ice-cold needles. It was winning, and humanity was losing.

And no Machine God could help them. Rick was standing at his post, remembering the events of the day and thinking. He was deep in thought, unhurriedly working through the ideas in his head which were gradually forming a unified picture. The picture still lacked many details, but the general outlines were already coming through. It was enough.

When the shift ended, he reported to the senior patrolman in the proper order, but then went along the Porch towards the Chorda instead of returning home. For some reason, he no longer had any fear of the Expanse. As he passed by the hole in the Porch, he slowed down. He saw something shine on the floor. Rick bent down and picked up a strange object. Then he remembered that he saw it in the ear of the captured girl when he helped her free her hand from the clamps.

By the time that Rick reached the Chorda, the cold of the Expanse had started to sneak under his clothing and bite at his face. He went out onto the balcony. He looked at the sealed gates of the sector—the same type of gate was open ten levels above. Rick calmly put his baton on the floor, walked five paces away from it, sat down, pulled in his legs and began to wait. It was getting colder. That meant that night was coming. Somewhere, the old man and his sister were waiting for him, but there were more important things to do.

Rick waited, ready for anything.

The main thing was not to fall asleep. Otherwise, he would never wake up.

The great Chorda silently floated in front of him, piercing the Expanse. Where did it begin? And where did it end? The Catechism, which was the main teaching of the Faith, stated that it was infinite. But what if that was not true? Dangerous questions. Thus did men fall into heresy.

Part of the Chorda was lit up with lights from the sector levels, but the rest was hidden in impenetrable darkness. Rick rose. The cold had thoroughly frozen him and it would be good to get a little warmer. Very slowly, he approached the edge of the balcony, looking above. His eyes got used to the dark. The Chorda stretched far out for several dozen levels and then disappeared, consumed by the darkness. Rick lay down on the edge and looked down, going numb with fear. The Chasm was truly bottomless. He thanked the darkness for hiding what was inside, for it would send any mortal man insane.

"It's rather deep over there," someone's voice said.

Rick jerked himself away from the edge. The baton! Too far. He was such an idiot. This would be the most inane death in the history of the Commune! A man stood on the edge nearby. He was holding a torch with one hand, and held on to a thin steel cable with the other.

"Who are you?" Rick whispered. He wanted

to shout, but his voice betrayed him.

"My name is Ahmed Cormancour."

"Two names? Are you a man or a spirit?"

"I'm just as human as you are."

Rick looked at his youthful face with wonder. It looked like the man was young, but his features were different to those of the people of the Commune—he had bushy eyebrows, thick lips and a large nose. His skin was so dark that it seemed black.

"Did you come from the otherworlds?"

"Yes," Ahmed replied.

"What for?"

"We are looking for something."

"We? You are not alone?"

"I'm alone right now. Since your people captured my friends," Ahmed eased the tension on the cable a little, "I saw everything. Which is why I decided to talk to you."

That meant that his eyes did not play tricks on him.

"Why are you looking over there? Take your stick, I'm not going to touch you."

Rick picked up the weapon. It made him sure of himself again, and he calmed down a little.

"The trial of your people took place today. One of them got sent into the darkness."

Ahmed's face fell.

"What about the others?"

"They are waiting for their turn. Tomorrow and the day after."

"Oh no, please, not that!" the newcomer whispered desperately.

"You speak our language," Rick pointed out.

"We have a common tongue. Does that surprise you?"

"I didn't expect..."

"Yes, I forget. Your sector has lived in isolation for so long, that you started to consider yourselves the only people in the world."

"Our sector?" Rick's surprise knew no bounds. "What are you talking about, barbarian?"

"Barbarian?" Ahmed chuckled, "So that's what you call us."

"That's what we call everyone that lives in the Expanse."

"I see. What is your name?"

"Rick."

"Can I trust you, Rick?"

Rick had completely forgotten about his duties and his status. He had to arrest the barbarian now, and escort him to prison. He hesitated, and Ahmed noticed this.

"I shouldn't expect anything good from you, is that right?"

"You're right. But I," Rick found it hard to

say the words, "have changed my decision."

"Why?" Ahmed asked with genuine curiosity.

"I don't want the girl to step into the chasm. Or that barbarian, either. You don't look like infiltrators."

Ahmed looked over Rick for a minute. Ahmed's wondrous torch was burning by itself and required no cranking. His face did not show any anger or low cunning. He looked Rick straight in the eye. Barbarians did not behave like that. But maybe this was some sort of trick, or some kind of game? Rick was wracked with doubt. Then, he made his final decision—let whatever happens, happen. He lowered his baton.

"Thank you," Ahmed let go of the cable and proffered his free hand to Rick, "You are the first of the ones from below that it's been possible to have a normal conversation with."

"No," Rick chuckled, "we are on the higher levels. The lower levels begin below level twenty."

"What did you say?" Ahmed's lips curled into a brilliant smile, "Level twenty?"

"What's so funny?"

"Rick! Our unit came from sector K — Kappa. It's on floor seven hundred and fifty and above."

7

TWO MEN walked along the radial corridor of the prison level—a prisoner and a guard. Everyone that passed them looked at the prisoner with great curiosity—they had never ever seen a person with such dark skin before. The patrolman was the personification of tension and readiness, ready to use his weapon at any moment were the prisoner to attempt an escape. The small convoy walked almost to the end of the corridor and stopped by the doors of the Commandant's chamber.

Rick knocked. The door took its time to open, and a sleepy looking gaoler stuck his head outside.

"What'd you want?"

"Brother Shaw, I caught yet another rat on the Porch," Rick pointed at the prisoner.

The gaoler stared at Ahmed.

"Where did you dig him out?"

"He fell on me from above by himself. He was going down a metal thread like a spider. That's when I got him. The scumbag tried to escape, but I calmed him down some."

Rick poked the prisoner in the side with his baton for added effect. The gaoler woke up completely at last and took a combat knife out of his belt.

"So, then. Very good. Wonderful! Well done, Rick. Thanks, I will take him to the Committee member on duty."

"That's fine, brother. It's just that..." Rick looked at Ahmed warily, "This devil is strong as a bull, you know? What if something happens..."

The gaoler sized up Ahmed with a glance and nodded.

"Yes, you're right. You can never be too careful. Come with me."

They walked back along the radial corridor towards the stairway. It was late. However, every floor was still being patrolled. They turned and started to climb the stairway. However, as soon as they passed just one flight of stairs, Ahmed tripped and fell prone upon the ground.

"What's wrong?" barked Shaw.

"My leg," Ahmed whined with such pain in his voice that it seemed that he had lost the ability to walk forever.

The gaoler bent down and put a knife to Ahmed's throat.

"You're not going to fool me with that trick! Get up, you little rat, or I'm going to break your other leg!"

Rick quickly raised his hand and struck Shaw on the back of his head. The gaoler made a noise like a leaking ventilation shaft. Rick hit him again, and Shaw fell on top of Ahmed. Breathing heavily, Rick helped his accomplice get out from under the massive body of the gaoler.

"What next?"

Rick panicked. His position in the Commune had completely collapsed and there was no way back. But immediately after, he felt as if a great weight had lifted from his soul and a great clarity about what to do next entered his mind. He immediately composed himself, quickly searched Shaw and found ring of keys. Together with Ahmed, they dragged the body to the wall and somehow forced it behind a radiator. One hand constantly kept falling out and refusing to bend.

"Enough! We have no more time," Rick gave Ahmed a shove. Someone could appear from above or below at any moment. Rick took Ahmed back into the corridor and led him to the cells where the barbarians were kept, continuing to pretend to escort him. A convoy was patrolling with their back to them at the far end of the corridor. Some prisoner was singing a gloomy song. They reached the cell they needed. Even though Rick did not know how to read, he had no problem with counting—cells eleven and twelve, if you came from the direction of the stairway. Here they were. Rick stared at the ring of keys in confusion, going through them in his hands. The keys looked exactly the same.

"Look at the number and look for it on the key," Ahmed whispered.

Rick obediently started to look for it. He went through a dozen keys, but the right looking one appeared at last. Rick calmly put it in the lock and opened the cell. They entered. The girl should have been in the cell, but there was a man there. Not a barbarian. They had made a mistake!

The prisoner expectantly looked straight ahead, past Rick.

"Who are you?" Rick could not resist blurting.

The prisoner made a gurgling sound with his throat. Rick looked at him closer, as the prisoner seemed to be familiar. He got up from the cot and blindly started at the light.

"Have you come to kill me?" he wheezed at last.

"No."

"So why have you come?"

Rick warily approached him. But the prisoner did not turn his head towards him. He really was blind. The man's face was covered with a gray beard up to his very cheekbones, his teeth were so stained that they looked dark brown and he smelled of sewage. A broken shard of a man.

And that was when Rick remembered. A family used to live near to them when Rick was just a little boy a long time ago, probably fifteen years back. The father was a rigger and the mother worked on the farms, as they do. They had a son, who was of an age with Rick. Then one day, the family was struck by misfortune— their little boy fell off the balcony and severely injured his back. The healer said that he would not be able to walk. Never. Because his spine had been broken. The father then went to the priests and implored them to pray to the Machine God to have mercy on his family. The priests listened to him, promised to pray, but this was beyond their powers. The rigger held his ground and spent day upon day visiting the Committee. The Warden kept meeting him, but did nothing in the end. Then, someone whispered to him that a cure could be found beyond the barrier, in the darkness of the Expanse. Without a second thought, the rigger prepared himself and left the Commune. His wife used to visit Rick's mother to sit at the table and talk. She cried and complained about her fate, and Rick's mother calmed her down, while Rick played with that boy. Months passed without news of the husband, and everyone decided that he had perished in the Expanse forever. His wife somehow got used to her sons disability and made her peace with it.

But the husband returned. Mother Darkness

released him from her grasping embrace. He did not just manage to survive—he brought some sort of complex device that had to be applied to the back of his son. The Warden personally descended to their level to visit their room to watch and see how the unusual device would work. The boy was turned to lie face down and a silver disk was placed on his back. The disk started to hum and glow red. Everyone watched silently. Once the disk turned green, the father pinched the boy on the heel and he yelled from the pain—his legs obeyed him once again. The Warden left without a word.

The returning rigger started to tell tales about the incredible things in the Expanse. He swore on the his most sacred things that he was telling the truth, even though it was at odds with the Holy Writ. His fellows from the commune listened to him with interest, but thought he was insane. The rigger came back to work, but he started to go blind after only a week had passed. Why this happened, no one knew. And then he disappeared. Everyone decided that he went beyond the barrier again. Only his grieving wife denied this, because the wondrous disk-shaped device that cured her son had also disappeared.

Rick could not remember what happened to them next.

"What do you want?" the blind man asked.

"We are looking for a girl. She should have been in this cell," Rick replied.

"A girl," the prisoner muttered. "A girl."

"Let's go, we won't get much sense from him," Ahmed called.

Rick shared his opinion. They moved towards the door of the cell.

"A girl. Screamed. Cried. Girl. They took her down the corridor. They said: he has ordered for her to be brought to him. They said: third time today... said they..."

The muttering became unclear and turned into a series of whistling sounds.

"I don't know about you, but I think I have worked it out," Ahmed said, "Thank you."

"Have you been to the edge of the world?" asked the blind man. "I have. There is so much light there that it hurts your eyes. I still see that light..."

"What light?"

The prisoner did not answer—he lay down on the cot, turning his back to them. When they opened the door to go back into the corridor, he suddenly loudly declared, "The sun came from behind the cloud, and with its rays on me shone proud."

And then, the prisoner was gripped with a paroxysm of insane laughter, laughing so hard that he choked, turning it into a series of grunts.

Ahmed and Rick had a look in the neighboring cell. The bearded barbarian was not there either. Without hesitation, the accomplices set off for the top level. That was where the rooms of the Committee members were located and where interrogations and court sessions were held. They played the same roles yet again. There were five patrolmen on the level—Rick even recognized a few of them, and nodded in greeting.

"Where are they interrogating those barbarians?"

"The ones with the girl? Over there," they readily showed him. "Bringing them a third one?"

"That's right!"

They approached the office. A patrolman was standing at the entrance. Rick lied to him in the same way as he did to Brother Shaw the last time. The patrolman glanced at Ahmed curiously, saluted with his baton and said "I will report this now."

Then he disappeared behind the door. Rick felt that his heart was about to burst out of his chest and his palms became slippery with sweat.

"What're we going to do?" he whispered.

"Whatever we have to. Push him back and rush them."

The patrolman appeared in the doors again, but did not come out.

"Come in," he offered indifferently, stepping

back inside.

Rick did not even have the time to act surprised. They entered. The room was rather large, with a window occupying the whole width of the opposite wall and a table in the corner, where a Committee member was writing something on a scroll. Another stood by the window, through which another room could be seen, where the barbarians were sitting tied to chairs, with two inquisitors working hard on them and striking them around the heads. The Committee member finished writing and got up from the table, putting his hands behind his back and approaching Rick and Ahmed.

"We've been waiting for you for a while. Welcome," he invited them to come closer to the window.

Everything looked like they had been forewarned. The accomplices slowly moved towards the window. They heard the sound of a charging baton behind them. Rick would not have mistaken that sound for anything else.

"Rick, thank you for your hard work. You have really proven yourself," the Committee member slapped him on the shoulder. "Warden Croesus recommended you as a very talented young man, but I never suspected that you were capable of this. Bringing this barbarian here without any extra hassle. I'm impressed. And what about you?" he turned to Ahmed. "Here you are, enjoy seeing your friends."

But Ahmed was looking at Rick, not at the glass.

"I don't know what he is talking about," Rick said.

"You lied to me," Ahmed replied.

"Oh, well," the Committee member said. "What an uncomfortable moment. Don't beat yourself up about it, Rick, this lie was for the good of the Commune."

"What lie? I am telling the truth!"

"Of course, Rick. The more convincing the lie, the more it looks like truth. A lie becomes the truth when you truly believe in it. You were so convincing to him, because you believed your own lie."

"You bastard!" Rick shouted at the Committee member, clenching his fists.

The smile on the face of the Committee member was replaced with a predatory scowl.

"Be careful, young man. I will forgive you the first time. But know your place in future!" he loudly slapped Rick around the face. "Remember, your whole pointless life, your whole body and soul belong to the Commune because it gave you your home, food, clothing and warmth. You should be happy that you were born here, and not beyond the barrier, like these animals. You whelp, you should spend every second of your life thanking the Committee and the Warden for your blissful childhood and youth. And you should fall to your knees in gratitude for becoming a patrolman and being worthy of the great honor of serving the Commune with a weapon in your hands! So think who you open your mouth to!"

Rick was looking at the floor, burning with the fire of hatred. He felt as if his face was inflamed, especially the cheek that had been struck, he felt that his ears were in flames and that his heart was hammering in his chest.

"You still have a lot to learn. And the first thing is to understand that you always have to sacrifice something for the greater good. You don't want the people of the Commune to die, tormented by cold and starvation, do you? The brothers and sisters of the Commune believe and hope that the Machine God will help them, and the Committee which channels his will shall save them. They cannot be disappointed. The Commune could die as a result of your actions. You must understand! These barbarians are our chance to find the divine flame, their lives are not worth a piece of stale bread in comparison to the life of the lowest cripple in the Omicron sector! Don't forget about your sister, either. Decide what is more important to you—her life, or the well-being of these... beasts." The Committee member turned to Ahmed, "And you, barbarian, look at your friends and prepare yourself."

Rick growled and punched the Committee member on the nose with his fist. It was a solid punch—the hours spent training in his free time were not in vain. The nose cracked like a nut. The Committee member howled. A bolt of electric lightning hit Rick's back with a hiss. But the guardsman's baton could not have hissed that loudly and Rick understood that something else had happened to the baton's discharge. A moment later, Ahmed caught him to stop him from falling over and shoved an unusual shell-shaped mask onto his face—he had one just like it on his own face. The room rapidly filled with clouds of caustic mist, drowning the agitated people inside. The guard behind opened the door and staggered out, but then fell on the floor after only taking three steps. The gas was seeping into the corridor outside. The Committee member and his assistant had already collapsed into unconsciousness. Ahmed and Rick hid behind the door. The shouts of running patrolmen could be heard from the corridor, but as soon as they reached the room, the shouts turned to groans and the thud of falling bodies.

"Sleep gas," Ahmed winked, "It's great!"

"Thank you," Rick replied, "I did not lie."

"Later. We need to free my people."

The torturers in the interrogation cell saw that something was amiss. As soon as they opened the door, Rick released all of his anger on them, masterfully laying about with his baton. The first of them fell, struck down without too much noise, but the second started shouting, desperately fighting back and throwing everything that he could get his hands on at Rick. Once he caught him and it was all over, Rick suddenly understood that he had just knocked out a strong adult man.

Ahmed put breathing masks on his friends. It was painful to look at them—the inquisitors had worked hard, marking their faces with numerous beatings, most of which were suffered by the bearded man. Rick draped him over his shoulders, while Ahmed was helping the girl get up from the chair.

"We need to get out of here!" Ahmed shouted.

"They are about to raise the alarm."

"Where do we run to?"

Rick brought the sector plan up in his head—the exits from the corridors were blocked. There was no way they could run in that direction.

"Downwards," Rick commanded. "We'll work it out once we get there."

A thick cloud of gas filled the corridor and

anyone that got caught inside fell to the floor unconscious. But the effect of the gas could not last forever. Rick tried to go towards the stairway, but he heard voices coming from that direction.

"We're trapped! The second stairway is too far away, and they will take us by the time we get there."

"Then let's descend using the elevator," Ahmed offered.

"Using what?"

"I see. Where is the long vertical tunnel?"

Rick thought frantically.

"The cable?"

The shouts of the patrolmen that were hurrying towards them were coming closer and closer.

"Yes, yes! Where is it?"

The escapees ran towards the open elevator shaft. The elders said that the cable had once worked by favor of the Machine God—it was a cabin, that moved up and down. But now, it had to be moved using mechanical force. The cable was only used when heavy weights had to be transported.

The gas had almost cleared. Patrolmen could be made out at the far end of the corridor— swearing terribly, they were waiting and were prepared to make chase. Ahmed opened a panel by the doors and quickly dialed a combination of buttons on the small altar. Something started to thrum in the mouth of the shaft. The altar blinked with green lights.

"It worked!" Ahmed breathed out.

"How did you manage that?" Rick asked with surprise, "Do you know how to talk to the Machine God?"

"I have no idea what you're talking about."

The patrolmen kept coming closer.

"Do you have any more of this magical gas?"

"Yes, one last capsule, but we should keep it for later!"

Rick thought of something to hold back their pursuers. He stuck the baton into one of the holes which covered the corridors and walls on every level, switched on the charge and fixed it in place. The baton crackled with electricity, chaotically throwing lightning bolts upwards. They reflected off the walls and ceiling and branched through the air at unbelievable angles. Rick directed the baton towards the pursuing patrolmen so that there was a barrier of dancing violet charges in their way.

"Rick!" Ivon shouted at him, his face contorted in anger. He was still far away. "What are you doing?"

Rick did not reply.

"This is rebellion! Stop, before it's too late!"

Rick quietly stepped back towards the cable.

The cabin had just arrived, and Ahmed was dragging his friends inside. The bearded man had got himself together and could now stand on his own two feet. Ivon kept imploring Rick to obey, but the escapees had already jumped into the cabin and Ahmed pushed a button. The elevator started to move downwards.

The doors were open everywhere. Levels flashed by them, and every corridor could be seen as well as everyone that was there. The icon of the Machine God was blinking with sigils at eye level. Rick guessed what it meant. The first five levels were left above them, the corridors were well lighted, clean and well decorated. The people there walked around in golden clothing. The levels of the fourth circle came next, which were not as well-kept, but still well lighted. People walked around wearing green here. The people of the third level, which was where his room was located, wore all red and the lights were on at half power here. Then the elevator entered the twilight zone—past the residential blocks of the workmen, who moved through the corridors as shadows, wearing all black. It seemed like the corridors were full of fireflies, because of the handheld wind-up torches that the workers used to light their way. And finally, the elevator passed the second circle of life, where the young generation only wore yellow overalls. It was a little lighter here, but not even half as bright as it was above. However, the cabin did not stop.

"Where are we going?" Rick asked, as he returned the filter mask to Ahmed.

"To the very first floor of your sector," he replied.

"But there's no way out of there!"

"There is a way out," the girl piped up. She had composed herself and sat on the floor in the corner of the cabin. "Every sector has an exit above and below, to the maintenance floors."

It was almost completely dark again. Only the orange dots of the lights occasionally glittered on the walls. The levels of the last circle of life were like the bottom of a huge and murky quagmire, with lights flashing and going out immediately here and there along the corridors.

"Who lives here?" asked Ahmed, with surprise.

"Those that have left the fifth circle. Old people. As well as the sick and crippled."

The elevator came to a stop. Ahmed turned on his torch. The ray of light pierced the darkness, catching huddled bodies. The living covered their eyes with their hands, while the dead lay along the walls, as if they were forgotten things. The girl and the bearded barbarian also switched on their torches. The escapees slowly walked on.

"How can you keep them here?" the girl indignantly asked.

"They have lived through their time. Would you keep a broken knife in your kitchen?" Rick calmly parried.

"A person is not a knife!"

"Enough!" Ahmed cut them short. "Enough arguing. How much time do we have before they get down below?"

"It is always easier to go downwards. Five or six minutes. We still have time to go above to get into the lower corridor."

"That's not an option. Look at our wounded! They can barely walk!"

Pushing the bearded man aside, Kyoto jumped out in front of them.

"Rick! What are you doing here?"

"I am a criminal now. There's no time to explain," he replied. "The barbarians say that there's a way out of here."

"That true!"

"What? You knew?"

The old man smiled happily, "Of course. Let's go!"

He took the escapees to a side corridor. They turned into another one there, which was much lower and without any lighting, so full of various junk that they had to walk in line. Kyoto opened two or three doors. The floor squelched under their feet and water dripped from the ceiling.

"The distribution station," the old man said.

"In every sector," the girl confirmed. "Are you an engineer?"

"Nope. A simple plumber."

The small corridor took them into an oval space which was two levels high. The whole ceiling and walls were covered with intertwined pipes, both large and small. Some of them continued further, while others were connected to huge tanks that stood on raised platforms. The smell was revolting—Rick would have happily put on a filter mask, but there was no time for that. A weak and diffuse light shone from somewhere below the ceiling and dust motes danced in the air.

"Here!" Kyoto pointed at a manhole on the floor.

Rick tried to turn the locking ring, but did not manage to do it. A thick layer of rust was left on his palms.

"It's stuck."

Ahmed and the old man helped him, and they pushed the ring together, barely managing to move it.

"It hasn't been opened for too long," Rick stomped on the manhole. "The metal has fused..."

"Try and use this as a lever," the bearded barbarian threw them a thick steel pin.

Ahmed grabbed it and put it through the ring, bracing the end of the pin on the manhole, pressing down on it—this time, the ring creaked and gave. Things went quicker after that, and soon, the escapees stood above a black hole. Ahmed shone the torch down there.

"It's not that high here, but it's totally dark."

"We're going down," the girl slid down the hole first.

The bearded man carefully jumped down after her. Ahmed lingered a moment.

"Thank you," he told the old man.

"You shouldn't."

"I'm waiting for you below," Ahmed nodded at Rick and disappeared into the darkness. The lights of the torches could be seen flashing there already.

"Well, then," Kyoto encouraged. "Jump."

Rick was lost for words, "But... I'm from the Commune."

"You are no longer a man of the Commune. You know that yourself."

"And what about Aurora?"

"I will look after her. She will be safe. I will look after myself as well, I have enough experience to deal with this. While your main task is to find the source of the divine fire and to save us all."

"Jump! What are you waiting for?" they

called from below.

Rick looked down into the hole—the Expanse awaited below, full of mysteries and uncertainty.

But the decision had been made.

"Until next time."

"Bye, Rick. There's a bolt on the other side which blocks the manhole from below."

Rick slid below, with a last glance at Kyoto. The old man said "Come back—with your shield or on it."

Then, he slammed the manhole cover shut after him.

8

EVEN THE SMALLEST and quietest sounds reverberated loudly in the emptiness. Judging by the distant echoes, the escapees had entered a very large space, but its true size was hidden by the darkness, which could not be completely dissipated even by the light of the torch. However, the darkness did gradually start giving way as their eyes adapted to it. The escapees walked a couple of hundred steps until they came upon a wall. Ahmed started to methodically examine it, moving to the right. The girl, who was called Maya, as Rick found out, moved to the left.

Rick and the bearded barbarian called Reiner were left to wait together. Rick crouched and vacantly stroked the floor with his fingers. The surface had an unusual feel to it—it was rough to the touch and not as smooth as the walls and floors of the Commune.

"Plascrete," Reiner told him. "An extremely durable, but light material."

"How do you know?"

Reiner was twice as old as his young companions. The inquisitors had turned his whole face into a livid bruise. He did not look too good.

"I studied the specs." Suddenly realizing, he added, "You probably don't know what that is, do you? It's a document that contains the main characteristics of a material, its weight, mass, chemical composition, density... Do you know how to read?"

"No," Rick admitted, thankful to the darkness for hiding his embarrassment.

"Ah, then that's what you needed to start with. Don't they teach you to read or write in your Commune?"

"Few have that right. The chosen ones."

Reiner grimaced and gingerly touched his side.

"You're good at beating people up though.

Looks like one or two ribs have been broken. It's painful to breathe."

"I am no healer..."

"Even if you were a doctor, you couldn't help me."

"I found it!" Maya shouted. "A door."

They hurried over to the girl, who was carefully reading the signs on a large double shuttered black and yellow door with a red circle right in the middle. Rick saw familiar symbols and glyphs, but they were combined in unusual ways. The largest glyph was "II".

"It leads to the cap of the second aeon. Can you feel it?"

They all leaned on the door. There was a strong draft coming from the gaps. The wind was howling. The touch of cold could be felt, a true frost which would not just turn water to ice, but turn a warm blooded man into a frozen mummy. Back in the Commune these frosts were considered to be the most terrible as they engulfed the sector for two or three weeks.

"That means that we are going the right way," Reiner declared tiredly. "Before we move on, I propose having a break for a couple of hours."

"They took our things with all of our food supplies," Maya frowned at Rick. "All of our packs of concentrates, medicines, equipment and maps!"

"I still have some water," Ahmed added and took out a flask. They all shared the water among themselves.

Maya worriedly examined the bearded barbarian, and even though the pain was obvious on her face she calmed down a little. The escapees sat down along the wall, too exhausted by pain and stress to try to sleep. The girl was grimly going through the contents of her pockets. Reiner was calmly sitting and staring in front of him. Ahmed was rearranging the contents of his backpack. Rick lay his combat knife on the floor in front of himself and closed his eyes for a second. He opened them and took another look at the weapon. The darkness suddenly burst into his consciousness, taking away his body, arms and legs, taking the world and the passage time away from him, replacing it with itself. A quiet conversation came from somewhere far away.

"Let's leave the savage. He'll return to his own and forget about us. He's just going to be a burden."

"Wasn't it him that saved you when you were stuck under the circular corridor?"

"I think he took me for one of his own."

"When him and Ahmed got you out of the camera, was that by mistake as well?"

"I don't know. I fear these people. I don't

trust him."

"I'm not talking about trust. He can be useful to us."

"He can kill us. These savages from the lower sectors are merciless and devious. They have no concept of mercy."

"But they are strong and hardy. We could use that."

"If he knew the lower levels, then yes. But he never left his box in his life!"

"Oh, yes. And you did that just a year ago. They are like that, because they were made to be that way. They are the same species as us biologically, and no worse than us. I did not see anyone who was mutated, infected or deformed among them. They're normal people—it's just that they are hungry, angry and stupid."

"Do what you think is right, Reiner, but I am against this."

Silence. A minute later, there was a rustling sound and Reiner said, "All right. Let's go."

Something creaked, metal hammered on metal and some sort of mechanisms that the Machine God filled the surrounding Expanse with started moving. The howl of the wind grew louder and streams of cold air touched Rick's face. Rick understood that he was alone and abandoned. Alone with the Expanse. Unable to fight off his lethargic condition, he lay there, helpless in the bosom of Mother Darkness. He wanted to wake up, but also wanted to sweetly drift away. This dichotomous feeling was familiar to him. Like a fish taken by a net from an aquarium farm, he lay prone on the floor, now unable to turn back and go home. A pathetic, pathetic whelp, that had ruined his life in the space of an hour. May he be consumed by the Expanse for all eternity.

"And what about your sister?" his inner voice whispered. "Aurora will be left all alone. You must fight for her sake. If they come for her, the old man will be unable to protect her. And when they take her and drag her above..."

Rick woke up with a start using an effort of will. The surrounding darkness started to clear, giving way to twilight, but he could have been mistaken and this could just be an illusion. However, once he concentrated, he understood that he could see the walls well without the help of a touch. Rick spent a while rubbing away the numbness in his body before he got up. The cold had sunk deep under his skin and thoroughly chilled his body, immobilizing his muscles. Rick knew the dangers of cold drafts—a third of the population of Omicron constantly blew their noses. In the worst cases, people became feverish and coughed pus for a long time, until they died from suffocation.

Rick pushed the fear away. Once he finally

warmed up, he stood up in front of the door, examining it again as if it was the first time he saw it. What if it was sealed with an incantation in the Machine tongue? Then he would never be able to open it. Rick was overcome with terror. He reached out towards the massive handle as calmly as possible. At first, it seemed like any attempt would be pointless. But no, the handle gave way and the door opened, releasing gusts of cold air. Without tarrying for even a second, Rick slipped inside.

The space was gigantic, around twenty living levels height and as wide as half a sector. Squares, rectangles and abstract multilateral shapes could be seen on the walls, floor and ceiling. Their surfaces were covered with various protuberances, complex devices and mechanism created by the Machine God. The walls and ceiling glinted with a dull, phosphorescent light. Rick stood upon a bridge under the very ceiling and could see how whole arteries of cables, pipes and chains extended into the distance. But the thing that surprised him was not just the Expanse itself, which was full of technical wonders—it was the even layer of hoarfrost that rimed every surface, evening out the many bumps and depressions.

Yes, it was cold here. Every breath steamed up in the air. The space looked abandoned, an empty and forgotten place. A man could never survive here for long. It was true that the deserts of the Expanse were abandoned and unsuitable for habitation.

Rick noticed a chain of tracks leading down along the bridge and running into the distance in the blue twilight of the Expanse, where the glitter of strange yellowish lights could be seen by the Chorda. The floor and ceiling of the hall was also bisected by a fat black line extending from the Chorda that could be made out as being a chasm. Here and there, there were small bridges across the chasm extending from the edges. Rick began to descend the stairs, carefully looking around himself. Predators make sudden attacks, so he had to be vigilant. As soon as he was down below, he understood that the lines dividing the floor into geometric shapes were cavities similar to furrows, half a man's height deep.

Rick jumped down into one of these. The tracks of the barbarians were clearly imprinted in the snow. Three pairs of feet. After a hundred paces, Rick noticed some other tracks by the side—they looked human, but the toes were extended. At first, he only saw one chain of tracks, then it became two and more and more appeared as he moved forward. Here and there, thick poles were stuck in the floor, garlanded by hanging bones, patches of fur and tufts of hair, with the very surface of the metal covered with drawings and scrawled symbols. Rick stood in front of one for a long while, trying to make out what was written on it. The symbols were nothing like anything he had seen before.

Praise be to the Machine God that Rick had his patrolman's blade with him. He thought for a while before he continued on his way. What could he do? Basically, the barbarians had abandoned him. That meant that their conversation was no dream.

He moved on. The lights ahead started to grow in size, and Rick understood that this was real fire. A jumble of large boxes and the dead machines that had lived in the Expanse once upon a time was chaotically stacked by the Chorda. He could hear ululating calls, laughter and shouts. When he managed to stealthily move closer to the fires, he hid behind a container and carefully glanced around the side.

His former companions were chained to the wheels of a huge and dead machine. All the demons of hell seemed to be communing around them. With a mixture of terror and curiosity, Rick could make out a collection of strange, manlike creatures in the glint of the fires, that randomly sat, lay, and walked around their camps. They were monsters, humans twisted by the Expanse and the reflections of its crooked mirror. Rick saw hypertrophied body parts decorated with stumps protuberating out of the flesh. Even those that looked normal had unhealthy skin, lumps growing along their spines, disgusting blotches, constellations of hairy warts and large pustules. There were dwarves, people with two heads, three arms, single legs, one eye, no ears, no hair or those with doughy, distended bodies. Disgusting, contorted creatures dressed in rags. All of them were gathered around the barbarians, poking them with spears, throwing stones and making noise. They howled with laughter when Ahmed swore after being hit by the latest stone. They danced by their prey, shaking their weapons— sharpened hooks and simple pieces of metal.

Rick was worried to notice that only Ahmed and Maya were chained. Around a dozen monsters sat further away by a big fire. They were happily consuming meat that had been roasted in the flames, that had a long spit suspended above it with the remains of their prey. Rick had to clamp his mouth shut so that he would not scream—the bearded barbarian was looking at him with glassy eyes, his head the only thing remaining on the spit.

There was another explosion of laughter. Some monster had poked Ahmed in the groin with a stick. Ahmed howled with pain.

"The birdie tweets!" a hairy one-eyed hulking

beast shouted, pointing at the prisoners with his finger.

Someone tried to irritate Maya, buy the girl lowered her head and did not react to the pokes. A hunchbacked crone ambled over to her and began to touch her red locks, cheeks and stroking her fingers over Maya's lips, neck, breasts and stomach, smacking her lips with pleasure. A bald and ugly horror covered in warts jumped up and gave the crone a kick that made her roll away like tumble-weed. The bald one hit his chest with his fist.

"Mine!" he raised a club above his head, "anyone who touches, I kill! She'll be my wife. Yarg needs good wives from above."

"Good prey must be shared!" the shouts came from all sides.

"If not for me, you would eat rats today!" he growled, swooshing his club through the air, "Away with you, vermin!"

The grumbling crowd stepped back. The bald one was obviously considered to be their chief. He bent down towards Maya and gripped her by the chin with his four- fingered hand, critically examining her.

"Get your hands off her!" Ahmed angrily shouted.

Yarg laughed hoarsely, shouted an order and a bandy-legged, fat and bearded creature ran up to Maya, took a ring of keys from his belt and opened the lock on the chain. As soon as the fetters fell, Yarg put Maya on his shoulders and loudly declared, "I am going to go and love my wife!"

"Let her go, you scum! Can you hear me?" Ahmed screamed at him, making a futile attempt at reaching the bald one with his foot. The chief proudly marched towards one of the larger containers. An ugly creature with his hands reaching his knees ran up to him.

"Check the nets on the eastern ray," Yarg ordered him.

Rick turned away, unable to keep watching. He felt very cold. The dead light coming from the walls and ceiling could not warm him and the fires were far away. Rick guessed at the distance to the leader and to Ahmed. Too far again. He had to get closer. He started to work out how to get to the container without being noticed, but suddenly felt someone's intense stare. He quickly turned around.

A dwarf dressed in rags stood only two steps away. He could be taken for a child, if it wasn't for the age obvious from his wrinkled face. They spent a minute looking each other over.

"Throw down your weapon," the dwarf said.

"No," Rick hissed. He started shaking.

"Don't be afraid. Where are you from? From

above?"

Rick nodded, lowering his knife but nor releasing it from his hand.

"Why did you come below?"

"To seek the holy fire."

The dwarf seemed to take an interest in that. He slowly and carefully lowered himself to the floor, pulling his legs under him.

"Why did you think it might be here? Take a look around."

"I don't know... Let's part ways peacefully. Let me leave."

"No."

"I will fight."

"I have no doubt. But I want to talk to you first. Tell me of the world above."

The dwarf seemed to have no interest in the feast nearby. His eyes reflected an internal strength, intelligence and cruelty.

"My friends are over there..."

"I am sorry, but that is the price of recklessness. What they did was stupid. That is a sign of weakness. And the weak do not survive here for long."

Rick had a disgusting feeling that something had made its way inside his head and started to dig around inside for unknown reasons, going through memories like tools in a box. He felt weak and could not move, unable to resist an alien will that had taken charge of his reason. Everything around him went dark, while the face of the dwarf, became closer and brighter, as if someone had shone a torch on him. This creature had unbelievable power.

"Let me go..." Rick mumbled, gathering the remains of his willpower.

"Wait. You are afraid of me. I am a monster to you. You chose to risk yourself by leaving your home. For her and everyone that you call barbarians and for the residents of the Commune pursuing you. You are also driven by a hunger, a terrible hunger to find out the truth and understand this world. That is a brave deed. Wonderful. Your life has great value. I always looked for ones such as you. But you are all mistaken. Your ideas are wrong."

"What are you talking about?"

"You will understand, with time," the dwarf pointed towards the camp with a crooked finger. Over there, on the other side, there are other villages, and that is where I came from. They don't touch me because I can do this inside anyone's head. On the first day, Yarg wanted to use me for cooking soup. Now he is afraid to even glance in my direction. His clan lives here since the times that the monsters came from the depths and started to hunt people. People used to live below before, many people. That was a very long time ago. Then the great Boom happened, and many people died from the fire and even more died slowly afterwards. Some hid in their homes, some ran away, and others remained. They knew that Death awaited below, but still stayed. Many died, and those who survived became like me and them over there. There were very few people. They did not understand who they were and what they were doing anymore. Then the monsters came and our tribes ran above, to this place. It is warm but dangerous below. It is cold here, but you can live. The monsters do not climb up here. Yarg's people catch anything that falls from above into their nets. The braves go down below to hunt in the jungles. This is the way we have been living for many days."

The dwarf closed his eyes and Rick felt his mind clear and there was no more alien presence and will in his consciousness. He was prepared to run without looking back so he would never be under such alien influence, but his mind hinted to him that this would not be a good idea.

"Do you want me to take you with me?" Rick asked, overcoming his fear.

"No. Because you won't. And because my place is here."

"Then why did you tell me all of this?"

"Because you will keep going and you must

know what is there below. No human has ever done this. You say that you are looking for the holy fire. Possibly that was what actually made the big Boom. Do you know how to use this fire? Of course you don't, as I've been inside your head and know everything. But you want to learn, and that is the main thing. Wait for the morning. They sleep in the morning."

The dwarf rose and headed to the camp. He moved with great difficulty, as if his joints were affected by a strange illness and every movement caused torturous pain. The dwarf suddenly stood still half-way—a small, black figure outlined with the red bursts of flame, and said, "The Omega is not the end, but a beginning."

And then he disappeared in the shadow of a container.

Rick waited a little and then sneaked ahead following the dwarf's tracks and crawled into a hollow under a container, drawing himself into a ball. His heart beat weakly in his chest, as if his blood had cooled and barely moved along his veins. For the rest of the night, he was in a drowsy reverie, shuddering every time that he woke up from his uneasy sleep from the screams nearby.

He had no watch, because every Omicron sector level always had a clock from which it was easy to find out the time of day. Now, he had to depend on his feelings. Once the screams calmed at last, the camp descended into silence. Someone would pass by the container occasionally, so Rick was wary of getting to the surface. He came out when the fires when out. The freaks of Yarg's clan had gone to their sleeping places.

Rick crawled over to Ahmed on all fours. Ahmed almost screamed, but Rick whispered just in time, "Quiet! It's me."

Ahmed was looking at him, but could not recognize him in the dark. Rick got up to be face to face with Ahmed, and then recognition dawned in the eyes of the prisoner.

"Get out of here!" he hissed, "Save yourself. They'll kill you!"

"Be quiet. Who chained you? Where are the keys?"

Ahmed started crying. Rick cuffed him around the head.

"Get yourself together! Where are the keys to the lock?"

The dark skinned barbarian pointed at one of the tents. Rick crawled towards it—the bearded fat man snored inside. Rick took out his knife and searched the rags, cutting down the ring of keys once he found it on the belt and returned to free Ahmed. They climbed underneath the dead ancient machine, and Rick demanded that

Ahmed tell him all that happened to the escapees when they left him. At first, Ahmed kept quiet and made whining noises, wiping away tears as he could not get himself together, but then told haltingly related everything that happened.

It turned out that once they entered this great hall, Maya started to argue with Reiner that they should turn back. However, Reiner completely refused to return as that would mean the failure of the exhibition. They were walking towards the Chorda and arguing amongst themselves and did not notice how they got surrounded by mutants. It was too late to run and too stupid to fight as the mutants outnumbered them. Reiner tried to negotiate, but Chief Yarg ordered for everyone to be captured and dragged here without any talking. Reiner tried to appeal to their reason, but no one listened to him. And then they did that to him...

At this point, Ahmed's lips started to shake and he started to make whining noises like a scared child again.

"Wait here," Rick said, getting outside.

He had noticed some fuel barrels by the container where the leader lived—anyway, they stank of fuel, like those that were in the Omicron sector warehouse. Kyoto had explained that fuel was very dangerous, pointing at a picture of fire on the barrel and some sort of writing. Rick got closer to the barrels and started to unscrew the lids on the bungholes. The smell became a lot stronger, and Rick even started to feel dizzy. He was unscrewing the lids and then slowly putting the barrels on the side, so that a viscous, strong smelling liquid poured out, making glugging noises.

An ugly creature got out of the sleeping space nearby, who was about Rick's height, but had a small and flat head with the eyes of a child, and started to curiously observe what was going on. Rick thought for a while that he should maybe kill the mutant, but then understood that he was harmless and started to quietly roll the barrels in different directions, leaving oily puddles on the floor.

Soon, there were three different ugly mutants watching him, and they started slowly but surely coming closer to him. Rick was hurrying, spurred on by anger and fatigue, wanting to get things over with this place as soon as possible.

"What you doings?" the small-headed mutant exclaimed, "Not allow!"

However, Rick ignored him and jumped over to the fire to pick up a glowing stick, blew on it and threw it into the nearest oily puddle. A flame burst upwards, which soon moved onto the barrels and spread across the floor. The fire sang, taking over the constructions, with the tongues of flame licking at the container and the ancient machines. Rick dove into the hiding place where Ahmed was waiting for him and started to watch sleepy mutants jump up from their sleeping spots, running around and screaming, trying to understand what was going on. The mutants quickly panicked. The hissing flames consumed all that they could reach. The surrounding hoarfrost rapidly melted and the puddles of water reflected the brightly flashing fires.

A disturbed looking Yarg appeared from within the container. His wart-covered face held an expression of absolute surprise. The chief threw himself into the thick of the crowd, generously giving out orders and kicks. The mutants milled around the camp in complete confusion. Rick went inside the container and almost tripped over Maya, whoa had been tied onto a bed. Nearby, on a higher point, there was a cage with a tiny humanoid creature that started to howl something in an incomprehensible language. The tiny, big-headed mutant continued screaming, while Rick cut the girl's bonds and helped her rise. That was until Rick picked a rock up off the floor and launched it at the cage, hitting the mutant on the forehead and forcing it to shut up.

He dragged Maya outside, and no one paid

any attention to them as they were all occupied with the fire. Rick got to the hiding place where Ahmed awaited them and they ran from the cage together. However, they had only gone a hundred paces when a rock lying ahead of them suddenly changed into the dwarf that Rick met. The dwarf silently pointed towards the Chorda, smiled ominously and suddenly disappeared.

As there was no time, Rick did not explain anything to his companions and led the group in the direction shown by the dwarf. Soon, they saw a two-leveled structure appear ahead, which looked a lot like the place of execution in the Omicron sector. There was definitely going to be a staircase there, Rick realized.

"Over there!" he commanded, and the runaways did not waste words, surging forward until they reached spiral staircase a few moments later.

The inside walls of the well which contained the Chorda were covered by four staircases of this kind, one for each sector segment. Just like his home sector of Omicron. The staircase was wide, but it had no railing. They were descending into the darkness, often tripping over. Their feet slid upon the steps. The bluish twilight filled the surrounding space, with a weak light coming from all around.

Once they had passed ten levels, Ahmed

could no longer take the pace and fell, lying still.

Rick and Maya stopped, breathing heavily and straining to listen—they heard noise and stamping feet coming from above. A burning torch fell downwards into the chasm by the side of the stairs.

"Ahmed, get up!" Rick growled hoarsely, "We must run!"

They helped Ahmed rise and continued their descent. Wind could not be felt inside the well and it was not as cold. Soon, the hoarfrost was gone from the surfaces, replaced by slimy black spots, fungal growths and furry mold that weakly glinted with green light. Some sort of plants hung raggedly from the edges of the steps. The smell of metal and rust changed to a smell of decomposition and flowering, which Rick was familiar with from the Commune farm.

They descended thirty-five floors, when Maya exclaimed, "Stop!"

The pursuit continued above. Rick worriedly looked at the circling chain of torch lights above. He was about to argue with Maya, but she just thrust her finger at the open doors of a radial corridor leading into the sector segment. The "π" glyph could be made out above the doors. Rick felt that there was danger below, and that they should not descend any further.

He nodded, "Let's run there!"

They threw themselves into the depths of the sector. It was good that Ahmed had miraculously managed to keep his torch, as it was now their only light source. The floor underfoot suddenly became softer and the air filled with particles in the torchlight—this was earth! Rick dodged some creeper strands hanging down from above. If there was earth on the floor here, that meant that the sector might be similar to the farm in the Commune. He noted many familiar details—the same doors, levers and glyphs, large and small altars of the Machine God, the same division into rooms and the width of the corridor. However, there were differences too—part of the corridor had transparent walls, where rooms emptied by fires or explosions could be seen.

They kept walking along the corridor, away from the center of the Expanse until Maya ordered a stop again. It was only then that Rick saw the grimace of pain on her face. With a sigh of relief, she entered a large room which was two levels high and had transparent walls. Rick and Ahmed followed her inside.

"Ahmed," she asked, "seal the room hermetically."

The barbarian shut the door tight. The room was full of beds, cabinets, shining metal tables and ancient machines.

"Help me lie down," Maya asked Rick, "no,

over here."

He put her on a large and wide table. Maya got her breath back.

"All right. Now turn the dial on that panel."

Rick shook his head, "I may not touch the altars of the Machine God."

"Ahmed!" Maya closed her eyes—she was probably in a lot of pain. "Please."

The barbarian opened the lid, blew the dust off the controls and turned some sort of lever. A deep thrumming noise started up.

"An autonomous generator," he explained. "A little weak, but enough for us."

The room filled with a soft white light. Ahmed was doing his magic with other instrument panels, pressing and turning something. Rick stood and watched his movements with an open mouth. These people knew technical magic better than any priest. Unceremoniously, Ahmed moved Rick out of the way and helped the girl undress down to her waist. Her wiry body was covered with ugly bruises and there was a torn, bleeding wound in her side.

Ahmed took some sort of needled device out of a cabinet and stuck it into the girl's shoulder. Then, he put a lamp above her so that he could see the wound, washed some terrifying looking instruments under the water and sprinkled some unknown powder over them and the wound—the blood around the wound started to bubble, and Maya started to groan from the pain. He cut away the ragged flesh from the edges and then took the needle and thread and sutured the wound with quick, obviously experienced movements. It took him another couple of minutes to apply the bandage. He rubbed a brown liquid over the bruises and grazes and bandaged them as well. Ahmed worked quietly and confidently, it was obvious he knew what he was doing. Once the operation was finished, Maya went to sleep. Ahmed looked at the walls and ceiling and cheered up.

"Everything's fine," he said, "the medical block is isolated. We can sleep."

He turned off the light and fell on the nearest bed. Rick sat down on the floor and spent a while in the darkness, examining the companions that had suddenly changed his entire life after their meeting.

9

"WE WON'T reach it."

The words sounded like the statement of an obvious fact. Maya sat on a table, dangling her legs, while Ahmed changed her bandage.

"It's impossible. We will die," Maya seemed to argue with herself.

"What are you looking for below?" Rick asked.

Maya never answered, distractedly looking through him and obviously thinking some thoughts of her own.

"First it was Dimitri, then Varg and then Roxana," she continued, "no. We should have already turned back when we reached the New."

"We knew what we were signing up for," Ahmed replied, "I could have been in their place. Or you."

"This is too cruel!" she struck the tabletop with her fist and suddenly started crying. Ahmed finished the bandage, threw a jacket over her shoulders and hugged her.

Once Maya calmed down, Rick said, "We must find food."

Maya stared at him with fury in her eyes.

"Barbarian!" she spat out, "No intelligence, no emotions, only instincts."

Rick did not know the meaning of the last word, but understood that it was an obvious instinct. He stepped in close to the table, and glanced at Ahmed and then Maya.

"We need to talk. Why did you come below?"

Both of the barbarians were silent.

"Tell me about your world. Who are you and where are you from? If she doesn't want to talk, then you should."

"Don't tell him!" Maya elbowed Ahmed in the ribs.

"Why not?"

"Because she doesn't trust me," Rick answered. "I heard everything while I slept. All of your conversation with Reiner. When you were persuading him to leave. Isn't it interesting, what would have happened if I didn't follow you?"

Maya began to take angry short breaths. Rick no longer felt unsure around her. These people were flesh and blood, just like him.

"Personally, I have nothing to hide from you. My Commune is dying of cold because our holy fire is growing weak and no one knows what to do. Even the Warden."

"Holy fire!" Maya laughed. "How stupid!"

"I don't understand what's so stupid about that."

"Maya," Ahmed interrupted, "he really doesn't understand."

She stayed silent for a minute, solving some sort of complicated problem in her mind. This was a strong girl, and Rick liked watching the way the emotions showed on her face.

"All right," she surrendered. "But first, you must know that I don't trust you and I will never trust you. You are a barbarian, a savage and an uneducated brute."

"Thank you for your honesty. You don't have to thank me for saving your life. Now tell me about your civilized world."

"It's not a world, but a sector just like yours. It is just higher along the Axis."

"Axis?"

"You call it the Chorda. That's the whole problem. You turn everything inside out..."

"Start from the beginning."

So Maya gave him a short description of their home sector—Kappa, which was the location of the so-called Order, a group of people that were the descendants of some sort of settlers and who had inherited knowledge that was considered to be the greatest treasure from them.

"I thought that there was nothing more important than a warm home and tasty food."

Maya chuckled at Rick.

"Yes," she said. "But neither is possible without knowledge. It is only thanks to knowledge that man knows how to make fire and grow food. The Order carefully preserved knowledge, passing it from generation to generation, until it became obvious that it was insufficient for the people and new knowledge was needed. The charge in the sector generator is running out, and it is unknown where to get more. The Archivist spent a long time studying all of the existing records, but the problem is that few of them survived the great fire. At last, they managed to find a diagram on which Kappa sector and four other sectors of the second aeon were marked. The Archivist carefully studied this document and came to the conclusion that other aeons and sectors exist. Before this, the Order had been sealed—the settlers made a vow to remain within the walls of their shelter until the Plague passes," she carefully looked at Rick. "Do you know what the Plague is?"

Rick shook his head.

"The Plague is a fatal disease against which there is no cure. This is why no one knew what awaited us outside—life or death. There was no choice. So we had to risk it. We opened the main gates, and the first unit went on an expedition to go above."

Maya paused and sipped some water from the glass Ahmed brought her.

"None returned. Then, the Order Council instructed for another expedition to be sent downwards. We have a week. If we don't come back in time, the Order will make their decision."

Rick was deep in thought. He remembered the execution after the Spring Run.

"All right. Now tell about this "gen-er-at-or"."

"It's a power source," Ahmed joined in. "To

understand how it works, you must know the foundations of physics and chemistry, areas of knowledge which are called science. How can I explain this to you? It's an energy like fire, but it is much stronger and burns in a different way. It is sort of like an internal fire."

"Does it burn according to the will of the Machine God?"

"You should forget about your Machine. Everything that surrounds us was created by man."

"This can't be!" Rick shook his head. "A man cannot create the whole universe."

"The ancients could. They were so powerful, that they could control time, space, matter and life itself. They created this world and lived in it, and it was a true Golden Age. People lived on every level, in every sector and every segment. It was a living world, filled with people. Then, the Plague started, and humans began to put up barriers, seal doors and isolate levels and sectors. Every sector saved itself the way it could. It was a question of survival. The Order has existed for twenty generations because our Founding Fathers sealed their sector in time. We would never have ventured outside, if it wasn't for the disaster."

"They would never have let us out," Maya corrected. "The thing is, that there is a group of scientists in the Order that wanted to investigate Outer Space, which is what we call the rest of the sectors, for a long time."

"We call it the Expanse."

"Whatever you like," she agreed. "These scientists had long dreamed of an expedition outside to understand how the world works and what is its size. And when the time came, they included one of us in their group... I mean, one of them."

"You?" Rick indicated Ahmed.

Maya nodded.

"You are more intelligent than you seem," Maya admitted. "Perhaps your ignorance can gradually be cured. Our Order is organized so that knowledge is inherited in scientific categories. Some inherit the knowledge of mathematics, some of physics. Ahmed is an engineer. Reiner was a physicist. I am a biologist and I know everything about plants. Everyone shares their knowledge with each other, so that all of society has a high level of education. They took a specialist from every category for the expedition. There were ten of us. You can see how many remain now."

"My condolences," nodded Rick.

"I loved everyone in our unit, because the Order is one family. We have no superiors and subordinates, everyone is equal and everyone's life is valuable. Our Order is the heir of great settlers and must continue its existence no matter what."

Rick had heard similar words somewhere before.

"Our scientists have managed to discover the main Axioms of the World. All children learn them from a young age, even though few now understand what they truly mean. Even I. However much I think about them, I still don't understand what they are about."

"So what do the Axioms of the settlers say?" Rick asked curiously.

"The world in which we live is the Thermopolis. It is a place that is composed of a huge number of aeons, sectors and floors. The Thermopolis is pierced by the Axis, and these things exist around it. The Thermopolis has an external border. It is unknown how tall and wide it is. The ancient documents were destroyed by fire during the revolt, because the ignorant decided that all misfortunes come from books and that they must be destroyed. But we know that there is something there, beyond the external border. Because that is where the ancients came from. Some of our scientists say that there is only emptiness out there and the Thermopolis is constantly falling into an abyss. Others consider the opposite—that we are at the center of Creation, and it rotates around us, and that there is such a huge enclosed space above that it is not even an enclosed space, for it has no ceiling. Could you even imagine a place that does not have walls or ceilings at all?"

Rick tried to imagine one, but failed completely.

"So what is out there?" he scratched his head ponderingly.

"That is the greatest mystery," Maya said with flashing eyes.

"That means that it wasn't a god that created the Expanse, the Chorda and the universe..."

"That's right. Your whole cult is a complete misconception. And the reason for this is lack of knowledge. Even if we have only retained grains of knowledge, your connection with the past is completely broken."

Rick thought about what he heard.

"We studied the mechanisms," Maya continued, "and the underlying principles of how they work. We study every artifact or item from the past, trying to understand its purpose. Every find is of great value to us, as it allows us to solve the mysteries of the past. When we set off downwards, we suspected that we would run into difficulties. We understood that the descendants of other sectors would be different to us, but we never imagined that they would want to kill us. We knew that we could come across monsters, but we never thought that the monsters could be humans. This world is a disgusting place."

Maya sobbed.

"Now that our unit has been destroyed, there's no point in our mission. The only one who could have worked out the way the generator works was Reiner. He dedicated his life to this issue."

"Was it him that decided that you need to head below?"

"That was the decision of the Order Council. Reiner merely suggested that there is a main generator that supplies all of Thermopolis and that it is switched off right now. Otherwise, every sector would be full of light and life. Look around you. Everything is dead. That shows that the power has been switched off and only the emergency generators are working."

"Every sector has its own gen-er-at-or."

"You're doing well. The machines in every sector where this sort of generator is turned on will work until the energy runs out. And then it turns off."

"Darkness and cold."

Maya nodded.

"This is why the Council sent the expeditions to find out where the generator is located, find out what happened to it, and..." she cut herself short.

"Not to turn it on. To save energy," Ahmed added, "and for safety reasons."

Rick, who was more experienced in such matters, had a different opinion.

"That is no reason at all. I don't know who are the members of your Council, but they want to profit to keep their power. People are the same everywhere."

"They are not like that. They think of the good of everyone."

"Let's get away from this subject. Now something is becoming clear to me." He remembered his ragged piece of paper, "Have a look. What would you say about this?"

The girl laid the sheet out on the table. All three bent over the diagram, holding their breaths. For some reason, it now seemed to Rick that this might not quite be the map of the Omicron sector.

"I would bet my liver," Ahmed whispered, "that we have the diagram of the Fifth aeon here."

He slid his finger down the drawing, reading out loud.

"Air Generator, sections A-D, Raw Material Warehouses. Waste Processing Plant. Water Station. Energy Station. Moisture Collectors, reservoirs 1-4. Sectors Phi, Xi, Psi, Aqua,

Omega... Where did you get this?"

"Kyoto, the old man that helped us leave the Commune gave it to me. What's an aeon?"

"As far as we know, it is a block that unites five sectors. Aeons are divided by aerial space. Like the one where those abominations live," Ahmed pointed upwards, reminding them of Yarg's camp.

"These aeons were probably once connected to each other," Maya replied, "using elevators. But they were sealed because of the Plague..."

She swayed and nearly fell off the table.

"We need to eat. We have become too weak," Rick insisted.

"I found something around here when I woke up," Ahmed stepped over to the cabinet and took out a clear package with yellow balls inside. "A universal vitamin complex. There's also food concentrate and energy capsules. We can last on them for some time."

They quickly swallowed the capsules, washing them down with the remains of the water in the flask and put the rest into a bag which Ahmed had thoughtfully taken out of the same cabinet.

"Turn the light on to full power," Maya asked him.

"You shouldn't," Rick shook his head. "As you constantly insist yourself, energy is a valuable resource. It would be better for you to listen to another story."

He gave a general account of his meeting with the strange dwarf and about his warning.

"Those are all mutations," Maya explained. "This happens because of the release of radiation. The Big Boom. Hmm, he was probably talking about the accident at the station. If that's so, we shouldn't go there. Even after many years, there may be high background radiation and we will get radiation sickness. It seems that your little friend was telling the truth—plants and animals have extreme reactions to such processes and also mutate. That means anything might await us below."

"Or nothing."

All three went quiet. Everyone was thinking of something of their own.

"So what is our decision?" Rick asked, "Up, or down?"

His directness seemed to put the agents of the Order aback.

"There are too few of us," Maya began, "and what can we do? The best thing to do would be come home, tell them about everything we saw here and send out a new unit with people who are better prepared."

"You are right," Ahmed nodded.

Rick kept looking at them.

"You're leaving something out. You shouldn't be afraid of me. We're in one room now."

"The problem isn't you," Ahmed scratched the back of his head shyly.

"Are you afraid of what is below? Me too. But that's no reason. Bridges are made to cross chasms, not to stand at the edge."

"We just don't know what to do when we find this generator. Reiner constantly talked about some sort of safety key, but refused to say what it was for, because he had responsibilities before the Council."

"Great. Now there is no Reiner, and no key of his," Rick stated. "Did the Council predict such a turn of events?"

No one contradicted him, but Rick was not trying to humiliate them.

And then Maya exploded, "I can't do this anymore! No need to hide, Ahmed. Let's tell him."

"Whatever you want."

"We are rebels!"

"Well, well. Now this, is interesting," Rick crossed his arms across his chest.

"Reiner was our teacher. He is the author of the Babylon theory. He had spent a long time looking for like-minded people and gradually gathered students into his ranks that had a sufficiently open and flexible mind to accept his version of the structure of the world as truth. He wanted to test it in practice, and when the generator charge reached a critical level, made himself indispensable to the Council. He was included in the expedition, as well as us upon his request. He didn't just want to find the main generator—he also wanted to reach the edge of the universe, and look beyond that edge."

Maya said all of this in one breath, and the relief on her face was so palpable that it seemed that the rest of the destiny of the rebel girl had depended on this moment.

"And what is Babylon about?"

"There is a legend," Ahmed replied. "It's more ancient than anything. The legend states that humans used to live on the surface of a really large level. Just one level, can you imagine that? They crawled around here and there like cockroaches. So, once upon a time, they decided to create a world with many levels. They started building it and it took a long time. They called this building "Babylon". But they never finished it. Well, Reiner thought that this wasn't a legend, and we all live inside this building and there's a huge and far extending surface outside."

"I see. So they finished building it."

"It looks like it. If we manage to prove this theory, those that follow dogma will be defeated. We will then take charge and put forth our conditions. We don't like the way they rule."

"And what if you lose?"

"Then, such is life."

Rick cheered up.

"I committed a crime, so there's a heavy punishment awaiting me at home. You are also blowing up the foundations of your society. We're all just a bunch of suicidal rebels!"

Maya snorted and started gathering medicines, instruments and bandages from the shelves.

"Why are you standing around? We're going on another walk."

So they started to help her. They found and put everything they would need for the road in the bag—a coil of cable, a set of instruments, medicines and a supply of water. Then, Maya took certain injectors with yellow markers and injected each of them with a portion of medicine.

"Against radiation," she explained.

"Excellent," Rick replied. "That means we have decided—we are going down."

"We will at least find the generator and examine it. Get that thing over there—it's a radiation detector, it is going to start buzzing or clicking when the background radiation will suddenly get too high."

They left the medical block and decided to continue using side paths, through the stairways going down from the large circular corridor.

"What did you see between your sector and Omicron?" Rick asked.

"Two sectors were closed. The third was open, but abandoned. Some sort of white creatures were running around there. We were moving as carefully as we could, but our group seemed to be cursed. One had his throat torn out by a white bloodsucker. Another fell to his death down the chasm. The third just disappeared—he probably got lost. Two of the others had an argument and nearly killed each other, while the other one closed off inside himself. I won't tell you their names, because they will tell you nothing. The name of someone you don't know is an empty word. The lower we descended, the harder it was to move. The walls just seemed to close in on us. I could not sleep normally anymore, even when we locked ourselves in rooms for which we had access codes. I always felt as if someone was watching us. I have that feeling now. I have goosebumps running down my back."

They reached the place were the temple of the Machine God would be in the Omicron sector.

"Let's have a look," Ahmed said.

Rick hesitated for a second, but still entered.

The room was filled with floor to ceiling with Machine God altar stands, a place for great sacrifices. Then Rick remembered that this was untrue and there was nothing supernatural about them.

"The operations room," Maya commented, "a control nexus. Do you have one too?"

"Yes, but it is forbidden for common people to enter,"

"I see you have a good setup. Let me explain something to you then."

She started to show him every button, level and panel, explaining their purpose. Rick did not understand much of course, but the main thing was knowledge: the girl knew machines. That meant that in time, he would know them too. Once he knows them, he can control them.

"This is a temperature monitor. It shows the state of the heat distribution network. Here it shows the voltage of the internal power network. See, everything is black. It is switched off. We can turn on the local generator if its batteries have not been drained by those that lived here."

"And there will be light and heat everywhere?"

"That's right."

"Then we can stay and live here in complete peace of mind."

"I have thought of this too."

Rick and Maya stood by the controls, trying to get used to this new idea.

"No. We can't do it," Rick finally countered.

"There are too few of us. This is a dead end."

"I also arrived at that thought," Maya smiled, as Ahmed nodded with approval, "but the limited resources also need to be taken into account. A sector generator is not eternal. A problem will arise in the future."

Rick noted that her earlier grim resolve was put on.

"We need a source of renewable energy," Ahmed replied.

"So many interesting words," Rick noted.

"It's fine, you'll get used to it," Ahmed looked through a cabinet at the far end of the room. "Aha! Just what we need! Now we've got good torches."

"You're an engineer. Does that mean you deal with the sewer system and water supply?" Rick asked with interest.

"Partly. I also study all of the com-mu-ni-cations—I mean all the cables, pipes and wires that go through the sector. You can't imagine how many of them there are in the walls. The Expanse is practically crammed with them."

They left the operations room.

"The ancient builders had planned for everything. Every mechanism has a safeguard. If there is an accident, the automatic systems turn on. Any part and any wire is universal. It can be easily disconnected and reconnected in a new place. This world is like a big construction set. Look at the wall. What do you see?"

Rick obediently looked at the wall of the corridor they were walking through.

"It's just a wall. There are signs and doors. There is the ventilation and some cabling under the ceiling."

"You surprise me. And what about the oval cavities and handrails, over here and over there? See, they repeat in a certain pattern. Pay attention to this line here. This is a seam that connects blocks to each other. See how it goes along at the level of your chest? Look, here it crosses with a vertical seam. Look at these frosted glass inserts. These rectangles here. Do you know what they are?"

"No," Rick admitted.

"I haven't found out either, yet. But none of these things are random, and they all have a purpose of their own."

"I see. And what about you Maya, do you work on the farm? It's not easy."

"What, do you think I crawl around the vegetable patches from dusk till dawn? We've got special machines called auto-robots to do that."

"What is it you do then," asked Rick incredulously.

"I breed new species of plant."

"Ugh..." Rick shook his head, "I'd never have

thought..."

"Our biologist caste constantly works on the issue of creating plants that would require little light, but would still be tasty, hardy and cold resistant."

"Is that even possible?"

"Of course. But it's a difficult task. We have only managed to solve one or two problems. We either get weeds, like this creeper over here, or we get tasty types that are too sensitive. Some of us also work on animals—hamsters, rats, chickens and pigs."

"What's a pig?"

"Haven't you seen a pig? If that warty freak went on all-fours and squealed he would look a lot like a close relative. Pigs can be eaten, but they require a lot of feeding. We don't have many of them, and we only eat them twice a year during great celebrations."

The three of them were moving along the circular corridor and quietly conversing amongst themselves. Ahmed was holding the radiation detector. The air was cloyingly humid, liquid was constantly dripping from the ceiling and the walls were covered with a layer of slime that exuded a thick and sickening smell.

"Do you think this all appeared by itself?" Maya pointed at some greenish gray growths, "These are overgrown plantations, and there are some hydroponics nearby. Our ancestors knew how to grow whatever they wanted. Did you know that plants create air as well as being food? That is called oxygen synthesis. The plantation system was so well thought through that no one ever starved. The sectors were supplied with food."

"And not only that," Ahmed added, "every sector received heat, light and energy for their machinery. There was a cycle of matter in this world. Our scientists also insist that there is a communication system, which people could use to communicate at any distance, through many walls and over many levels. It is switched off now. There were many wonders in ancient times, and we don't even know a tenth of them."

"We had communication in the Commune, but only the senior patrolmen had it," Rick chimed in, "the Ether Voice is what we called it..."

Maya and Ahmed exchanged glances, but stayed quiet.

The corridor led them to a large spiral staircase, which was overgrown with creepers. They slowly started to descend, carefully examining every step. The counter in Ahmed's hands started to emit weak clicking sounds. The walls gradually hid under a thick carpet of creepers and the steps were covered with a layer of soil. It was as if they were stepping into a labyrinth of plants. Nature ruled here. By the time they reached the bottom floor of the sector, the floor, ceiling and walls were thickly layered with a reddish green layer of plants. The radiation detector emitted a steady stream of clicks.

"We need to determine the source of the radiation," Ahmed said, "let's go along the radial corridor from the beginning to the end."

Rick and Maya agreed. The time for talking was over—now they silently studied their surroundings in the world below.

"There's light ahead," Rick noticed.

"Let's see what it is."

The corridor was becoming lighter as they approached the center of the world. They had to tear through thick lianas to get through to an open space by the entrance to the balcony of the main well. Light was pouring in from below. The next sector was fully illuminated. They came close to the edge of the platform and saw that the sector floors around the Chorda flickered with a diffused white light. Rick thought that it would fall into darkness lower down, but distant lights could be seen glinting far below.

The Underworld turned out to be a place of light.

Ahmed passed his detector over the precipice. The clicking was not as fast as at the bottom of the staircase.

"The source is at the edge," Ahmed looked puzzled, "and the radiation is too weak. I was expecting the detector to tear itself to pieces."

"Is that good or not?" Rick asked.

He could not understand them—these people from up above behaved strangely, seeming concerned when they should have been happy.

"Yes, that's good."

Rick approached the spiral staircase and almost fell down below. The stairwells were disconnected. Maya took the cable from Ahmed, skilfully tied it around herself and moved Rick aside.

"Look out for me!"

Before he had a chance to say a word, the girl jumped. She softly landed on the organic layer and immediately got into a defensive stance. Rick and Ahmed descended after her. They spent a while examining the balcony and walls of the next sector. The outlines they were used to seemed unusual and strangely shaped when the even white light of ceiling lights working at full power fell on them. The light had a greenish, diffused aspect to it because the lights were covered by greenery. It was rather painful to look at.

"Whoever lived here, they definitely had no problems with a power source."

"Energy is life," Maya said. "This sector is habitable. We must be ready for anything."

They started to descend using the large spiral staircase of the main well. The greenery covering every surface was succulently green, with fat stems and thick leaves. Multicolored flowers bloomed and spread a tangy smell. Rick sneezed. His eyes started to water. This sector had a somewhat different design to the two previous ones. There were no rooms, and each floor had high walls that extended over two or more levels. It soon became obvious why—he saw that behind the transparent thick walls, there were tall plants with long and thick stems reaching as far as the ceiling, with a crown of leaves at the top.

"Trees," Maya explained, sounding just as surprised. "I thought they don't exist anymore."

They were looking around, and all they could see were masses of greenery that had filled all the levels of the sector. This was a real jungle. A collection of wild, untended plants, that had overgrown and taken over the surrounding space. The glass could not resist the pressure in some places, and the leaf-covered branches had broken out, trying to grab on to emptiness. It was hard to breath. This was not just because of the thick smell of flowers, but also the intoxicating air that filled their chests and tickled their nostrils. They passed the ten upper floors of the sector, and the growth became increasingly thick, making it even harder to move on ahead. They were no longer going down the stairs, but stepping over interwoven roots as thick as a human leg. Something was constantly clicking and crunching, as if it was imitating Ahmed's detector. Dried branches and fruits fell from above. The leaves seemed to quietly rustle by themselves, making them feel uneasy. However, Rick guessed that it must have been the incoming streams of warm air that were moving the surrounding plants. It was much warmer here, so much so that his overalls were drenched with sweat and he had to constantly wipe his face.

"Hey!" Ahmed shouted from the back once they passed another stairwell. It looks like I've got stuck.

Rick and Maya returned. Ahmed was unsuccessfully trying to get his ankle out of a knot of roots. Rick tried to help him, but it was as if Ahmed's foot was caught in a vice. Next, Rick tried to lift up the root. This was no easy task.

"Pull!" he shouted, pulling with all his strength, until he suddenly felt a contraction in his hand, as if he was handling something with the muscles of a living creature.

Ahmed sprung out of the trap, but his dark

face had gone pale with fear. Rick's legs got tied up and constricted, and the prehensile tentacle branch started to crawl upwards along his calf.

"Watch out!"

Rick immediately understood what had grabbed him, drew his knife and hacked at the dark green joints. The branch broke in half with a loud crunch, and thick juice began dripping from the stump.

"Run as fast as you can!" he screamed at his companions, but it was too late. The predatory ivy had already grabbed Maya and Ahmed, locking their arms and legs in its embrace and slowly dragging them upwards. They desperately fought back, trying to tear the hard stems apart, but the ivy was far stronger. While Rick hacked at the stems that had engulfed one leg, three other tendrils had slid around his waist, shoulder and other arm. Ahmed was already twisting in the air like a fish that just got hooked. A huge flower bud opened above him, filled with rather sharp spikes.

Rick knew this type of plant from up above. There was even one growing on their farm for experimental purposes. The children often played with it.

"Maya!" he shouted. "We need fire!"

"What?" She had almost no strength left.

"Do you have any fire?"

Maya somehow managed to slide her fingers into her pocket.

"No!" Her eyes radiated hopelessness.

"There!" Ahmed, who was covered in intertwined leaves up to his shoulders pushed out a hand holding a dully shining silvery object.

"Light the fire!"

Ahmed flicked the lighter open and struck the wheel, so that a small flame similar to that from a candle appeared. He put the fire to the stem.

"Throw it on the ground!"

"Why?" he asked incredulously, but then threw the lighter on the floor when he understood Rick's idea. The lighter fell, bounced and clicked shut. Rick threw himself towards it, but the ivy had already covered him up to his waist. He fell on the ground and crawled towards the lighter.

The ivy started to rustle loudly. The screams of his companions began to falter and sound tired, while Rick had no more strength left and breathed heavily. With a desperate thrust, he stretched out his arm—he was a hair's breadth away from the lighter. Ahmed screamed horribly—the spiked part of the flower had started to swallow him. Rick remembered his knife and used it as an extension of his hand. He hooked the lighter and pulled it towards himself, flicked it open and struck down on the wheel. He managed to make the fire appear on his fifth or sixth attempt.

Rick felt that he could not breathe. The plant's predatory embrace was crushing his chest and body. He carefully laid the lighter on the side and watched, with fascination, how the little flame slowly crawled onto the dry layer of fallen leaves and desiccated plants, how it lazily and hesitantly burnt through them and then got the taste for them, gathering in strength and consuming them. Soon, one of the steps on the staircase was engulfed in flames, and the fire crawled on, consuming the dry matter. The embrace of the ivy weakened.

The fire licked at the stems, twisting the leaves into black rags. Something fell to the floor—it was Ahmed, who fell prone right onto the ashes, looking like he had hit his head so he lay still without moving. Maya jumped down next. Rick stabbed the stem with his knife, but the ivy was already letting him go. Rick hacked off the last of the tendrils and was finally free. The fire continued to crawl up and down, jumping over to the level itself. The air was full of acrid smoke. Rick and Maya grabbed Ahmed under his arms and dragged him downwards, as far away from the fire as possible. Everything hissed and crackled around them, but they no longer paid any attention to the jungle. Rick was counting the levels, as the hydroponics sector would be over after they passed twenty floors.

"We need weapons! We can't do much with this knife!" he shouted.

"We need a rest..."

They collapsed in the stairwell, breathing heavily. Soft white fruit lay all around them, and Rick used one as a pillow under Ahmed's head. He slapped him on the cheeks, and when he began to groan, he finally breathed out and touched Ahmed's forehead.

"He's burning up. Something's wrong with him."

"It's poison," Maya said. "The ivy injects it into its victims. It did not manage to do that to me, but Ahmed was unlucky. One moment..."

She took an injector with blue markings out of their camping bag and stuck it into Ahmed's shoulder.

"He needs to lie down for at least a day," Maya's said shakily.

Rick understood that she would be unable to take another loss.

"I will carry him."

"You won't manage."

He had no strength left to argue with her, he just chuckled, looking up to where the fire was burning ever stronger.

"Wherever we go, we leave a fire behind."

"Let this world burn to ashes!" Maya spat out viciously.

Rick looked at her with reproach.

"Is that what you really want?"

She did not reply. Her eyes were full of pain, exhaustion and melancholy.

"Do you think we can really burn everything down?" Rick refused to stay quiet.

"No," she shook her head. "Watch."

He looked up again. Nothing was happening. The fire methodically consumed level after level. Smoke rose upwards up the well of the Chorda. Perhaps his kinsmen would probably smell the smoke as well. Then, something wailed loudly, machines started to hum in the entrails of the walls and a loud hissing and crackling sound could be heard. Streams of filthy water mixed with ash fell onto their heads, washing away the remains of the leaves, branches and other dirt. And the fire went out above.

"Understand now?"

Rick nodded. He needed no explanations. He began to understand this world and its second hidden layer without the glazing of religion. The ancient machines worked and put out the fire. This is what happened. The ancients had foreseen such an eventuality.

The water flowed away. Maya swallowed a tablet of concentrate and gave one to Rick.

"The central elevator..." Ahmed muttered, without opening his eyes. "We must activate the system..."

"He's delirious. It's the fever." Maya bent over Ahmed, opening his eyelids. "If there is too much poison, his body will not be able to deal with it even with the help of an antidote."

"Maya..."

"He will lose consciousness and die in a delirious fever. His heart will stop."

"Maya!" Rick raised his hand.

"What?"

"Stay still."

She glared at him angrily, but then anger turned to fear—she finally felt it.

"What is it there?" she wanted to put her hand behind her back, but Rick stopped her with a gesture. "I can feel something. Tell me!"

Rick looked around and picked up a large stick, taking careful aim.

He said, "Don't move, I beg you."

He swung and threw the stick at whatever it was that was sitting on her back. He hit the target, and an unusually large insect flew away into the darkness. Maya immediately jumped away. They stared at the walls of the level and noticed that the radial corridor leading to the edge was overgrown with porous rust almost up to the ceiling. The rust was filled with holes where white eggs could be seen being rolled around by insects with powerful mandibles.

"This is..." Maya began and suddenly yelled.

Dozens of huge six-legged insects the size of a well-fed rat were crawling towards them. The mandibles of the creatures clacked threateningly, while their red abdomens twitched nervously. The insects were obviously preparing to attack.

"By the powers of Omicron! What are they?"

"Ants," Maya mumbled, and then looked over at Ahmed, who was only steps away from the first rank of the insects. "And we have disturbed their nest." She pointed at the white fruit lying around everywhere. "We touched their eggs."

"Let's get out of here!"

Rick rushed over to Ahmed, gripped him by the shoulders and dragged him downwards. Maya picked up a long stick and started to defend them.

It seemed that the ants were coming from everywhere. Rick started to growl in anger and desperation, as the unconscious Ahmed was incredibly heavy. After five levels, Rick's strength was completely spent, so he slowed down and listened—the clacking sounds behind him had not stopped.

"We must hurry!" Maya shouted.

"Take my knife," Rick ordered, "you're going to cut through the brush ahead."

They kept moving in this way for the next several minutes. Rick prayed that there would not be something large and impassable in their way. He began to understand why Yarg's vermin were so afraid of the jungle—if they came across an ant nest by the Chorda, then what sort of things could be in the depths of the hydroponics sector?

"Maya!" he moaned. "I'm exhausted."

"Just another two levels, Rick!" she shouted back. "We are almost through this sector."

He gathered the remains of his willpower into a fist and moved on after her. If he had a good idea of what the sector would be like, they would come across a missing stairwell with a platform below.

Rick turned out to be right, and they managed to get some distance on their pursuers. Without breaking stride, Maya jumped onto a liana that hung down like a rope over the platform below, swung like a pendulum and found herself on the edge of the stairwell. They tied the liana around Ahmed and Rick jumped down onto the platform and ordered Maya to lower their wounded companion as he would catch him if anything went wrong. Every second was precious, but the liana could not take the weight and snapped, so Ahmed fell right on top of Rick. They fell onto the floor. Maya jumped down by their side, and then an ant fell right on her shoulder, immediately biting into her neck. With a squeal of pain and fury, Maya tore the insect away from her and threw it into the chasm. The ants fell from above like hailstones, pattering onto the floor like nuts and bolts spilled from a toolbox.

"Further, Rick, let's run further!" she shouted. "We can't stand still!"

Overcome with terror, Rick and Maya started dragging Ahmed downwards. This sector was also covered in hydroponic jungles, but it was not as brightly lit. There was no time to take in the details, but Rick felt the presence of someone or something there. They continued their descent, now just dragging Ahmed along the floor, having reached the limits of their strength.

"No more..." Rick fell to his knees.

Maya lowered herself by his side. The quickest ant jumped up to them, and Maya hacked it in half, but then one more appeared and then another. Maya was slashing at them with the blade while Rick kicked and stamped them until he hit a liana that stretched above the floor. There was a loud whistling sound from the side, then a rustling sound and then Rick and Maya were covered in a net. Both screamed when they were dragged up into the air, waving their arms around, but soon Maya's voice was cut short. Rick noticed a shadow move off to his side, turned his head and the last thing he saw was the end of a thick club.

The strike landed right on his temple, and the light went out.

10

THE DARKNESS went gray and then fell apart into separate fragments, that stretched out into lines, lines which suddenly became the bars. This was the first thing that Rick saw when he woke up, but everything started to blur in his eyes again and his head started to pulsate with growing pain. Rick shut his eyes, looking at circles which exploded and went out... Where was he? Where did he end up? Where were his companions?

He opened his eyes again. He could see the outlines of a human figure through the haze. Only the stranger had a tight-fitting mask over his head with round lenses, rimmed with metal like a pair of goggles instead of eyes. The stranger approached the bars. The lenses stared at Rick, reflecting the light of the lamp.

The floor on which Rick was lying suddenly started to swing and the stranger disappeared somewhere above. He managed to somehow raise himself up on his elbows—the pain in his head became somewhat less. It turned out that Rick was inside a cage hanging on a cable which was being lowered now. The question was, where to?

The cage shook with a clang, and all was still.

He had arrived.

With difficulty, Rick sat up. He head was spinning, and started to see double—he kept being unable to focus on the figures standing outside. He lay down and closed his eyes again. He could not tell how long he had lain like that, he could have possibly gone into a reverie or fallen asleep. When he came to, he heard the creaking, clacking and humming of mechanisms and he heard voices nearby. Somewhere, metal struck metal. Rick lay there and thought about where he had ended up. Judging by the sounds, it was a workshop, but a very large one.

Suddenly, a great stream of water hit his face. Rick tried to jump up, but they continued to drench him, not letting him get up properly. Then, they stopped just as suddenly when they switched off the water.

He sat up, spluttering and wiping his face—it took him around a minute to come to his senses and get his breath back until he could take a look around. A man wearing an orange jumpsuit and a tight black mask over his head was standing in the cage. Two round lenses, rimmed with metal, were stuck in the place where his eyes should have been.

So it was no dream, that first time when the cage was being lowered. Rick waited. The stranger threw the hose which had just been spraying water onto the floor and moved a bowl full of a grayish green mass towards Rick with his foot. Rick took the bowl, sniffed it and swallowed. Food! His belly betrayed him by growling loudly—he hadn't eaten for a long time. Forgetting about everything, Rick quickly swallowed the nutritious mass. Then, the stranger picked up the hose once again, opened the valve and filled the bowl with water. Rick drunk the water too. The stranger picked up the hose and the bowl and left, clicking the bar on the cage shut.

Thanks for that, at least. Rick got up on his feet and looked around.

The massive cage with thick bars in which he had ended up stood in the middle of a spacious hall. A production unit—Rick remembered the word that he heard in the Commune. That was what they called the separate, large rooms in the workshop. This production unit contained lines of mechanisms that had manipulator arms hanging above them. Machine tools and other machines that were used for unknown purposes stood by the wall.

People stood everywhere behind the machine tools, manufacturing something. The production unit was around five levels in height.

The stranger in the orange jumpsuit approached the cage again, accompanied by a stocky man who did not wear a mask and walked with a slight limp. His eyeballs were light, almost white, while his skin was weather-beaten. However, the feature that struck Rick the most were his frosty steel-gray eyes, that immediately seemed to radiate cold. A pair of round glasses made of darkened glass rested on the man's forehead.

He was a welder, Rick decided for some reason. These were the glasses that welders wore in the Commune, anyhow. The black shirt of the light haired man was torn in several places and knotted muscle could be seen underneath. The man crouched by the cage and started to observe with great interest.

Rick wanted to talk, but the dryness of his throat betrayed him and he started coughing. The stocky man laughed uproariously and left.

In the end, Rick sat in the cage for several hours, trying to guess what might have happened to Maya and Ahmed, while watching those around him. No one approached him anymore or paid any attention to him. The people in the production unit looked strong and healthy, without any abnormal behaviors or mutations. Many of them sported beards and mustaches, as well as many having ritualistic tattoos covering their faces. All of the workers spoke a language Rick could understand, but with some sort of strange accent where they rolled their R's. Each of them carried a knife or a cleaver with a wide and long blade. They occasionally glanced over at Rick, but it was obvious that they considered him an object or an animal. One of the workers threw him a piece of toast as he passed by.

While he was watching, one group of workers changed with another. Then, when the second shift had completed their allotted work, some people left, while some stayed behind. Finally, the light haired man that Rick had tried to talk to appeared in the production unit. He was accompanied by the stranger in the orange jumpsuit and skintight black mask.

"Hey, boys!" the stocky man called over as he walked in. "Want to have a bit of fun?"

He was answered with a chorus of assent, as the rest of the people started to gather around the cage.

"We had a curious catch yesterday. Some plague monkeys rolled down from above. Take a look!"

He banged a wrench on the bars of the cage.

Rick got himself ready. He was not afraid—

there was no point to be scared ahead of time. This was something he already learned back in the Commune.

"Hey, monkey!" the stocky man shouted. "Do you know how to talk?"

"Yes."

"You're so well trained!"

The workers started laughing. The silent stranger in the orange jumpsuit brought up a tub full of nuts and bolts, and the stocky man started throwing them, aiming at Rick and saying, "Do you know how to walk on your hind legs? Can you do tricks?"

"I'll show you a trick," Rick muttered through clenched teeth and threw his bowl at him.

The bowl would have definitely hit the stocky man in the head, but it was too wide to get through the bars of the cage and bounced off with a loud clang.

The stocky man recoiled inadvertently, and the workers laughed even louder.

"Not bad," he said. "I will give you a chance. But not today. Tommo!" he addressed his companion in the orange jumpsuit. "Bring him something to eat, he looks like he could be broken in half with one finger."

Tommo nodded. Rick noticed several people that wore similar masks and jumpsuits to

Tommo in the crowd. All of them wore gloves on their hands, without exception.

"But not now," the stocky man warned. "Later. Let the boys have their fun."

He smiled a predatory smile, showing two rows of strong and even teeth and left, leaving Rick alone with the workers, who did not leave him waiting and started to throw dirty rags and pieces of machine parts while shouting insults.

Rick tried to angrily answer back, but soon worked out that it was exactly what was expected of him—helpless aggression gave special pleasure to these people. Then he stayed quiet and turned his back on them. The workers soon lost any interest in him, as they understood that they wouldn't get anything from him. The noise in the production unit gradually quietened down and everyone went on their way. The bright lamps on the walls went out, a pair of red emergency lights came on somewhere far away and Tommo appeared in front of the cage. He put his hand between the bars and threw a concentrated ration briquette inside, as well as putting down a mug of water.

Well, food was strength. Rick nodded his thanks and started to eat. He would definitely need his strength tomorrow. Once he finished the ration and drunk the water, he sat for a while, staring straight ahead with unseeing eyes, the thoughts in his head crawling around like cockroaches until he stretched out on the floor and quickly went to sleep...

The next day was empty of any events. Tommo brought bowls of gray mass or concentrated ration and water, while Rick ate everything he was given, carefully observing Tommo and the workers. He tried to talk to Tommo once, but was unsuccessful, he just never answered questions or reacted to taunts. One time, this strange quiet man in an orange jumpsuit jumped on a wall and crawled along it to the ceiling to free a chain stuck in a lifting crane. Rick could not believe his eyes—Tommo scrambled up the wall like a large spider, quickly moving his hands and feet.

Next morning, he was woken up by a metallic clang. The light haired man stood by the bars and banged on it with his wrench. Rick suddenly remembered the speeches Croesus made about infiltrators from above. Now he understood what the barbarians from the higher sectors that were caught by the Patrol must have felt.

"Good morning, monkey!"

The stocky man opened the door of the cage, stepped aside and made an inviting gesture.

"If you please."

Rick stepped out, trying to be impassive,

and they set off through the crowd towards the gates leading out of the production unit. There was another production unit behind the gates, which differed to the previous one through the placement of the machine tools and the lines with the manipulator arms. After passing through, Rick guessed that this was a typical radial corridor. There were narrow windows in the floor, through which the rooms below could be seen. Everything was full of life. People in dirty yellow robes were hard at work on something, with cargo carts wheeling by.

They exited the tunnel into a spacious hall, where the light of the lamps dissipated under the high ceiling. The walls of the hall were covered with galleries and observation platforms crowded with people. There was a column in the center of the hall, crowned with a bust which was the height of two men, cast of metal and partly covered with red at the top, with a mouth painted into a toothed maw and a third eye scrawled on the forehead. Women danced a ritual dance around the column, bare down to their waists with necklaces of nuts around their necks.

"Hail to the Red King!" the stocky man shouted.

The women interrupted their dance.

"Hail!" an uneven chorus of voices replied.

The spectators on the observation platforms

lowered themselves onto their knees and bowed down to the floor. Having completed the greeting, all rose, and an old man stepped forward towards the stocky man and shouted "We greet you, Cornelius!"

The stocky man raised his hand with the wrench over his head and exclaimed, "The Reactor must live!"

"Must live!" everyone around shouted back.

"The Reactor must be fed!"

"Must be fed!"

"It needs the souls of sinners! Let the Red King judge who has sinned on this day!"

"Let it be so!"

Cornelius jumped up onto a raised platform. The crowd stepped back, looking at their leader.

"All are equal in our Brotherhood. Everyone has the right to live. And everyone has the freedom to die. We can make a great choice. Who is ready?"

A dozen tough looking young men and women stepped forward, their grim and concentrated faces full of determination.

"Excellent! Now, look at him," Cornelius pointed at Rick. "Answer, are you a human?"

"I am a human," Rick replied.

"And are you a righteous man?"

Laughter and whispers.

"Yes."

"If that is so, we shall test this. Only the righteous achieve victory before the eyes of the Red King. You have two roads out of here—life or death. Make your choice."

Rick smiled grimly. The people of this sector did not know him and did not know what he was capable of. This was his advantage.

"I choose life."

"Excellent!" Cornelius seemed to be happy with the way things were going. "Had you chosen death, it would have been immediately obvious that you are a righteous man. The sinners always choose life."

Rick lost his patience.

"Enough talk!" he shouted. "What do you want?"

"To be sure which of us is right. Only one wins in a dispute. Choose your opponent!"

"Choose me," a toothless old man wheezed from the crowd. "I will give you a quick death!"

An explosion of laughter.

Let them laugh, it was obvious that they were not seeing this sort of spectacle for the first time. These people were looking at him as if he was already dead, as if the result of the combat was already assured. Men, women, grandfathers and grandmothers—at least they had the sense not to bring children here.

Rick could help but shudder when he saw

Maya among the crowd. He barely recognized her—her hair had been cut short, she was wearing a filthy robe and silently looking at him. Her eyes were full of worry and the desire to help.

"If you are a righteous man," Cornelius added, "then you have the right to be with us. But you must earn your place. Choose!"

"Then I choose you." Rick pointed his finger straight at him.

"Think well, if you want to survive even a minute!" someone shouted from the crowd. "Cornelius will tear you to pieces!"

"I choose him, and that's that!" Rick paused. "Or are you afraid of me?"

A sharp breath reverberated around the entire hall. Cornelius' steel eyes glinted coldly.

"Excellent! Before the face of the Red King we shall start and end this dispute here and now."

Everyone immediately backed away from the place of the coming battle. Someone threw Cornelius a chain, which he caught and started to spin around above his head, swinging his wrench in his other hand.

Rick understood that he would not get help from anywhere. Even Maya was helpless to do anything. He threw a quick glance in her direction. Maya was choking back tears, crushed between the onlookers in the crowd that were supporting Cornelius with shout of encouragement.

"End him!"

"What're you waiting for?"

"Come on!"

Cornelius made a couple of feints and then rapidly attacked head on. The chain crashed into the place where Rick had been a moment ago with a loud clang. He managed to jump away into a roll just in time, and then get up, to immediately crouch down again. The chain whistled above his head, ruffling his hair.

"So, come on then, monkey! Come on!" Cornelius yelled. "Brave monkey!"

They continued to circle on the platform, piercing each other with eyes full of hatred. Someone tried to trip Rick up, but Rick felt the threat and jumped to the side, almost getting caught by another strike from Cornelius. Then came another failed attempt to knock him off his feet, which sent Cornelius into a rage. A series of strikes crashed down upon Rick, but none of them hit the target.

The crowd howled in ecstasy. Cornelius was so furious that he growled. Rick began to run out of breath, took a misstep and barely stayed on his feet. However, this saved his life—the wrench cut through the air where his head had been a moment ago. He jumped up and struck Cornelius with his fist to the body. He put the remainder of his strength into the punch. Cornelius grunted and jumped back a pace, rubbing at his side, giving Rick time to catch his breath.

The crowd suddenly quietened, entranced as they watched the opponents. Cornelius did not keep anyone waiting, and attacked again, which was met with shouts of encouragement. He was very strong and no longer gave Rick any time to rest, even though he still could not reach him with his chain or wrench.

"Tear his head off!" the most impatient spectators shouted.

"Gut him, Cornelius!"

"Smash him to a pulp!"

Sweat poured into Rick's eyes and his lungs were burning. He wheezed, breathing out every time that he dodged and attack. And he got more and more tired... A moment—an attack. A miss. Another lunge. He tripped over himself and this was the moment Cornelius appeared right by him, crashing the wrench into his shoulder, making him fall to his knees and cry out in pain.

Rick frenziedly struck back, hitting Cornelius with his hand on his hip, but he never even noticed, threw down the chain and struck out with the wrench again, this time to the face, crushing Rick's nose and lips. Then he grabbed him by the neck with his hand and jerked him upwards so that he was hanging above the platform.

Rick was ineffectually jerking his legs, unable to move his broken shoulder and trying to get out—but Cornelius had a powerful grip. He was slowly crushing Rick's neck with his strong fingers.

"Finish him!" the spectators screamed, clapping their hands and whistling. "End him!"

Cornelius bent forward, looking Rick straight in the eye and quietly said, "I will keep your girlfriend for myself."

Then he brought his hand sharply downwards, smashing Rick's head into the floor.

The world drowned in a red haze. He did not even have the strength to get up and only managed to turn onto his back.

Cornelius grabbed the wrench with both hands, raised it above his head and froze.

"In the name of the Red King!" he addressed the crowd. "Brotherhood of Sigma and Tau! I give this sacrifice to the Reactor!"

Rick looked at the ceiling dully—this was it, this was the end. There was no point in begging for mercy. He was saying his mental farewells to his sister and to the Commune. What was Aurora doing right now? Maybe she was listening to old Kyoto's fairy tales. Or maybe the Committee had come for her and... His sister needed him, and he promised to return! A horrible premonition forced him to try moving his healthy arm—he had to at least try. Rick turned his head and his hand felt the chain that Cornelius had dropped.

This was his chance!

The crowd was overjoyed. Cornelius started to lower the wrench, when Rick rolled onto all fours and swung the chain, wrapping its links around the neck of the big man. Cornelius still completed his strike, but the wrench slid along Rick's arm without causing any harm. The eyes of the huge man went wide and he instinctively grabbed the chain, trying to loosen its grip, and that was his mistake.

Rick rammed a knee into his stomach and then headbutted Cornelius in the nose, which immediately started to bleed. He jerked his opponent so he would have his back to him and struck him in his midriff, forcing him to bend his knees.

Cornelius started choking, and both fell onto the ground, with Rick pressing down on the big man with his body and not allowing him to breathe. Cornelius made a desperate attempt to turn and throw Rick off, but with no success.

The crowd roared. Rick raised his head for a moment—there was a serious fight going on around him as some wanted to stop him from killing Cornelius, while others were stopping them from interfering. Then, Rick pressed his knee into Cornelius' back, stretched the chain tight and loudly exclaimed so all could hear, "What do you choose? Life or death?"

Cornelius made croaking sounds.

"Tell me! What do you choose?"

The surrounding people went quiet, stopping their scuffle.

"L-let me go…"

"Do you want to live, or not? Tell me!"

"Live! I want to live!"

Rick threw down the chain and rose, with great difficulty. The world swam before his eyes, but his business was not over. He cast his dull eyes over the crowd and shouted, "Hey, you! I give your Cornelius as a gift to you! Take him."

The people of the Sigma and Tau sectors looked at him silently. Contorted with pain, Rick raised his hand and his eyes found Maya. She was smiling happily and wiping away tears.

And elderly man stepped out towards Rick and said, "You have achieved victory. The Red King saw it all. Cornelius shall be given to the Reactor. You shall take his place. Such is the law."

They were looking at Rick with a new expression on their faces. They admitted his strength, even though they mocked him and openly wished for his death but a minute ago.

Rick despised them.

"Who was Cornelius?"

"The Chief Reactor Operator."

"Then I want to see that place."

"Let's go. You will have your own room and a personal prole. This is Tommo, and he is now yours." The man pointed at the quiet creature in the orange jumpsuit and black mask. Tommo came closer and stood still, a couple of paces away.

A tall and tough looking youth stepped out of the crowd, followed by another paid. The youth declared, "This man is an outsider! He is a damn mutant, born of filth! A monkey from above! He must be banished from above! He is no one to us!"

The man was supported by some voices here and there. However, Rick was not taken aback.

"You have some objections? Then let's settle this dispute here and now. Well?"

The youth stood still, considering his chances. Rick slowly moved towards him.

"What're you waiting for?"

The youth inadvertently stepped back. Then Rick addressed the crowd.

"I acted according to your law. I proved that I am human. What else do you need?"

The people stood silent.

"He is right," said the man who had first

accepted Rick as the winner. "This was an honest dispute, the Red King bears witness to this."

It seemed that this was the decisive argument and the crowd made approving noises. The man stepped up close to Rick.

"My name is Arcadius. I will show you our Brotherhood."

"This girl," Rick pointed to Maya, "came with me. I want to take her for myself."

"Of course." Arcadius respectfully inclined his head. "She was victorious in a dispute with another woman yesterday, and the Reactor took the loser."

"We had another with us, a black skinned man called Ahmed."

"We thought that he would die from his wounds, but he opened his eyes and spoke yesterday. This means that life is strong within him and he can challenge for a place in the Brotherhood in the future. We are monitoring his condition."

Rick thought that Ahmed could have been thrown into the chasm like a piece of garbage. There were some in the Omicron sector that did such things, motivated by higher ideals. Even though they had obviously barbaric and pagan customs, the people obeyed certain rules here.

Before Arcadius took them down the corridor, Rick was given help. They used an injector on him that made the pain in his shoulder go away and his head clear. Maya rewarded Rick with a grateful look, silently took him by the hand and walked alongside him. The corridor obviously led to the Chorda. They came out onto the balcony and crossed the stairway to the neighboring segment, descending to a lower level. There were elevators moving in the niches by the entrances to the radial corridor of the segment. There were similar niches in the Omicron sector, but they had always been unavailable to the people of the Commune.

"We are going to go down the stairs," Arcadius guessed his thoughts. It's not far.

Rick considered him more carefully. Hair streaked with gray, short but broad-shouldered, small gray eyes. It looked like Arcadius played an important role in the Brotherhood and definitely had a degree of power.

Tommo the prole quietly followed Rick two paces away.

"He will follow any order you give him," Arcadius said, noticing Rick's curious glance. "It's a privilege afforded to the Chief Operator."

Rick stayed prudently quiet, even though he really wanted to ask a huge number of questions. They descended lower and lower, and the staircase and walls surrounding them shone with cleanliness. Rick watched the numbers signifying

178

the levels: 315, 314, 313...

"Floors," Maya said. "We will soon be on floor three hundred."

Rick could barely remember the number of the floor on Omicron's main level—it was probably five hundred and forty. He said that to Maya, and she quietly explained, "That's too high. Your sector is far higher, and ours is way more so."

However, Arcadius also managed to overhear their conversation.

"You descended from above? We thought that there is nothing up there apart from jungles and mutants. How high up do humans live?"

"It's difficult to say," Rick admitted. "It's not long since I thought that there was nothing below my sector apart from emptiness. And Maya lives even higher up."

"This is amazing. Sometimes outsiders come down here, but they are either monsters, or bloodthirsty barbarians."

"Haven't you tried to go upwards yourselves to find out what is going on above?"

"This was a long time ago, and it ended with a lot of blood," Arcadius replied. "The jungle was smaller back then and it was possible to pass through safely. No one has gone there since then. We have all we need to live. And we are satisfied with this."

He sounded completely sure of his last words.

The corridor led them to the edge of a huge shaft filled with a blue glow. The source of the glow was at the bottom of the shaft—a huge sphere, which shimmered with a million points of reflected light.

"The Reactor," Arcadius explained.

The stood still on the promontory that went over the shaft and spent a while observing the sphere. A powerful hum came from the below, so strong that it even blocked their ears. Rick felt a dry heat emanating from the sphere. It had been a long time since he felt this warm.

Arcadius led them along a walkway around the wall, towards a semicircular rule with panoramic windows.

"The Chief Operator's Post."

A significant proportion of the room was taken up by tables with machines that flashed with multicolored lights. The black squares of monitors were positioned equidistantly from each other. One of the large monitors on the opposite wall displayed a strange diagram, which Rick perceived as a drawing of an urn with a ball at the bottom. The shape of the urn was highlighted with a silvery light. Messages and signs flashed. Arcadius pointed at a large armchair, located by the tables.

"From now on, this is your place. Take it, as is your right."

"Thank you. What must I do?"

Arcadius intoned with great import, "The Chief Operator observes the Reactor."

Rick waited for him to continue, but it was in vain.

"And is that all? I must sit here and watch this thing down below?"

Arcadius looked reticent.

"The position of Chief Operator was hereditary. Cornelius took it after his father Angus, who replaced his father, and so it went. No one had ever challenged the Chief Operator and won a dispute about life. I believe that Cornelius must give his position to you. Yes. I will take care of it. To be honest, I thought that the people from above were intelligent enough to use amulets."

He looked at Rick questioningly as he said it.

"We know how to operate machines," Rick said confidently, "but there are so many of them in the world, that each one requires skill and knowledge."

"Of course."

"And what is your position, Arcadius?"

"I am the Brotherhood Mentor. The First Brother. Please excuse me, I must go. Stay here and look around. We will talk more later."

Arcadius respectfully nodded and left before Rick had the time to ask a new question.

Tommo continued to stand in the middle of the room, doing absolutely nothing. Maya fidgeted as she stood, and touched the chair of the Operator.

"Rick..."

"Maya, I am incredibly happy to see you."

They looked at each other for a second and then locked each other in a tight embrace. Rick was uncomfortable with Tommo's presence, so he ordered him to leave. The prole obeyed and quietly stepped out of the room to the walkway

"They kept me in a cage like an animal..." Rick began.

"And I was put on a chain. Then they took me into a hall, a different one to the one where the Red King stands, a smaller one with a well in the middle. They forced me to choose whether to fight, or to jump into the well."

"You won."

"You did too."

"And Ahmed is alive."

"I was so worried about him!"

They went quiet, looking at each other in confusion. Suddenly, there was no need for words and they just held hands, taking pleasure in each others presence and the feeling of being alive.

182

"So what do you think of all this?" Rick asked, indicating the machines.

"This looks like a generator, but Reiner described it as a cylinder, not a sphere."

"This Arcadius said that it's a Reactor. Is there a difference?"

"Yes." Maya furrowed her brow, carefully picking her words. "A reactor produces something, while a generator turns this something into energy."

"I don't understand anything."

"Reiner could explain everything in a simple and understandable way, but I don't know how to do that. Basically, this is not a generator."

"Are you sure?"

Maya walked over to the observation window and looked down for a minute, pressing close to the glass.

"No," she replied. "They have light and heat, but it is not produced here."

"Then what is happening here?"

"We need to take a closer look." Maya approached the control panel and consulted some sort of data on the screen. "The radiation is at a normal level. This means that we can come closer to the sphere."

They came out onto the walkway and stumbled into Tommo.

"Who are you?" Rick demanded. "Tell us

about yourself."

Tommo stayed silent, standing there and looking at them.

"Maybe he is deaf? Or he can't speak?"

"Or maybe he is not human. I saw the way he crawled on walls like a spider. So, who are you?"

But Tommo continued to stare wordlessly at them with his round lenses.

"Our scientist say that in ancient times they were able to make machines that were similar to people. Maybe this is one of them..."

"He is very strange. I would like to know what is hidden under his mask."

"And I don't want to see that at all!"

"I would bet that if he has even a grain of intelligence, he could tell us many things about the people here. What are you looking at? It seems that there is no point to you. Get out of the way, we want to go down below."

Tommo inclined his head to the side, and motioned for them to follow him. Rick and Maya glanced at each other in confusion, but they complied. They whispered to each other behind Tommo's back as they walked.

"We mus be careful..."

"He might have been attached to us to spy on us..."

Meanwhile, Tommo entered the elevator

cabin at the other end of the walkway, waited for his companions and pressed a button, sending the cabin downwards. The cabin crawled slowly, so they could examine the shaft in detail. Weak lights shone around the edges, there were walkways circling the shaft at even intervals and platforms with elevator entrances could be seen here and there. It was becoming not just warm, but hot. The air here was very unlike the moist heat of the jungle—it was more akin to the dry breath of a red-hot oven. The cabin reached the bottom. The sphere looked much bigger from here than it had seemed from above. They followed a stairway into the hall, covering their eyes from the bright shine of the sphere, which was quietly rotating around its axis.

Tommo pointed at a control center identical to the one installed in the room above. Rick and Maya approached a table. The screens shone with pale diagrams and columns of data. A green notice was flickering on the main screen. Maya read it out loud.

"Sleep mode. Awaiting activation using the Omega protocol."

"What does that mean?"

Rick tried to press a button but nothing happened, just a sentence that appeared on the screen.

"Enter access code," Maya read out loud.

"What?"

"Something like a spell, if I speak using terms you would understand. In reality, these are just security passwords. The ancients had them. There was also a book of passwords in our sector, but it burned in the great fire. The scientists remember no more than a dozen."

Maya tried to enter something on the keyboard, but the machine refused.

"It doesn't work."

They started to examine the screens, control panels and the readings on dozens of devices, going from one table to another. Everything was covered with a thick layer of dust. Maya suddenly yelled, knocking over a chair and a large and dusty mass that was in it. There was a crunching sound. Rick rushed over to her side and understood the reason for her alarm—a desiccated mummy lay on the floor. Its clothing had turned to rags through which bones could be seen.

Rick and Maya looked around more carefully—several other mummies could be seen in the chairs and on the floor nearby. An oblong object with a lever and handle at one end and an opening on the other lay by the side of one of them. Rick picked up the object and turned it around in his hands.

"I wonder, what is this?"

"Please be careful!"

"What's the matter?"

"This is a weapon. It could be loaded."

"I saw our Committee members with something similar."

"The ancients used to use these." Maya took the object away from him, looked at the mummies and grimly added, "Rather successfully, so it seems."

Rick was consumed by curiosity. He examined the remains one by one, while Maya was busy at the far end of the hall.

"Look at that. I found it around one of their necks. It's just like my talisman!"

However, Maya was not listening to him, she was entirely engulfed in studying the ancient papers strewn around the table. Rick could not help but think that it was time he learned to read.

"Come over here, quick!" she exclaimed triumphantly. "I think I found it!"

He came closer. Maya unfurled a sizable sheet with a large and incomprehensible diagram. The diagram was divided into five parts, and each part was split into another five. Rick immediately noticed some familiar sigils. He took out his own piece of diagram that he got from Kyoto and put it by the side of the canvas.

"Here!" Maya combined the two diagrams,

and it turned out that Rick's drawing was almost identical to part of the large diagram. They bent over the papers, trying to make out the details and understand their purpose.

"They spoke of the people of Sigma and Tau. And these sectors," Maya tapped her finger on the diagram, "are exactly above Rho sector. There's a label here—"Hydroponic plantations and farms". And opposite Sigma and Tau there are the "Machine production plants. Biotechnology plants". Everything matches. It's so great that I know how to read!"

"So we are moving in the right direction?"

"Yes. And this drawing supports what I guessed—the generator is still a long way away. Here, look, Epsilon sector follows Tau sector, and they have written that it is the "Material synthesizer. Particle accelerator.".".

"What is that?"

"I don't know," Maya shrugged.

Without conspiring, they looked over at the sphere rotating behind the window.

"That is either a synthesizer or an accelerator," Rick said. "There is no third option."

"Brilliant! You're such a genius. But that's not enough. We must find out the details. All of this is in the fourth aeon. The Generator is located in the fifth." She drew her finger to the segment at the edge of the diagram and silently mouthed some words. Then she compared it to Rick's drawing. "Well, that's right. The same symbols. We will need to descend another one hundred and fifty floors."

They had a quiet moment, getting their heads around this fact.

"You know, the more I look at this drawing, the clearer the difference between the aeons is to me," Maya noted. "The lower aeon has a different energy supply system. It is more powerful and advanced."

"The light is brighter," Rick nodded, "and there are more machines."

"It looks like the core of this world."

"The Expanse is full of mysteries..."

"And we stumble into them like blind men, unable to solve them."

"But we will definitely find it all out," Rick said with assurance.

"Are you serious?" Maya seemed to lose all her will and determination.

"Of course! Look at the number of levels we passed already. It sounds strange, but over the last few days I felt... How can I say this? That we can do it. We've got the strength, you understand? We overcame our fear and gone too far to turn back."

"You have changed, Rick from Omicron," Maya looked at him with a new expression. "I must admit I was wrong about you. You could have abandoned us many times, but you didn't do that. I am starting to..."

"No. It is too early to talk about that."

Rick noticed that Tommo came to life and started making signs at them.

"What do you want?" Rick called out in irritation.

Tommo stayed silent and kept making the gestures, first pointing somewhere upwards and then to the side. Rick did not understand what he wanted to say. Meanwhile, Maya started to collect all of the papers she could find on the table, excitedly muttering to herself under her breath.

"These are priceless treasures. Many would give their lives just to read these manuscripts. We must take them with us!"

"You won't be able to take all of it."

"I will take what I can. It seems I can't rely on the help of a certain someone."

Rick breathed heavily, but started to help her with the papers. They raised a whole cloud of dust and started coughing. Rick was rolling the papers into tubes and grumbling.

"Don't forget that we are now members of the Brotherhood and we need to think what to do about that. We can't just get up and leave. I suspect that the traditions are a little strict here.

Come on, what do you actually want?" he got distracted by Tommo again.

The prole was jumping in front of them, getting in their way. Something had alarmed him. Only now did Maya and Rick hear the noise coming from above. It sounded like rats scurrying through the ventilation shafts—still far away, but the sounds were getting louder and louder.

"Damn!" Rick slapped himself on the forehead. "I think I understand. We have left the post."

"Time to return."

They wanted to return to the walkway by the sphere, but Tommo kept stubbornly pointing in the opposite direction to the door which led out of the room on the other side. The noise became louder. Maya jumped out onto the walkway anyhow, and looked up.

"Someone has come to the post. They are busily running around. They are coming down here."

Logic dictated a simple solution—to walk up to meet Arcadius and his men. But something in Tommo's gestures said the opposite. Rick's inner sense suggested that the prole was worried for a reason and that he was trying to warn them.

"Rick, we must go back."

"Yes, but first, we must find out what's over there."

"Where are you going?" She looked at him in astonishment.

Rick did not waste time on explaining. He followed Tommo into a narrow rectangular room, which mostly looked like a storeroom. The room was filled with identical gray cabinets with a sign and number on each. Tommo slid along them so quickly, that Rick almost lost sight of him. He ran after the prole and found himself on a small platform with a chair in the middle. It was an unusual chair—it was large, massive, and fixed on a rounded raised area, with a powerful back and armrests, full of complex devices. But the most amazing was the helmet, which hung down from the ceiling right above where the head would be.

Tommo indicated the chair.

"What is this?"

Tommo stayed silent. Rick sighed. It was pointless to ask. He approached the chair, touched the cold plastic, the metallic joints and the coils of wire. The device did not look broken. It was only that it was covered with a thick layer of dust, like all the other surfaces. Rick stroked the shaped plating with his fingers and he was overcome with the feeling of something familiar, as if his hands had muscle memory and had already once interacted with a complex device of this kind. But in which way? Rick looked at his hands, and did not understand. Shouts could be heard from the large hall. Maya ran into the room.

"They're already here!" Then she stood still. "What is this?"

They had no more than a minute. Rick jumped into the chair. He did not know what he was expecting. He just felt that he was doing the right thing, imagining himself in the place of the unknown ancient operator that said his technical spells here and entered mysterious passwords to command the machines. His hands found the niches by themselves and the back softly adjusted itself to the form of his body. Rick brushed the remains of the dust away with his elbows and stared at the small screen in front of him. A dot appeared, which quickly grew into a red semicircle and then closed into a full circle which turned green just as fast. Then, the circle disappeared and the outline of a human palm appeared.

They heard approaching shouts: "Where are they?", "They're here!", "Look for them!", "I warned you!". Rick placed his palm inside the shape on the monitor. A blue line ran upwards across the screen, the screen blinked green and a notification appeared.

"Maya! Hurry and write what's written here!"

""Genetic code confirmed". How did you do

this?"

"No idea. Here's another sentence. Hurry and read!"

Their pursuers had already burst into the storehouse and ran past the cabinets, shouting, "This place is forbidden!" "You mustn't!"

"Chronos program in operation. Select or modify program: Gaia, Chronos, Uranus."

Rick thought for a moment and then tapped on "Uranus".

"Uranus program selected," Maya read out hurriedly. "Recharge of batteries, generators, air supply stores and water completed. Activate external shell? Yes—No."

Rick had already guessed that a red square meant denial, while the green meant confirmation. He pressed the green one.

"Maya! Be quick and read!"

Burly men in dirty yellow robes ran out from the rows of cabinets and pushed Tommo away. Their fierce faces turned to the chair.

Arcadius screamed from the door, "Stop them!"

"Launch particle accelerator? Yes—No."

And Rick pressed on the green square before he was dragged out of the chair and thrown to the floor. Arcadius was red in the face from his run, and stood opposite them, breathing heavily. It took him a minute to come to himself—his hands trembled and his cheeks shook.

Suddenly, a low rumbling sound started to grow behind the wall. Arcadius grabbed Rick by the front of his suit and shouted, "What have you done? Answer me!" He shook Rick furiously in a moment of rage, but quickly ran out of breath and threw him down. "It is forbidden to enter here! This is the holy place of the Reactor, and you have desecrated it! It is all my fault. I should have left guards with you. What have you just done? Tell me! Just tell me!"

Arcadius was almost begging in desperation.

"You have committed a crime! Now god's wrath awaits us all! We will have to punish you and this trollop. Pray, pagans, to all the gods that you believe or don't believe in. You will beg me for a quick death. The test before the Red King will seem like child's play compared to what I will do to you! Ah, ah, ah! Oh, oh, oh, mighty Reactor, forgive us!"

Arcadius had finally completely lost control. He ran around the chair, but then gave his clothing a sharp tug to put it in order and calmed down, addressing Rick again, who was by then being held tight by the elbows.

"Listen. I have allowed myself a weakness. Let's forget about it all. Of course, there is no reason for us to give you to the Reactor, if you put everything back. Tell me, what did you just do? Tell me all you know about machines. I give my word that I will let you go."

The room fell silent. The rumble of the sphere behind the window changed, growing quieter, but having a more intense quality to it than before, as well as being a tone higher.

A worker entered the room and said, "Mentor! The amulets are all lit and they blink with holy lights. The Reactor has become brighter, and everything is full of light!"

Rick saw that it took Arcadius a superhuman effort to remain calm.

"Good." He turned to Rick. "I am listening."

"I will tell you everything, but let's go upstairs. The Reactor will be fine."

Arcadius was about to open his mouth, but Rick added, "I give my word, the same as you gave to us. The Reactor is safe."

The Mentor glanced at him dully and motioned for everyone to leave.

11

"SO," Arcadius said, looking at Maya and Rick, "I am listening to you carefully."

Around an hour had passed since they were taken out of the underground storeroom. Rick demanded food and water, as well as a meeting with Ahmed. Only once he was sure that the dark skinned engineer was held in decent conditions and nothing was threatening him did he agree to talk.

Rick's tale was short and to the point. He told the whole truth. Arcadius obviously did not think so. Eyes full of doubt, with his arms crossed on his chest, he listened to the story of Rick's escape downwards with his new friends, Yarg's camp, the empty levels of sector Pi, the wild jungles and their denizens and the way that the runaways finally understood that they will reach their target.

"And that is all."

Rick took a glass of water from the table and downed it.

"Fine. What were you doing in the storeroom?"

"I just sat in the chair. I suddenly really wanted to."

Arcadius watched him intently.

"I sat down," Rick continued, "touched the buttons, and then this thing started to blink. I was afraid, so I tried to switch it off, but I never did it in time, because that oaf," and Rick pointed at the guard standing a step away from him, "threw me down on the floor and pulled my hand behind my back. He left a bruise, by the way."

Rick demonstrated his bruise to everyone present. The guard grinned with pleasure. Arcadius looked back at Rick, whose only desire was actually to get some decent sleep.

"You are lying," Arcadius said. "Tell me true, what did you do and why?"

"I am telling the truth."

Arcadius gritted his teeth. He looked at Maya and back at Rick.

"Let met tell you about our Brotherhood, so you understand where you have ended up and why we are so worried about this issue."

According to Arcadius, the history of the Brotherhood stretched over many centuries and began at the moment of the great epidemic of an unknown disease. The safety system turned on and separated the worker's sectors from the upper and lower aeons, and the residents of these sectors knew nothing of the fate of other humans since then. No one tried to communicate with them for a very long time. This is why the workers of Sigma and Tau considered themselves the only survivors. Fear of the unknown infection became part of their consciousness. The aeon survives due to the great Reactor—it provides the people with heat and light and sustains the machines that produce food, transport cargo and passengers and do a lot of other important jobs. The wisest men were selected among the workers, who started to call themselves Mentors and solve all of the most important issues, from food supplies to pipe repair. The aeon survived without any significant events for a while. Several generations of people changed.

Then, the machine responsible for heat distribution in Pi and Rho sectors got damaged as a result of one of the internecine wars. It was a disaster. Many died. Even more suffered as a result of burns and a terrible illness that seemed to dry a man out from inside—their hair fell out, their bodies quickly lost moisture and the affected person turned into a walking mummy. The zone around the accident became forbidden. Some escaped upwards, and some downwards. The Brotherhood attempted expeditions above several times, but all that returned later became sick and died from the same illness. The higher levels started to be considered cursed. No one went there anymore. The life of the Sigma and Tau Brotherhood was entirely dependent on the machines and the Reactor. If the Reactor would break down, everyone would face slow agony and death.

"Do you understand our concern now?"

"Completely. But my Commune and Kappa Order are in a far worse situation. The people of my homeland are already dying of the cold and going blind in the darkness."

Arcadius nodded, with a look of concern, and asked, "So what did you do to the Reactor?"

"It is not a reactor, it is a particle accelerator."

"What?" Judging by his facial expression, Arcadius did not understand.

Rick patiently repeated himself.

"The true source of energy is located far deeper, on a lower level. That is where we are going, to switch it to full power and bring our whole world back to life. Then we can forget about the issue of the cold. There will be enough energy for everyone, do you understand? Everyone will have as much heat and light as they want. We passed through the jungle, we managed to do that, so we have nothing more to fear. All the peoples of the world must unite to achieve one aim."

Arcadius, who had obviously cheered up, was listening and nodding along. Once Rick finished, he asked, "So how do I control the Reactor? Teach me how to do that."

"I only managed to do it randomly. I have no idea how it happened."

"Maybe we should go down there and try again?"

Rick became wary of Arcadius' insistent requests, but he tried not to show it, turning to Maya, then glancing at the guard and back at

Arcadius.

"Do you think I can do it?"

"I have no doubt!" Arcadius declared.

"And what about Cornelius? Does he know nothing about the Reactor?"

Arcadius waved dismissively.

"All he thinks about is fighting and entertaining himself. He is rather stupid. Well then, shall we go?"

"Not now."

Arcadius motioned to the guard, who separated himself from the wall. Two others that were waiting by the doors also came into the room.

Rick understood that he had made a mistake by calming the Brotherhood Mentor, as Arcadius was now sure that the Brotherhood was in no danger and that he did not need those who came from above. Rick nodded to Maya and said, "Fine."

He made an approving gesture and assessed the situation in the room at the same time.

It would all be a matter of seconds now.

"Now, that's better." Arcadius arose from the table. "Don't forget that we are looking after your third companion. We don't want to do evil to anyone."

"Neither do we," Maya replied. "Which is why you will let us go, right now."

"And why would we do that?"

Maya took the weapon she picked up below from underneath her clothing and pointed it at Arcadius, "Because of this. A single movement, and your brains will spatter the walls."

Arcadius laughed.

"Where did you pick up this toy? Down below? It is a useless piece of metal."

"I don't think so," Maya pressed a lever on the handle and the room was lit up with a flash of light, as a crackling bolt of lightning hit the wall by the Mentor.

Arcadius face immediately changed.

"Now, all of you must go to the far corner," Maya ordered. "Quick!"

Rick watched out that they would have a free path to the door, and stepped towards the exit—there was no one in the corridor apart from Tommo.

"What are you going to achieve?" Arcadius spoke up again. "Where will you go? Up above? There is nothing below apart from emptiness and monsters. You have nowhere to run."

"That's none of your business," Maya countered. "Stay in place, and count to a hundred. Slowly."

Rick waited for her to leave the room and barred it from the other side.

"Run," Maya whispered.

Tommo immediately followed them.

"How did you manage to use the weapon?" asked Rick on the way.

"I just entered all the codes I could remember in advance. We were lucky."

They took a turn at a junction, and Rick came to a sudden stop, turning to Tommo.

"Can I trust you?"

The prole, who stood still opposite him quickly nodded, but Rick had no time to say anything to him as a siren blared in the corridor. Red emergency lights started blinking and a mechanical metallic voice began intoning, "Alert! We are under attack! Alert! We are under attack! All workers must gather in the main halls. Defense forces must occupy the top level!"

The worried residents of the sector started running around the corridors. Rick ordered Tommo to take them to Ahmed and they ran after the prole. The siren continued to blare, inspiring fear and putting pressure on their eardrums. Rick and Maya nearly lost each other in the commotion and the push of the crowds at another junction. They once mistook another prole for Tommo and had to double back, but it was fine in the end, and the three of them continued on their way.

"Alert! There has been an attack!" the metallic voice sounded again from the ceiling.

"There are infiltrators in a sector! A young male accompanied by a red haired woman! Apprehend them and terminate them! I repeat..."

Tommo turned at a junction, taking the escapees into an empty corridor.

"Hey, you! Halt!" they heard behind their back.

Rick looked back to see two men rushing after them.

"They're here!" the first of the men shouted. "Get them!"

The two men threw themselves towards them. Rick met the first with a fist to the jaw, but the second was faster and tackled them both to the ground. It turned into a brawl. Maya rushed to Rick's help, but the locals were joined by several other men. The situation was becoming desperate. Tommo tried to help, but got quickly pushed away as they started to beat the escapees. Rick covered up with his hands, shouting to Maya that she should no resist—they had no way of getting out of a narrow corridor filled with that many people.

Suddenly, the strikes came less often and they heard worried shouts. Rick managed to get up—new participants entered the struggle. Several proles quickly cleared the space around Rick, Maya and Tommo in perfect coordination. Cornelius stood behind the proles, swinging a sledgehammer.

"Get out of here!" he shouted at the workers. "Get lost, if you value your lives!"

This worked, and the men ran back behind the corner, freeing the way.

Cornelius glanced at Rick.

"I owe you something. Your life in exchange for mine. And I always pay my debts."

"Thank you. How do we get down below?" Rick immediately moved on to the main issue.

"Follow me."

Cornelius flashed a predatory grin. Rick could not understand whether the former Operator was happy because he got into a fight with the workers, or just because he could spite Arcadius.

They ran after Cornelius, who led them through empty corridors, constantly turning to get them away from busy places.

Rick finally managed to orient himself—they were running towards the periphery, where the air became colder and there was a perceptible draft. They could hear the wind howl in the ventilation shafts. Cornelius stopped at the end of the radial corridor.

"This is where we need to go," he said, pressing a button on the panel with a Tau sector glyph. The door panel on the wall slid to the side, opening a cargo elevator.

"Get lively!"

People appeared in the corridor far away, screaming as they ran.

The escapees entered the elevator, and the cabin rapidly surged downwards as soon as the panel closed. Rick only just managed to grab a railing, while the prole saved Maya from falling. After passing around ten levels, Cornelius gave the lever on the panel a sharp tug, making the elevator come to a smooth stop and they ran outside. There was a corridor which was nearly identical to the previous one, save for the two paneled gates blocking entry. Cornelius approached the control levers on the panel. Rick thought that he started to understand where they were.

"Does this door lead to the edge of the Expanse?"

"What?" Cornelius did not understand. "It leads to the parapet. Let's get a breath of fresh air!"

Rick had no time to reply, when Cornelius pulled the lever. The panels slid open, letting gusts of wind and snowflakes into the corridor. Frosty air blew into Rick's face so strongly, that he could not even normally breathe out at first. His eyes and nose were immediately covered in snow. The bright white light was blinding. Rick shut his eyes—the radiance beyond the gates was brighter than a hundred of the most powerful lamps and was painful even through his tightly shut eyelids.

"Move your asses!" Cornelius roared and gave Rick a sharp pull on his sleeve. "Take this and put it on. Hurry up!"

He threw Rick a thick jumpsuit and a pair of gloves and got another for Maya from the locker by the open panel. Then he took coils of cable, carabiner clips and torches for everyone and started getting changed himself.

"Wait!" Rick shouted to him. "We have another friend! We can't leave him behind!"

"That black one?" Cornelius zipped up his jumpsuit with one swift movement and took up the cables again. "My proles will take care of him!"

Cornelius gave each of them a torch, explained how to use them and ordered them to put the torches in their pockets. Then, he attached the carabiner clips to Rick and Maya's belts, passed the cables through them, and silently disappeared into the white mist. Tommo followed suit.

"Rick, I'm afraid!" Maya shouted.

"Me too! Let's do this together!"

They held hands and stepped into the unknown.

12

RICK THOUGHT that they were about to fall and plunge into eternity. However, he felt a hard surface beneath his feet, and Maya and Tommo were also by his side. Far away, they could make out the silhouettes of Cornelius and the rest of the proles. Rick caught his breath and looked around.

His eyes no longer hurt as much—something was strange about the surrounding space. The three vertical flat surfaces, the walls that he was used to, were not there. The ceiling could not be seen either. It was like an unfinished sketch of the world, as if some unknown creator had not completed what they started, having only created the floor and the wall behind his back. The thought of them simply not existing made Rick's head spin. He held onto the wall and stood still, not daring to move on. The wind fiercely threw handfuls of prickly snow in his face, but this did not stop him—the platform ahead ended in twenty paces, and ended in a looming abyss. Rick looked into the unknown beyond the edge, and the white Expanse seemed to be laughing at him. Maybe there was so much snow that the ceiling and walls could not be seen? That's what he wanted to think. It was probably just a very big internal space, greater than all that he had seen and all of them put together, but which definitely had a normal floor, ceiling and walls. Yes, there was definitely no doubt about it.

The panels hummed behind his back and closed.

That was it, there was no way back.

"How are you?" He turned to Maya.

Her face was covered in snow and her eyes were two narrow slits.

"All right." She barely moved her lips.

Cornelius returned and worriedly examined them."What, haven't you been outside before?" he shouted over the wind.

Rick shook his head.

"Stand one behind the other!"

Then he dragged Rick after him, while Tommo helped Maya detach herself from the wall and follow them. They crossed the platform and jumped down onto the ramp, walking along for a while until they met two of Cornelius' proles. The proles were standing beneath a massive vertical cutaway section, which went away from the wall and downwards at a sharp angle. The cutaway looked a little like a gigantic, vertical fin. A fragile looking ladder led to the spine of that fin. One of the proles was already hanging from it, using the carabiner clips to attach the cable to its bars. Another was laying wide metallic plates on the ground.

"Here!" Cornelius pointed at the place where the wall met the fin. "Let's rest."

The whole company rested against the wall, waiting for the gusts of wind to subside.

"Now what?" Cornelius spoke again. "Are you going to descend? This is the quickest way. The proles once tried it out, and we followed them. The mechanism is simple—you take a plate, stand on it, fix your feet to it with belts and slide downwards. Then it all depends on your dexterity and reaction time. The main thing is to brake in time."

"How do we do that?" Rick asked.

Cornelius showed them a large hook attached by a carabiner clip to the coil of cable behind his back.

"There are large loops attached to the wall at even intervals. You must catch a loop with the hook as you go and turn to the side. The table will be taught and jerk upwards, so you will hang on it. You must immediately hook the nearest loop with the second hook, or you will fall off and fall downwards. All understood?"

"Have you ever gone down there, to the very bottom?"

Cornelius roared with laughter.

"Do I look suicidal? Death is below. Any fool knows that."

"But what is there?" Rick continued questioning.

"Nothing! A desert!" Cornelius laughed. "That's the thing!"

Rick stared into the white mist in disappointment.

"The final frontier is at level two hundred and fifty. There is a smooth surface beyond, with no windows, doors, ladders, nothing. Then, that vertical cutaway," he indicated the proles on the ladder, "veers off and goes far from the wall. Only the cutaway is connected to the wall by a narrow walkway. You must stop when you see the walkway. As soon as you see it, you must brake, or you will fly into the abyss, from which there is no way out. There is a ramp by the walkway, and my prole will wait for you below. Watch and learn! Hey, Thomas, are you ready?"

The prole, who had climbed onto the spine of the fin, had already jumped onto his plate. He turned and gestured to confirm his readiness.

"Onwards!"

The prole crouched and started to slide downwards on the plate. At first, he went slowly and then started to speed up more and more. Everyone tensely watched him become smaller as he receded into the distance, an orange spot flying along the spine, until he disappeared in the mist.

"Did you see that? There's a snowstorm right now, otherwise you would see him anchor himself."

"There's no way we will manage this..." Rick moaned.

"Your choice. But I'd advise you to hurry up."

Maya took Rick by the hand.

"Listen. I had no time to say this earlier..."

"What are you talking about? Take a plate."

"No, Rick, wait."

"What?"

"When we were there below, when you activated the external shell and particle accelerator and then got apprehended, I managed to read a message on the screen."

Rick froze.

"What message?"

"There was a question there—"Activate full generator power? Yes—No."

"Right..."

"But that's not all. There was an addition— "Activation is synchronized with the Control Center." "Synchronized" means at the same time."

"The Control Center?"

"Yes. I looked at the maps." Maya took a folded diagram out of her suit and showed him a fragment. "The Control Center is at the top. Do you understand? At the very top!"

"Are you sure?"

"Yes!"

"What are you talking about?" Cornelius asked. "Why did you even need to descend?"

Rick gave him a quick account of the purpose of their journey.

"So why don't you stay here? I will break the neck of that upstart Arcadius and everything will be fine, as before!"

"And what about my people? And what about Maya's kinsmen?"

"We'll work something out!" Cornelius stated confidently. "Let them move and live with us. Together, we can defeat the mutants and destroy the monsters in the jungle."

For a moment, Rick though that this was the right solution. Why go through many problems, trials and dangers? They could unite with the people of Sigma and Tau. But how would Croesus react? What would the councilmen of Kappa sector decide? Would the people of these sectors even want to go off on this journey, when even going beyond the barrier on their own level fills them with terror. And even if you allowed for everything to pass without casualties, and there was enough energy for their lifetimes, what would be the fate of their descendants? What would happen when all of the generators of the world would run out, sending the Expanse into cold and darkness?

"Everything sounds so easy when you say it. But my answer is "No". If we need to go up, then this is the way it will be."

"You're really strange, guys," Cornelius shrugged his shoulders. "But it really is more fun this way! I like you. I wanted to tear you to pieces in the morning, but you are full of surprises, Rick from Omicron!"

"Excellent, I'm really glad. Now show us how to climb upwards."

"Wait. You want to know how to get to the very top? Did I understand you right!"

"Yes!" Rick exclaimcd.

"You really are completely insane!" Cornelius yelled. "That's amazing!"

He called the snowstorm to witness, but it only answered him with a wistful howl and new gusts of wind.

"Hey, Bram!" he shouted to the second prole that stood by the ladder to the spine. Take them up the ladder to the end of sector Pi and show them the entrance. When you come back, I will be waiting behind the airlock. Don't even think of crawling up all the way on the surface—you will turn into icicles. Good luck! And I have to deal with someone. I shall wash the face of the Red King with his blood. I swear by the Reactor!"

They immediately understood that he was talking about Arcadius.

"Thank you, Cornelius!" Rick offered him his hand.

Cornelius spat to the side and gave him a firm handshake.

"We're quits," Rick smiled. "If you cross me again, expect no mercy."

"That's a deal."

They disconnected their carabiner clamps from the cable. Bram the prole took them along the fin to the edge of the abyss and opened an inconspicuous lid on the wall, rummaged around inside the niche and a secret panel opened in the wall. The prole called them over with a wave of his hand, disappeared into the opening, and they followed him inside. They found themselves in a narrow corridor that pierced through the fin under the spine. The prole had already opened an identical panel on the other side, and calmly walked along the ramp, as if the snow, frost and piercing wing did not bother him. Rick noticed that the ramp had a barely perceptible bend to it in the distance, which supported the theory of the world being round yet again. He got a little used to the wrongness of outside space and thanked the snowstorm for hiding the truth from his eyes.

They soon passed some protruding five level

high signs with the letters "IV". Rick was examining the detail of the wall, noting every seam, cavity and other useful detail. At last, the prole stopped and pointed up at some rungs that were fixed to the wall, and started to climb them. Rick followed, then Maya, and Tommo followed at the back.

The ascent seemed easy to Rick at first. However, he started to feel tired once they had passed twenty levels. One look below was enough to make him press himself into the rungs—the wall stretched away into infinity. Rick was overcome by his fear of heights, just like he felt during the Spring Run, when he was with his opponents were on an open walkway bctwccn sector segments.

Mother Darkness, but that was so long ago!

He looked down again. Maya was looking up at him with concern, with Tommo visible behind her back.

"What happened?"

"I just need a little rest! That's all."

"Good."

He continued the ascent, but his fingers grew increasingly numb from the cold with every level. The cold penetrated through his gloves and turned his hands to ice. Soon, he had almost stopped feeling his fingers, his feet felt like logs in his boots and his fear of falling grew, but Rick clenched his teeth and kept climbing, looking at the prole ahead.

All of a sudden, Maya cried out. Rick turned around, pressing his body close to the rungs. Tommo was holding the girl by the belt. If it was not for the prole, Maya would have plunged into the abyss. Tommo helped her grab onto the rungs again and start moving ahead, and their company continued the climb.

The cold inexorably did its job. Rick's consciousness started to wonder and he no longer felt the frost, but wanted to just stop and go to sleep. His movements slowed down. Rick yawned, wanted to smile, and then suddenly slipped. Understanding only returned when he collapsed downwards but a strong pair of hands grabbed him by the scruff of his suit and dragged him upwards.

Bram the prole took him onto an even platform and helped him get onto the platform with Maya. The proles moved them over to the wall and started to rub their extremities, and that is when two minutes passed and Rick felt a terrible pain. He groaned loudly, and continued groaning until he felt his strength return. The proles continued to rub at their numb arms and legs.

Rick turned his head towards Maya and asked, "How are you?"

"Better. A lot better."

"Do you think we are there yet?"

"I don't know..."

After a few minutes, the proles helped them to get up and pointed at a ramp which was covered in snow. They needed to walk. For some reason, it started to get colder and darker.

And again, a procession along a ramp. There was a place where they had to climb over a snowdrift as high as two men. The snow lay there in a thick crust, which made it difficult to get onto the crest as their hands and feet kept slipping. That is when the proles saved them again, tying the cables as safety harnesses around them and dragging them upwards. Rick and Maya armed themselves with hooks so that they could stab them into the snow and ice and not fall off.

The ramp soon grew significantly wider and the going became easier, as they could walk around the snowdrifts instead of having to climb over them like a wall, but the snow was so deep in some places that their feet got stuck in it as if it was mud, so fatigue eventually took its toll.

"Wait!" Maya shouted.

Her echoing cry came back from all sides.

Bram stopped and Rick turned around. The girl was stuck to her waist in a pile of snow. Tommo tried to get her out, but managed to get himself truly stuck as well.

"I'm coming!" Rick shouted in reply, but then stood still, listening.

A distant rumble coming from above made him wary. Rick raised his head and saw a cloud of white dust coming quickly headlong at them. Rick never had the time to get scared—Bram sprung up to him and grabbed him by the sleeve to pull him to the side, closer to the wall. Tommo managed to get out of the snow at the last moment and protect Maya with his body, when the ramp was covered with an avalanche of snow.

Rick realized what happened when Bram used his back to push through the heavy layer of snow above them, helped him get to the surface and immediately started to dig into the snow nearby.

"Maya!" Rick called out. "Where are you? Maya!"

Bram kept digging at the snow, and Rick started to help him. They dug deeper and deeper, going in different directions, but they still could not manage to find Tommo or Maya.

Suddenly, they heard a piercing whistle— that was Bram signaling that he had found a boot. Rick went over to him, and Tommo soon appeared out of the pile of snow, who then carefully got Maya out onto the surface. The girl was unconscious. They took her closer to the wall where the wind was weaker, and Bram started to massage Maya's chest.

Rick prayed to the Machine God, squeezing his talisman in his hand. He would have agreed to become a slave, walk into a chasm or let any monster kill or tear him into pieces so Maya would survive. And then a miracle happened— Maya coughed once, then twice, then again and again. Bram quickly turned her onto her stomach and the girl vomited, but then started to take quick, hoarse breaths.

The snowstorm continued, but the wind started to lose its strength and stopped throwing handfuls of snow into their faces. The snowflakes now softly fell, dancing around in circles.

The company had to take a long break. Maya was only able to get up after half an hour and they continued on their way when the light had almost gone. Now Rick was always close, supporting her by the arm. They carefully walked along the balcony, and Rick was afraid to talk about what would happen once darkness came.

The proles soon stood still by a pile of snow by the wall—the outline of a door could barely be glimpsed just above. The proles started to clear the snow, with Maya and Rick immediately joining in. Rick wanted to get behind the wall as soon as possible, far away from the ice cold air. Together, they quickly finished the job. The proles opened a wall panel and started to try to force a massive lever, trying to move it from an upward to a downward position. They finally managed, as the frozen metal squeaked plaintively and gave, turning with a crunch—the panel on the wall drew back with a loud hiss and then moved aside.

Maya and Tommo stepped into the dark opening. Rick paused.

"Thank you," he told Bram, who stood inertly upon the platform.

"There is something I forgot to tell Cornelius," Rick continued. "Please, tell him my words, as it is very important. Tell him that we will definitely return and that he should prepare to meet us." He remembered that proles could not speak and added, "Try and explain my words to him."

He heard a click nearby—it was Tommo, who turned the switch on the wall so that the panel returned to its rightful place, cutting Rick off from Bram and the external Expanse. They were enveloped by darkness, but Maya lit a torch in a few seconds. Rick remembered that Cornelius also gave him one and was about to get it from his pocket, but Maya proposed conserving the light and he agreed. Tired, he sat down against the wall, getting used to his surroundings.

Rick's eyes hurt, which was all because of the unexpectedly bright light outside, which initially blinded him as he was not used to it. However, once darkness fell, he felt normal again. He bent his legs, hugged them and rested his chin on his knees. He closed his eyes. Maya was doing something by his side, trying to arrange a place by the wall. Rick could clearly hear Tommo walk off down the corridor—he probably went to reconnoiter what lay ahead.

Rick never noticed going to sleep, and when he woke up he spent a while in silence, blinking and staring at Maya. She was sitting by his side and studying papers, lighting them with the torch.

Rick coughed, and heard, "Good morning."

Maya smiled at him sadly. The lines of her face became more expressive in the light of the torch. Her eyes were shining.

"Can I have a look too?" Rick asked, moving closer.

"Yes."

Maya turned the sheets to him, which had blackened at the folds. Some looked strong and smooth, but time had erased almost all the glyphs from them, turning them into smudged spots of ink. However, the paper was good at retaining drawings and letters, but it was very fragile, so they handled it very carefully to prevent tearing. Maya carefully went through the pages, holding them by the edge, raising them to the light and quietly reading out the ancient words.

"Generates any element of the periodic table... Works using the same principles as a 3D printer... The computer calculates the required proportions of a substance according to specifications... Control data is entered. Right. Particle accelerator. Distributes energy throughout the external and internal shells... Intended for the completion of the Uranus program. Technical data... Power, acceleration speed, core... Next."

"Anything interesting?"

"Wait. I need to work it out."

She continued to read, quietly mumbling under her nose. Rick sat alongside her for a while, but he soon got bored and started to examine the corridor, which turned out not to be that long after all.

"Has Tommo not been back for a while?" Rick asked.

"I haven't seen him since I went to sleep," Maya continued to be busy with the papers and did not even lift her head.

Rick got a little worried.

"Did we sleep long?"

Maya only shrugged.

He understood. Rick turned away and got his torch out.

The room in which they had found themselves turned out to be a spacious airlock that was obviously there for a technical purpose—the walls were covered with wires and communication lines. Rick opened a familiar panel on the wall and managed to understand the symbol above one of the switches, which let him easily open the internal door to step through into an extremely long tunnel. The walls floor and ceiling ran far away to become points, with the pillar of the Chorda visible far ahead. This was the space between aeons, the home of mutants. The same hoarfrost and the same familiar blue light. A human shape suddenly appeared ahead and he heard the sound of footsteps.

Rick almost cried out, but he recognized Tommo and breathed out in relief.

"How are things?"

Tommo stood by his side and looked back in the tunnel. His ocular lenses glinted like two red dots.

"Let's consider that everything is fine," Rick decided.

He intently listened to the shining cold twilight, but nothing disturbed the hollow darkness apart from a depressing draft. He did not seem to hear the voices of mutants anywhere, or the sound of fires or steps. It seemed like the mutants had abandoned this place. They might have gone to war down below. Rick wondered if the dwarf had followed them, or whether Yarg had abandoned the old and weak to the vagaries of fate. Rick remembered the dwarf's words—"The Omega is not the end, but a beginning!"

The sound of a closing door distracted him from his thoughts. Tommo still stood by the panel, flicking the switches, so the room was soon full with the light of the lamps.

Maya looked up at the ceiling in surprise and turned off her torch. Rick only shrugged.

"I have studied the papers," she said. "And something has become clear."

"Tell me," he got excited and sat down by her side.

Maya pointed at a large diagram, which was carefully laid down and smoothed out.

"We are extremely lucky that we came across a diagram of the whole world." She pointed her finger between the third and fourth segments. "We are here. Here, where the base is wide, is the ground. The very first level."

"So the chasm does have a bottom."

"Don't interrupt. Now look over here, at the opposite, narrow end—this is the top. The top of the world. This is all of Thermopolis. And it's absolutely gigantic. The floors and levels are shown here on the side. There are one thousand, two hundred and fifty floors in our world! Just imagine this number. Thermopolis is divided into five large parts, called aeons, each of which contains two hundred and fifty floors. Every aeon contains five sectors, with fifty floors per sector. And all of these floors are pierced by the Axis from the bottom to the top. We suspected that every sector is called after a letter of some ancient alphabet, but now we have documented proof. And the main thing is that we know where everything is located. Do you understand?"

Rick carefully examined the diagram.

"Here is your Omicron sector, for instance. Let's read what it says: "Residential sector. Avenues and park zone.""

"It looks like they are talking about our farm."

"Of course! Your ancestors dug plots in the parkland throughout the sector. This saved your lives. And now my sector, Kappa. "Residential sector," and nothing more. But we have warehouses of ancient supplies, which I will tell you about sometimes."

"I see. And where is that Control Center you spoke of?"

"Here!" she pointed at the highest point of the diagram. Gamma sector. "Control Center.""

"Is that all?"

"What else do you need? I could not find detailed descriptions. The rest of the papers describe the structure of the particle accelerator and material synthesizer. Formulas and clusters of numbers everywhere that even I find hard to understand. I am sure we will be able to find out much more once we get there."

"All right. Let's say that we know where we're going. But before we set off, you must teach me two things. Firstly, reading and secondly, how to use that ancient weapon that you carry in your pocket. If I don't know these things, it could cost us both our lives."

Maya nodded. First, she explained the inner workings and principles behind the weapon which fired bursts of energy. Rick quickly caught on and overcame his fear of technology. His hand easily laid on the handle and his finger wanted to touch the trigger. Yet again, he felt a feeling of familiarity, the same way as he did when he sat in the Operator's Chair. He hurried to share his thoughts with Maya.

"This is curious," she said. "I can't say for sure that I have the same thing, but sometimes I somehow manage to understand the inner workings and mechanics of ancient artifacts that I study without any outside explanations. This always surprised Reiner, because I often described devices using words which were the same as those used in ancient sources. This was possibly the reason he took me into the unit. He sometimes spoke about some sort of mission or purpose for humanity, but he formulated it in such an abstract way that it was difficult to understand. All I understood was that people like you and me were chosen for something. That is exactly what he said—the future of humanity is in the hands of the new generation. He said that we were far more intelligent and able than older people."

Next, Maya started to teach Rick the basics of the alphabet. She spoke the letters and Rick kept diligently repeating them. They spent half a day studying, while Tommo stayed silent and stood by the instrument panel by the door all of this time.

"Well, then," Maya said at last. "That's enough for today. We should set off."

She looked at the prole. He seemed to have been waiting for the order, as he turned off the light and opened the door.

They left the airlock and stepped into the space between the aeons. They walked along, as the hoarfrost crackled underfoot and the walls lazily blinked their bluish reflections.

"This is amazing," Maya said. "Just imagine, how much effort it took to create all of this."

"For me, it's hard to imagine that our word

never existed once upon a time," Rick admitted.

"But that's the truth."

And they moved along and quietly thought about everything they found out over the last few days. Rick told Maya about the last words that the dwarf said to him, about Omega.

"Not the end, but a beginning," Maya repeated thoughtfully. "The end, because it is the last letter of the alphabet. The next sector is called "Aqua". The water reservoirs are located there. Why is it a beginning, if the letters start from the top? Hmm..."

"Maybe he was making fun of me or wanted to confuse me."

"We must consider every option. We can't discard any version until we prove it wrong..."

Suddenly, Rick froze in place. Just before, he had glanced aside and noticed a huge sitting human figure with its head lowered in the gloom that filled a large niche. The figure was five levels high and Rick would have barely reached its ankles. Maya also noticed the figure and suddenly went quiet. They stood there for a minute, trying to understand what this giant signified. The figure remained still.

For some reason, Rick remembered the bust of the Red King at the top of the column. Everything was different here, but... The fear had gone, and Rick was now looking at the armored giant with great curiosity. There was a helmet on the giant's head. The metal gave off a midnight blue shine. Time passed, the giant never moved and Tommo calmly approached it, stood by its feet and waved to his companions.

Rick pulled Maya by the hand, saying, "It's just a metal statue. Don't be afraid."

They stood before the sculpture, looking up from below. The face of the giant was hidden behind a visor, with a narrow slit in place of eyes. Its hands were covered in fingerless gloves, making the hands into claws.

"I know!" Maya said, and smiled. "I know what this is."

She fearlessly climbed up the leg onto the giant's knees and started to read the words inscribed on its chest.

"EXOMECH C30010Z. It's an ancient machine. A man used to get inside and control it to carry heavy loads."

Rick imagined a monster like that coming to life and shuddered. On the other hand, it was logical—the walls surrounding them could only have been built with the help of machines such as that one. He helped the girl get back down to the floor. They stood there a while longer, and continued on their way.

"The ancients were as powerful as gods," Maya said. "There's yet more proof."

"Maybe they actually were gods," chuckled Rick.

They saw piles of trash ahead and quietened down. The place that they entered reminded them of an abandoned camp or settlement belonging to the mutants. The bonfire had long gone out. Bones, pieces of cloth, furs and other garbage was strewn around everywhere. Rick dug into one of the piles with the point of his boot and came upon a pale hand sticking out from under a piece of sackcloth. He almost retched...

They were looking for something that looked like food or weaponry. It was all in vain. All Rick managed to find was a bent steel rod, sharpened at one end. It was a rather poor find, but still a weapon.

Soon after, they had looked through it all and continued on their way. The Chorda was coming closer. Its fragment grew in size ahead, piercing through space.

The travelers finally reached the end of the tunnel and stopped. Far below, they saw flickering lights, heard a cracking sound and then a rhythmic knocking which faded into silence. Rick got out the cables and hooks which Cornelius had given them and looked upwards. Maya was observing him expectantly.

"We have two options," Rick said. "The first is to climb the walkways along the walls and then we crawl around under the ceiling looking for an exit. I doubt we will be successful as Omicron would have been taken over by guys like Yarg a long time ago. The other option is to look for a way through the well of the Chorda. What I mean is that we find some way to go upwards along the Axis."

Maya was examining the well, lost in thought. Powerful and very wide radial beams stretched from the segments to the axis of the world, but the Axis itself looked smooth and unscalable.

"Maybe we shouldn't have come to the center. We could have looked for a way in at the periphery..."

"I am not going outside," Rick abruptly cut her off.

They sat on the edge and started to think. Rick played around with the cable in his hands.

"What was it that was written on the plaque below the Red King?"

The girl frowned, trying to remember.

""Archimedes", and then something else. I can't remember."

"What is it for?"

"The Red King or the plaque?"

"Both. Why make an idol's head?"

"It's a sign of remembrance that such a man once lived. Idols, as you called them, are created in honor of famous and exceptional people. This Archimedes did something important."

Rick gazed into the chasm, deep in thought.

"Tell me something about your world," Maya asked.

"What?"

"I don't know. Something. How did you become a soldier?"

"I'm not a soldier. We have no army," Rick explained. "We have a Patrol, and internal and an external one. Only the strongest, bravest and most agile get in—those that complete the Spring Run around the Circle of Life."

"How interesting. And what does it all mean?"

Rick started to patiently explain the nature of the trial when a new level of life was reached.

"Life levels. Your society is organized in such a complex way. Not a life, but a constant series of trials."

"Just five. So what," he snorted. "Once every ten years."

"And what are the following trials?"

"Well, upon the third circle, a man goes through the Ides of Summer," Rick replied. "For men, it is a fight. It is something like the dispute about the right to be a man where I managed to overcome Cornelius. Two people fight each other. Weapons are forbidden. The result can be different and it does not have to be fatal, it depends on the choice of the participants. You can surrender at any time, but the loser always has to go to the worst level of the sector that have bad heating, food and lighting. Which is why everyone fights until the end. And it does not matter what was your place in the previous circle."

"And what about women? How do they go through this trial?"

"In different ways. It can be a trial by cold, by hunger, or by darkness."

"Please continue."

"What, do you want to hear about the fourth and fifth trials? Doesn't the tale sound too barbaric to you?" he glanced at Maya. "Well, all right then. The fourth trial is the Autumn Harvest. This is when a person passes from the fourth circle to the fifth. The point of this trial is to find something valuable for the Commune in the outer Expanse. The hunters go beyond the barrier and search. And the last trial is the Winter Night. This is a group trial. People split up into teams and compete in riddles, puzzles, charades and other intelligence based tests."

"Hey, wait, so what is the very first test?"

"It is the passage form childhood to the second circle. Nothing special happens there."

"But still?"

"Hey, look!" Rick got distracted, pointing at the Chorda.

They took a closer look. At first, it seemed that nothing was happening, but then the Axis started to fill with a soft, but brighter light. The blue reflections that fell upon it first changed to purple, which changed to shades of red. The blueness finally disappeared, and was replaced by a pale magenta shine. Then they heard a deep sound—a rumble coming from the depths of the world. This rumble kept sounding on the same note and then Maya showed Rick the part of the Chorda where vertical white stripes quickly ran across it closer to the right edge—they were so thin and quick that it seemed that the stripes distort the pillar of light in those places. Then, a similar stripe flashed on the left edge. And in the center a moment later.

"What is this?"

The question hung in the air. Neither of them knew the answer. They sat around a little more, observing the Chorda, until Rick felt that he was getting hot. He took off the top half of his jumpsuit, tying it around his waist. Maya followed his example. Tommo just stood by their side and silently looked ahead. Rick was surprised that the prole was being so still and quiet that they forgot about his existence for a while. He moved his eyes from Tommo to the beam leading towards the Axis. Tommo followed his gaze and suddenly walked over to the beam, nonchalantly stepping on it and walking towards the Chorda.

A minute later, the prole calmly approached the Chorda—it seemed that if he took a step further he would burst into flames, without even leaving a pile of ashes. However, the prole kept walking, and once he had reached the end of the beam he froze for a moment, stretched out his hand and touched the Chorda. He did not burn. Nothing happened at all. Then, Tommo put one leg on the Chorda, lifted himself up, put another leg on it, grabbed on with his hand, straightened his back and began to climb upwards.

"By the Machine God and the Great Expanse!" Rick exclaimed, so excited he nearly fell off the edge. "How could I forget about his abilities? Tommo!"

The prole looked back and signed that all was fine.

"How do you do that?"

It was a stupid question—Rick had seen the way proles moved along the walls and ceilings like spiders.

The prole pointed up.

"Will you return?"

An affirmative nod. Tommo continued his ascent, and Maya and Rick held their breath and watched him, until the figure in the orange jumpsuit disappeared behind the lower edge of the third aeon. They continued looking up for a long time, not knowing what they expected to see there.

"You know, he might not come back," Maya pointed out.

"Let's not think about that. I propose we sleep a little. We can take turns standing watch. You lie down first, and I will sit down nearby."

Maya nodded and they moved over to the wall, further away from the edge of the platform. Maya laid her head on his knees and quickly fell asleep. Rick was watching the Chorda and the way that its light changed everything around him.

The hoarfrost and snow melted away before his eyes. Water dripped from the ceiling... Spring had come to the world.

13

RICK AWOKE with a scream. His nightmare had been so realistic that he spent a while thinking that the space around him was filled with water, that fish-men with bulging eyes were swimming away in fear and that Croesus was a monster with pimpled, violet skin and tentacles for arms. Croesus' body was also bloated to the size of a sector and his vile belly filled the main assembly hall, while his tentacles stretched through all the corridors to grab people and drag them into the beast's maw. While this was going on, Rick had somehow managed to get out of the sector with Aurora under his arm and swam upwards, higher and higher past the other sectors until he reached the surface. Some air still remained at the top, and Rick rushed headlong towards it, not knowing why, like a moth flying towards the light of a lamp. He saw a hook and grabbed onto it, only understanding that it was a trap when it was too late. There was no way to get off the hook now, he jerked from side to side, but it made the cold steel sink further into his flesh. And when he was taken out on the surface, he saw the fisherman, the mutant dwarf that knew how to dig around in the thoughts of others. The dwarf was smiling and it was this smile that made Rick wake up from feeling the presence of another.

Rick jumped up, without immediately working out where he was and almost fell into the chasm off the platform. It was only then that he looked around and assessed the situation. Everything was calm, Maya had just fallen asleep at her post. He decided that he would not wake her and decided to keep watch himself for now—

he doubted he could get back to sleep.

His stomach growled, irritatingly. Well then, he did not know what was best—to sleep and go through the nightmare or to fight off hunger? Rick walked along the wall, looking at the seams between the segments where the fur of the mold could be seen. At last, he found what he was looking for—mushrooms, which he brought back to Maya's sleeping place and started to carefully cut up with his knife. He had seen mushrooms everywhere he had visited in the Expanse—the main thing was to have sufficient heat and moisture. Not all of them were edible, of course, but some were not bad at sating hunger even if they were watery and bitter to the taste. Risk would not risk to look for firewood to start a fire as he did not want to leave Maya alone. In the end, he ate a couple of mushrooms raw, knowing that his stomach would ache in the future.

Two or three hours passed. Maya started to move, stretching herself with pleasure. Rick waited. The color of the Chorda became light magenta with a dose of orange. Now, the bright lines of the discharges jumped through the Chorda all the time. It kept emitting a low, energetic rumble.

"What's the time?" Maya roughly got up, realizing that she fell asleep on her watch and things could have ended badly for them both.

"I think that it's the evening. Don't worry, I didn't sleep and stood the watch for you. Here you are." Rick offered her some mushrooms. "I already tried them. As you see, I'm still alive."

He smiled weakly. Maya nodded and started to eat.

"I dreamed a strange dream," she said after a minute.

"Me too. But I don't want to talk about it."

"Hmm," she looked back at him. "I don't think I want to either."

It seems that they were thinking about the same thing. The Expanse had somehow affected their minds and consciousness. Rick did not know whether that was good or bad.

They continued to sit at the edge of the precipice, each thinking their own thoughts.

"He won't come back," Maya said suddenly.

"Why do you think so?" Rick understood her completely—she was talking about Tommo.

"He's either been killed or taken prisoner."

"I doubt it. Those guys are agile as anything. I still don't quite understand what they are."

Maya thought for a little and offered, "Maybe they are artificial humans, not machines?"

"How can this be?" Rick did not understand.

"They are not born the way we are. They are grown like flowers in a pot. Or assembled from different parts. Basically, they are made. Which is

240

why they are completely different to normal human. They have different thoughts, desires and requirements."

"Do they die?"

"Probably not. I can imagine that they break, hibernate or go insane. But dying means ceasing to live, but can their existence be called life? That's the question."

Rick asked Maya to tell him something about herself in the same way as he did. This is the way he found out about life in the Kappa sector and about the traditions and customs of another small people. Some things genuinely amused him. He found the strict ban on eating in front of others especially funny—the people of the sector considered it to be sacrilegiously amoral behavior. The society of Kappa sector was strictly divided along gender lines—men and women lived apart. The Assembly, which was a long celebration of life, labor and love took place during special months, usually once a year, and united representatives of the whole sector.

The family did not exist as a social unit. It was replaced by brigades, teams or units, that were formed from people of one gender, but different ages. For instance, in a unit which was formed from the male half of society there were always children, youths adult men and a male elder. These groups were formed for exactly one year and all of their members bore collective responsibility for each other's actions. Maya herself had gone through several such units. Being part of a unit did not mean that there was a strict band on interaction with peers or other people, but the residents of Kappa sector had no private life. It was even regulated by the Mentors of the Order.

Work was distributed by lot and was also assigned for one year. At the end of the annual celebration, the Order organized a lottery, where everyone drew their lot and chance determined the fate of the participant for the following year.

"I got assigned to work in the greenhouse," Maya said, "for the third time in a row. This is probably why I am the best at botany."

"And what about hard labor which the children and the elderly can't do?"

"The Order has thought of that too, so they organize a separate lottery for every age category. This tradition has persisted for hundreds of years. They say that it was started at the very beginning to exclude the possibility of the usurpation of power and social stagnation. Machines help us a lot." Maya was silent for a while and then added, "We also have one important custom. Every person in the sector must compose and sing a song about their whole life. It is considered that the song contains their

242

very soul. Everything that the person has lived through in their years is included in that song— their work, those close to them, their victories and defeats, all of their achievements and all their most important actions. A person might be composing the song for their entire life, but if they do not sing it, then they are struck out of every chronicle and forgotten forever. This is why our elders sing the Song of Life every year, and we enter these songs into the sector chronicle."

"What, every single song?"

"Yes," replied Maya with great seriousness.

"Are you already composing yours?" Rick asked with a smile.

"Of course!" Maya exclaimed. "But only the first line."

"Sing that one at least."

"No." She firmly shook her head. "I can't. Maybe later."

Rick decided that he would not insist. Maya continued telling her tale, while he lay on his back, put his hands behind his head and started examining the ceiling. The light falling from the Chorda gave a strange color to all imperfections, protrusions and depressions. At first, it seemed that the relief of the floor was composed of chaotic combinations of lines, shapes and dots, but the eye could not help finding some sort of order, some unity or harmony, as if it was a mosaic that combined different elements.

Maya spoke, but Rick no longer listened with the same attention, consumed by hi study of the view that lay before him. Every figure and every line carried more than it had originally seemed. For instance, the circular shapes—their half circles were parts of more complex forms. They were crossed diagonally by lines that turned out to be the sides of a square that completed two other in itself. Rays radiated from the dots in some place, but they were also the sides of triangles, that built up an even more complex figure, and so on, to infinity. At one point, Rick realized that he saw the shape of a man, but this image soon fell apart into formless parts. Then, it seemed that a face appeared on the ceiling, with clearly visible lines forming its eyes, nose and mouth.

Rick felt uneasy.

"Are you listening to me?" Maya elbowed him in the side.

"Oh, yes," he snapped out of his reverie, finding it difficult to tear his eyes away from the ceiling.

"What did you see?"

"I..." Rick looked up again.

And he was struck dumb.

One of the dots in the center of the circle opened like the bud of a flower and a cable flew

244

throw the torchlit opening. Then, a figure in an orange jumpsuit appeared there.

Maya also noticed the prole. They jumped up, grabbed their things and hurried to the place where the cable was hanging.

Rick figured out that Tommo had no intention to come down and that the cable was meant to bring things up. He tugged on the end, checking that it was secure, and then asked Maya to lift up her arms, skilfully making a loop which he fastened with a carabiner clip across her chest.

"Take her up!" Rick waved to Tommo.

And Maya started to smoothly go upwards. Rick stood there, looking up, amazed at the strength of the prole. It was unbelievable—only a machine could pull on a cable without stopping, like a windlass that has a motor and a spool, but even the strongest man would require rest, and a man would raise the weight by fits and starts...

Tommo pulled Maya into the opening and threw the cable back. Rick quickly tied himself to it, clicked the carabiner clip close, shouted to the prole and set off upwards.

Soon, he could see a view of the space of the fourth aeon. He looked won at the abandoned mutant settlements, tamps and ladders, corridor entrances—everything did not look the same as he was used to. He would normally observe the world from the side or from below, and now he could see it from a different perspective. This must have been the way that the Creator saw the world.

Tommo grabbed him under the arms and dragged him through an opening in the bottom of a well, which had walls covered with a furry layer of mold and dust. The air in the well was dry and warm. Rick realized that they were in a ventilation shaft. Tommo looked at them, waiting for orders.

"You're a true friend!" Maya happily declared and tried to hug the prole, who quickly moved out of the way.

"He's just a little wild," Rick added and smiled at Maya.

He stepped forward and looked up.

"We will need to go up again," Maya said. "And I don't seem to see anything apart from darkness up there."

Tommo took two excellent torches out of a backpack that he had procured somewhere. Maya clapped her hands.

"What else have you got there?"

Tommo showed them his spoils: a pair of unusual goggles that had a compact battery like a torch but did not emit light when they were switched off, offering the ability to see in the dark instead. The prole showed how to use them in great detail and then put them back in their case. Then, he took out a pair of flasks of water, a box of tools and two breathing masks. Rick and Maya told him that they knew what the masks were for and how to use them. Which is when Tommo started to coil up the cable.

"I would like to know where you got all of this," Rick admitted, as he accepted a flask of water from Maya. "But you won't tell us anyway, will you?"

The prole nodded.

Rick took a swig from the nozzle and fastened the flask to his belt.

In a few minutes they were climbing up. A yellow line which fluoresced weakly in the darkness could be seen around the walls of the well at different distances, and there was always a ledge that followed the circle of the well over the line. Narrow branching pipes were placed symmetrically above it.

These narrow pipes probably provided ventilation to rooms in the sector. It was a shame that it was impossible to squeeze through them and confirm his suppositions—even Maya would have got stuck.

They quickly learned to use the cable and the safety harness, quickly attaching the carabiner clips to the rungs on the walls and then moving their bodies upwards and repeating the process. Just in case, Rick went first and Tommo went last. The prole could react quickly and he was very strong, so if they were both to fall, Rick had no doubt that he could catch them.

Maya was counting the floors. After every ten floors, the air shaft was connected to horizontal air ducts that were waist-length in diameter. It was easy to get through there, so they made short breaks to drink water and rest for a few minutes.

"We're going up through your sector," Maya said suddenly. Do you want to say hi to anyone?"

Rick did not reply.

"Floor five hundred and twenty," Maya reported a little later. "If I have counted right."

They were drenched in sweat and breathing heavily from fatigue.

"Let's go up to five hundred and thirty and have a long rest," Rick offered. "I want to eat."

They continued the climb, knocking their feet against the ribbed walls of the well. Rick looked down—the entrance was a tiny dot of light somewhere far way. What a climb! It seemed that they were separated by such a huge distance that this little dot was a little... star?

"Maya," Rick called out once they had sat down in the niches at the crossroads with the horizontal air ducts. "Do you know what a star is?"

Maya looked at him with a strange expression on her face for a while.

Then, she asked, "Where do you know that word from?"

"I don't know." Rick rubbed at his temple with his fist. "It just came up in my head, and that's all."

"Have you ever heard it somewhere before?"

"No. Nowhere."

She was looking at him intently, as if she was trying to read his thoughts like the mutant dwarf.

"Are you sure?" Maya asked as doubtfully as before.

"No, I'm telling you. So do you know what that is?"

"I heard or read about it somewhere, but I don't know. It's an ancient world, and it means an object from the outer limits."

They finished another flask and chewed on another couple of pieces of the mushroom that Rick had saved.

Maya spat it out and said, "How disgusting!"

"When you woke up, you didn't complain," noted Rick and chuckled. "When you want to eat this isn't the only thing you'd eat. What do you eat in your Order?"

"Food concentrates. The Councilors issue them from the warehouse, where they are defrosted after the freezer. We have a giant freezer, filled floor to ceiling with various supplies. The Councilors do not say anything about the levels of supplies, but someone had a look and less than half remain. This is why we try to grow some things ourselves. We also breed baby fish in baths."

"You're lucky," Rick offered a friendly smile. "When Omicron was established, we barely had enough supplies for a few years. The First Warden launched the generator and ordered for seeds to be planted in the ground. It was he who developed the plan to save the sector. If it wasn't for the inventiveness of the Warden, our people would have died out long ago. Since then, we live according to the established plan that forms the Circle of Life. Spring is a time of sowing. Summer is the time for collecting moisture. Autumn is the time for harvesting. And the winter is the worst time. The main thing in winter is to survive. This winter ended later than all others."

"Oh, really? Did you see the snow in the outer limits?"

"Yes," Rick admitted unhappily.

"Then you understand everything yourself." Maya grimaced. "It's time to move on."

They put their supplies away in the backpack and gave it to Tommo. Rick started to climb and Maya followed him. The prole followed behind them, as usual. They soon passed the fourth dozen floors of the Omicron sector. Rick was sadly thinking of what Aurora and Kyoto might be doing and what Croesus and his former Brothers in the Patrol were worrying about. It would be funny to tell them about the way he climbed through the sector, if that moment would ever come...

Rick had a sudden urge to go two floors back down and get into the air duct, knocking out the grille and going home. He started shaking and his heart started to beat faster and stronger in his chest. Let them arrest him and throw him in a cell, but at least he will be inside the walls of his homeland and will probably get to see Aurora and old Kyoto...

However, the urge went away as quickly as it arose.

"Floor five hundred and forty," Maya offered from below.

"I already guessed that," grumbled Rick.

He didn't even want to get distracted by her reports about the floors.

"Then you can count for yourself next time!" Maya declared.

Their climb continued in grim silence. When they stopped at yet another crossroads for a short break, they heard distant shouts and noises coming from the air duct. Rick listened and determined the direction. A crying woman and the shouting of men could be heard. Someone was being forcibly led along the corridor. The woman was begging for mercy, but it seemed like it was pointless.

"Don't even think about it," Maya said.

"The thought never even crossed my mind," he lied and let out a quiet sigh.

They set off again. The Omicron sector was long behind, and they entered the space of the Xi sector. There was a technical floor between the sectors which was more a lot like a storeroom that was used for the dumping of minor garbage, tons of dust, huge rolls of moss and mold. The light of the torches outlined huge insects that crawled away in a panic. The sight of them made Maya shiver violently and she barely restrained herself from screaming when Rick took a fat woodlouse off her chest.

"Don't be like that," he told her. "Beetles are a good source of protein. When they are fried with oil, salt and herbs, they combine rather well with..."

"Stop it," Maya demanded.

"Oh come on, I was only joking," Rick lied to her hurriedly.

Beetles and larvae really were a source of protein, and a great one, at that. This was something that old Kyoto told him and taught him how to cook them as well. It was really tasty. It's a shame that there was no way to properly explain this to Maya.

"Listen, Rick," she said to him. "I didn't want to tell you, but take a look at the ceiling."

They looked up together. Hundreds of carrion bats hung off the ceiling, looking like little bags of nuts, holding on to the ledges with their tiny claws. Most of them were asleep. Some of them poked their muzzles out from beneath their wings and let out quiet squeals.

"Mother Darkness," Rick could not help whispering. "We are going to wake them up with our talking. We need to get up."

"What are they?"

"Quiet," Rick bent down to Maya's ear and whispered. "Haven't you ever seen them? Those are carrion bats, it's just they're really small for some reason. The ones we have on our level can be the size of a baby and if they attack in a swarm, a man won't survive. They're vampires. They quickly drain all of your blood!"

Maya's eyes went wide and she quickly pushed towards the well, implying that he would go first as usual and they lost no more time in continuing to climb up. The creatures hung by the opening over the ledge and it would be difficult to get past without disturbing them. Rick managed to somehow hold on to the ledge pulled himself up higher. Maya repeated his movements, but still managed to squash one of the carrion bats, which immediately started to squeal and beat its wings. It was as if a wave passed over the rows of creatures.

"Faster!" Rick barked, and gave Maya a leg up, letting her go ahead.

A few of the small bloodsuckers sped upwards through the well in terror. The rest still hung in their places, raising a wave of squeals and squawks.

Tommo stopped by the opening of the air duct where his companions had just rested. He got out his toolbox and bent over, hidden from sight by the ridge.

"Rick!" Maya hissed from above.

Rick did not reply as he was watching Tommo. Once he was done, Tommo quickly climbed up the wall and grabbed him by the scruff of his jumpsuit to pull him up to the level at which Maya was hanging. Something unexpected happened next. A fine mesh suddenly slid out of the sides of the well from the ridge and closed it off. The bloodsuckers started to squeak even louder and tried to fly upwards, but another mesh slid out there to separate the creatures from the humans.

"Wow!" Rick exclaimed and turned to Maya.

"That was really great!" She nodded in

amazement. "Well done, Tommo!"

They took a relieved breath of air and started to calmly ascend without fearing an attack by tiny bloodsuckers.

They did not encounter any other dangers on the way. They kept moving upwards and resting in the air ducts, spending their time studying the ancient papers. Rick also got to practice his reading. Following another completed task, Maya looked at him with an expression of true admiration and respect. However, all it did was annoy Rick—he had not achieved anything special yet, he just learned how to put letters together into words, so what?

"I'm sorry. It's just you learn too fast," Maya understood what he was thinking about. "A man that never knew how to read is basically unable to learn that quickly."

"Well, I'm able, so let's continue our studies."

"All right."

Still, he never expected a reaction like that from Maya. His abilities in everything that was related to knowledge and science obviously made a serious impression of her. Maybe she believed in him at last? Believed that he was both able to fight and protect people and understand complex sciences?

Tommo never particularly expressed himself

during their breaks, he just waited while his companions talked and rested. Rick also realized that the prole could see in the dark, because Tommo would sometimes go to reconnoiter side passages impenetrable to the eye leaving the special goggles and torches with his companions, but always returned without any issues. One time, he came back with a human skull that had a clump of slime colored long hair attached to it.

"We should be more careful," Rick said. "Night crawlers might be around here somewhere. They fear the light as if it was fire, but they are very quick and they always attack in packs, especially if the victim is surrounded by darkness."

After being told this, Maya spent a long time moving in silence with her torch switched on to her power. It seems that this was how strong an impression Tommo's find and Rick's tale made on her.

They climbed higher and higher. The structure of the well did not change in any way, but they increasingly kept coming across streaks of slime, that shook in the wind and stuck to their clothing in watery lumps. It also had a caustic, sweet and sour smell that caused dizziness.

"Five hundred and sixty..."

The rhythmic knocking of their boots on the

ribbed protrusions and the clicks of the carabiner clips never stopped.

"Five hundred and seventy," Maya kept counting.

Their hands grabbed at rungs that we covered in slime, their feet kept sliding off to the side, but the companions stubbornly advanced leaving floors behind them.

"Five hundred and eighty..."

"We have almost passed the sector!" Rick noted. "Is it inhabited?"

"Probably in part," Maya supposed. "Judging by the sounds coming from the pipes some sort of psychotic barbarians are living in the rooms. The sector has probably been long abandoned by intelligent people."

"I see." Rick nodded. "Floor five hundred and ninety is coming soon. Let's get there and have a break. Then floor six hundred will be just around the corner."

"Yes..."

However, they did soon need to stop for a while, hanging on the cables in the well so that they could put on their breathing masks—the stink of the slime became unbearable and made their eyes sting. Once they reached another milestone, Maya moved the mask onto her forehead and coughed. Then, she said, "We could suffocate here..."

"Just a little longer," Rick decided against taking off his mask, so his voice sounded muffled. "There's only a little left."

"I'm getting double vision. We need some rest and sleep."

Maya lay day on her side in the air duct. Rick glanced over at her, and almost cried out. Forgetting his fatigue, he firmly asked her, trying to be as calm as possible, "Maya, please don't move."

"What's the matter?" She yawned and drew her legs up to her stomach, getting herself more comfortable.

Tommo noticed what was worrying Rick and whistled quietly.

"I'm a bit uncomfortable..." Maya tried to hesitantly move to touch her neck, but her hand stopped half-way and fell to the floor.

Rick was watching the creature that had latched on to the girl's neck and tried to work out what to do. A large, greenish white polyp the size of a fist was slowly swelling from the blood that it was sucking from an artery. It could not be torn off, as it would then leave a proboscis with drops of deadly poison in the neck. Tommo brought a lighter close to its pulsating body and lit a fire. The polyp immediately fell off. Rick resisted his desire to turn the creature into a fine paste on the ground. If he did so, he would spatter everything with blood and the smell would attract far scarier creatures. He threw the polyp down the shaft and examined Maya looking for other parasites. Nothing. He asked Tommo to examine him. Clean. Then, he had a careful look at the walls of the well, slowly moving his torch, and noticed polyp nests just over their camping place—pulsing garlands of pimpled balls with hungrily questing sucker trunks.

Rick shuddered.

"Let's climb further up," he told Tommo.

They somehow managed to wake Maya up, having to splash some water from the flask into her face, but that was fine. A sleepy Maya, who was weak from blood loss obeyed them and started to climb up. Tommo watched out for her from below and Rick from above, not forgetting to pierce the parasite nests with his knife along the way. Every time they passed a side air duct, they could hear a loud reverberating sound—whatever it was, Rick had no intention for looking for its source.

Finally, they reached another technical floor between levels. Nu sector was located above. They had overcome the milestone of six hundred floors. Falling out of the shaft into the air duct, Rick and Maya removed their masks and lay there motionless for a long while, inhaling air without the smell of slime. Tommo just waited, sitting on the edge.

Rick wanted to drink, but decided that he would ignore it. He got out his flask and forced Maya to open her mouth, pouring a double dose into her. Then, he somehow wiped the slime stuck to her neck and shoulders and looked over at Tommo, but he was gone. He probably wanted to do some reconnaissance as usual.

There was a lot less dust and rubbish here than in the air ducts on the lower floors. Rick slowly massaged the muscles of his legs that had gone numb from the climb, and noticed some details that he had not seen before with an increasing sense of alarm. There were crude symbols scrawled on the walls with faded paint, balls constructed out of garbage hanging on strings from the ceiling, uneven circles laid out on the floor out of dead insects, small bones and stones. And the main thing was the tracks. Lots of tracks.

The absence of the prole was already starting to be worrying. Rick got up on his feet and started to shine his torch into the surrounding darkness. He wanted to call Tommo, but then, someone's hand clamped his mouth shut. Rick spun around, about to draw his knife—the prole stood nearby, holding a finger to where his mouth would have been on his mask. Then he pointed at the torch.

"What do you want to say?"

Tommo abruptly gestured with his hands and suddenly grabbed Rick's torch and put it out, and then did the same to Maya's torch. They were in total darkness. Rick understood that it was best to keep his mouth shut and keep quiet. An invisible Tommo put the goggles with the special filters on his head and did the same to Maya.

"Tommo, what are you do..." she began.

"Shhh!" Rick whispered. "Quiet!"

He felt the danger. The smell also soon reached his nostrils. An animalistic, thick smell of filthy diseased flesh. The world turned into a collection of gray-green shadows.

Tommo approached one of the drawings on the walls, rubbed it with his hand, covering it in paint and returned. Rick did not resist when the prole daubed this thick and foul smelling goo on his cheeks and forehead and then did the same to Maya. The time for talking was over. The girl had sensed that there was something wrong had also stood up straight and was looking around with concern.

And then they heard a rustle.

Someone was slowly sneaking up on them, and small pieces of rubbish quietly rustled under their palms and feet. The creatures stepped out of the greenish darkness like ghosts—white, scrawny and crooked. Even though they were obviously similar to humans in their body shape, they had lost any reasonable behavioral reactions. They approached slowly, as if they were sliding along the surface, sometimes going on all fours, bent over and tense. Their faces were cut up with wrinkles and cuts, looking like fearsome masks of hungry death, with hollow cheeks, moist jagged slits for mouths and shining eyes. Clumps of hair hung down from the skin that was stretched taut over their skulls, but their bodies were hairless and naked, with extremities that were longer than those of normal humans, some of them even having joints that bent in the opposite direction. The creatures moved with unusual grace and flexibility, like caterpillars, while still managing to stay quiet, even though many of their fingers ended in long claws. Rick noticed primitive bone daggers in some of their hands and slowly reached for the handle of the knife in his belt.

There were many of the creatures—around a dozen. And they obviously knew how to act as a well coordinated group, so there was not chance for only three people to fight back.

As they approached, a thick smell of unwashed bodies started to be felt. Rick, Maya and Tommo froze in the middle of the air duct and watched the approach of the pack of night crawlers. Here they were, but a few paces away, sniffing at the air. Some of them made gurgling noises in their throats, but the pack continued moving on.

Rick could barely stop himself from stabbing out with the knife in his hand when the face of one of the night crawlers was close enough to almost touch him. The creature glanced him over carefully and then stared back into the darkness. The rest did the same as they slid past. One of them sniffed Maya's cheek and even licked the place that Tommo had marked with the paint. Another touched the wall, turned around, looked at Tommo and hurried after his packmates.

An incredibly long minute passed before Rick could breathe out and let go of his grip on the knife on his belt. Maya wordlessly sank to the floor, shaking. Tommo made a calming gesture, implying that the crawlers had gone and that they needed to be on their way.

"You're right, my friend," Rick whispered and made a hungry gulp from the flask. "We were definitely lucky. We must get out of here."

He passed the flask to Maya and asked her to gather the strength they would need for the ascent.

"These beasts have excellent hearing," Rick whispered in her ear. "But I hope that by the time they return, we will already be high up."

"Ask your Machine God for that," Maya said seriously.

"Are you all right?" Rick prepared the carabiners and the cable.

"Couldn't be worse."

"I wouldn't say things like that. You understand that..."

"I only understand that we need to get out of this well!"

"At the next junction," Rick assured her.

After a while, they crossed ten sector floors and crawled through a side air duct to the nearest ventilation grille. Rick spent a while carefully examining the corridor through the bars while wearing his special goggles and reported that he saw nothing suspicious. Maya immediately ordered Tommo to break the grille open.

In a moment, all three of them jumped down onto the floor.

14

IT TURNED OUT that they did not arrive in a corridor but in a very long and spacious room, which was also rather unusual. Rick had never seen anything like it. A standard residential room looked different. It also did not meet the description of a room full of "wonders" as Patrol Commander Ivon called them. There was nothing to compare it to.

First, the companions made sure that they were not under threat. Then, they tried to switch on the lights and were successful—Maya touched a little actuator by the entry door and oval lamps started to slowly light up under the ceiling.

"The power is on!" Maya exclaimed in a quiet whisper.

The room looked abandoned. Most of the space was taken up with rows of chairs turned towards the wall, which featured a large and very dusty light rectangle. Rick sank down into a chair and understood that he had not felt this tired for a long time. The incredibly soft back and seat of the chair embraced him and his hands lay on the armrests by themselves. Rick spent another second distractedly observing Tommo replace the ventilation grille and then his consciousness abandoned him to sleep.

His dream was short and confusing. He dreamed of his home, but spring still had not come. Rick had to deliver an important message, which was apparently destined for another friendly sector that had made its presence known and called for help. So Rick went on a distant journey through the cold and dark, but the most unusual thing about it was his route. The destination of the journey was beyond the Expanse. Rick stood by the Omicron barrier and the whole Commune was watching. The last source of light was in the hands of Aurora, who was seeing him off—an oil lamp. And then, Rick stepped beyond the confines of the sector and an inhuman cold immediately gripped his body. But there were still days of travel ahead, full of nights without a roof over his head, monsters and obstacles... Rick turned for the last time so that he would remember his sister's face as well as possible, and suddenly understood that the face was Maya's.

"Wake up," she said.

"What happened?" Rick was blinking, unable to think clearly.

"We have worked out the situation a bit," Maya looked calm and satisfied. "Do you know what this place is?"

"How would I know?" he grumbled, suddenly working out where he was and that he had just been woken up.

"Hey, stop being grouchy," Maya looked at him with reproach. "I have suffered no less than you and I want a rest too, but first I must tell you this. Do you know what that white thing is?"

She pointed at the wall with the rectangle and Rick shook his head.

"Living pictures appear on it," Maya grandly

announced.

"I want to eat something," Rick was not impressed with the information about the pictures. He stretched languorously, getting rid of the remains of his sleep.

Maya gave him a flask of water and a briquette made up of a yellow mass in clear packaging. Rick did not bother finding out where the briquette came from, tore away the packaging and tried the concentrate—it turned out to be tasty. He started chewing, without even asking what it was, while Maya hurriedly explained things to him. It turned out that the ancients used to watch living pictures on the white rectangle. Special projection equipment was in the neighboring room as well as shelves full of disks with these sorts of pictures. Any disk could be selected, put into a special device and watched. She showed Rick one of the cases. Rick carefully read the name, letter by letter: "Indians of the Amazon". Maya gave him another pair of cases. He read: "The Sahara Desert" and "A Year in the Alps" and looked at the girl questioningly.

Maya, happy as a little kid, shrugged her shoulders.

"I have no idea what's on them!"

Tommo calmly sat in a chair nearby and ignored them as usual. Once he finished the briquette, Rick followed Maya into the disk storeroom and started to read names which said nothing to him. The meaning only seemed somewhat clear to him once—the case was labeled "History of the Olympic Games". He thought it was about some sort of competition.

"Why don't we check this one out?" he offered.

Maya nodded, took the disk out of the case and put it inside an oblong machine. They went back into the hall. The dusty rectangle lit up and some writing appeared on it.

And then the rectangle came alive!

Rick could not help but flinch—it was as if a large window opened in front of them, so clear was the image and the sounds coming from all directions. They saw a huge space, something like an oval hall that was surrounded by rows of benches covered with a huge number of people making a great amount of noise. Half-naked competitors ran one after another along tracks on the floor of the hall.

Suddenly, a pleasant male voice spoke over the noise, "The history of the Olympic Games starts with the Ancient Greek myth of Olympus and the competitions that the citizens of Athens organized in honor of the gods in their pantheon..."

Rick and Maya watched, completely frozen in place, until the rectangle on the wall went dark and a message saying "The End" appeared. When that happened, Tommo loudly clapped his hands a few times.

"Did you understand anything?" Rick uttered slowly.

Maya, who had been leaning back hard into her seat turned to look at him with difficulty. Her eyes were full of delight and admiration.

"This is an incredibly valuable find," she finally found the words. "This is a treasure. We have found a treasure trove!"

"I am talking about this picture in particular."

"I think so. It looks like some sort of ritual or trial. Testing human ability."

"Did you see their faces?" Rick asked. "It was as if they were alive... They were alive! True techno-magic."

They watched another pair of pictures—one was about a gigantic aquarium which was called an "ocean" and the journeys people had through an unbelievable mass of water, and another about a big farm and jungles that had trees as high as ten, or fifteen or even more levels. Rick especially came closer to the screen to watch the moving picture, touched the surface, ran around the hall trying to change his perspective, felt the walls but did not manage to be particularly successful in his research.

"You can't see the ceiling in any of these pictures. Where is the ceiling?" he said, completely perplexed, when Maya switched off the projection machine. "Where were the walls? Now, that's a mystery."

"Well, they had that really large and very bright lamp there," Maya suggested. "That means there must have been a ceiling."

"That's right," Rick agreed. "Now what? Shall we go further up?"

"I think we should take a few cases with us."

"I knew you wouldn't be able to leave this place empty handed," he smiled.

All three of them went out into the corridor and started to examine the surrounding sector space. This place had high ceilings and mainly transparent walls. The space was like one large, complex gallery, with balconies, stairways, connecting corridors and many auxiliary rooms. Columns and arches decorated with protruding drawings were everywhere. There was a mosaic on the floor. Everything bore the mark of chaos and abandonment, and there were pieces of broken furniture and unknown machines strewn around in different places around the corridor. Some of the structures in some of the rooms were twisted or melted by fire.

They walked through a spacious hall, past broken windows, piles of trash and benches and tables overgrown with cobwebs. The hall reminded Rick of both the dining hall and the gathering hall in the Commune. He imagined how the ancients walked around here, busy with their own matters, discussed various issues, solved problems, became happy or sad, loved or hated each other. This place was once full of vibrant life, but now only emptiness lived here.

A large rat sat enthroned on the parapet in front of them. Once it saw them, it raised its muzzle and sniffed, without even a thought of escape.

"They are the masters here," Maya said, nodding at the rodent.

Another rat appeared on the parapet to their side, and two more a little further along. The long-tailed creatures were carefully observing their guests with their red, beady eyes.

"They're so big," Rick whistled.

"And fearless." Maya checked her weapon, just in case.

The companions made their way along a wide corridor towards the Chorda, curiously looking around. Even though everything was seemingly abandoned, they could not help being pursued by the feeling of an alien presence and someone's implacable gaze. Rick kept glancing at the upper balconies, but saw nothing there apart from the hanging remains of rotten fabric and broken structures. The corridor changed into a wide bridge, which ended in a wide stairway. They walked up, and a wide archway appeared before their eyes, framing the Chorda that glimmered in the distance right at its center. All three of them stopped in their tracks. And it wasn't because the color of the Chorda had changed from magenta-orange to bright yellow.

There was a man standing beneath the arch.

He was no barbarian, mutant or any of the creatures they had come across on their journey. A rather elderly, tall man with a carefully groomed beard and silver-streaked hair who held his back straight and looked down at them from above with an obvious expression of superiority. Something in his gaze reminded him of Croesus— this was the gaze of a man that was used to issuing orders, a man that was in power. The only clothing he wore was a light toga that hid his legs down to his ankles. The stranger held a rather large and fearsome looking weapon.

"Put the blaster on the floor," he told Maya in a calm voice, as if he knew her for a long time. Then he immediately turned to Rick, "Put your knife away. It cannot harm me."

Rick and Maya obeyed, putting their weapons on the ground.

"Than you for understanding. You may approach."

The stranger lowered his intimidating cannon. They came closer and Rick could not believe his eyes—the strange had the Omicron sigil tattooed on his neck. Rick looked at his absolutely unremarkable face and...

"Warden Drachus!" he breathed out.

"How is the Commune doing?" the former Warden replied.

"We have problems with the holy... We have energy supply issues."

"So it did happen, in the end," Drachus replied sadly. He had to go into exile many years ago.

He was considered dead, like everyone that had gone into the Expanse before him, but there he was, standing in front of Rick, hale and hearty, but aged by time.

"I apologize, we didn't introduce ourselves," Maya said respectfully. "This is Rick from Omicron. I am Maya, from Kappa sector."

"You are probably hungry, aren't you?" Drachus asked with a smile. "If you like, I can invite you to my humble abode for a cup of tea."

"Oh," Maya respectfully touched her chest with her hand, "we would be very obliged."

Rick looked at her enviously—how did Maya manage to speak in such a beautiful way and use body language to make a good impression on people?

Drachus led them up along one of the side stairways behind the arch. They ascended three levels and stepped onto an oval platform that supported a rounded wall on one side where entrances to several rooms could be seen. A view of the Chorda opened up on the other side of the platform. A large aquarium which had long dried out stood at the center of the platform.

The former Warden led them to one of the doors, entered an access code and let them in. Inside five minutes, they were sitting behind a table and warming their hands with mugs of a hot aromatic drink, while looking around without hiding their curiosity. The most interesting was the transparent wall that had a view of the Chorda well. Drachus walked over to the glass and nodded at the pillar of the Chorda that had become a lot lighter than it was before. The Axis of the Expanse was heating up like a metal that had reached a high temperature.

"I would bet my future bald patch that this is your doing," Drachus said.

Rick glanced at him sheepishly.

"The very fact of your presence here says a lot." Drachus crossed his arms on his chest. "And don't tell me that you've been banished."

"No. We are escapees and criminals," Maya reported.

"Seriously? So it's like that..." the former

Warden looked at both of them with reproach and then spent some time examining the prole with great interest. He finally uttered, "So what did you do?"

Rick started to tell him about how he met Maya and about their escape, their adventures and the final goal of their journey. Drachus stroked his beard, sometimes glancing sideways at the Chorda behind the glass. When Rick reached the point of describing the hall of living pictures, Drachus stopped him.

"Enough."

Then, he went quiet, thinking about something.

"How did you manage to survive out here?" Rick could not resist asking.

"Very easily." Drachus shrugged, as if he was talking about everyday matters. "The Expanse gives a man all he needs to survive. It was created for this very purpose. You just need to know where everything is. I have lived here for many years, and I have been waiting for someone like you. People who are brave enough to overcome the barriers and survive in the corridors of Thermopolis. People who will come to me one day, and start asking questions."

"And do you have answers to them?"

"Unfortunately, not all of them," Drachus shook his head. "You are going upwards. I am too old to accompany you, but I will try to help how I can."

"Even for that, we are grateful," Maya replied.

"It's nothing. Does your friend not know how to talk?" he nodded at Tommo.

"No, he doesn't. He only listens and follows orders."

"Interesting. I have never seen one of them."

"He is from the lower sectors."

"I see. So, you are saying that you need to get to Gamma sector."

"That's right," Maya confirmed.

"But that is incredibly high up! You can't even imagine how high."

"Oh no," Rick interrupted, "we definitely can. We have a map of the world. Show him, Maya."

The girl unfurled the Thermopolis diagram. The old Warden was examining it, walking around the table, his jaws tense with concentration.

"Well now," he concluded. "I saw a copy once, a long time ago, during a border war between sectors. Paper was considered to be excellent fuel for lighting fires back then, and no one looked at the little shapes that covered the sheets. But what can you ask of idiots? And now you have found one of the last copies to get into the Control Center and start up the generators."

"Yes," Maya and Rick said in unison.

"How are you going to do that?"

"We'll act according to the situation," Rick replied.

"You mean that you don't know how to start up the generators."

"No."

"Do you have access codes and passwords?"

"I know several, but I don't know if they will work up above," Maya admitted. "We will have to check them all."

Drachus started to slowly stroll back and forth around the room. After a couple of minutes he stopped, and said, "Your idea is doomed to failure."

"We will not step back," Rick declared.

"I am not making you turn back. You will just smash yourself against a wall. That's all." The old Warden paused. "This is why, before you stick your noses into the Control Center, you must get right here."

He stabbed his finger at one of the sectors of the first aeon.

"Delta," Rick read out, syllable by syllable. "La-bo-ra-to-ries. Ar-chi-ve, Lib-ra-ry. Da-ta-ba-ses."

"That is where all of the valuable information you require is held. All of the knowledge that the ancients had when they created this world. Their sciences, their art, poetry, history and cultural records. If you want to understand what the Thermopolis is, your road lies that way. Endless vistas of thought will be open to you. Under the condition that the repositories have survived, of course."

"Have you ever been up above?"

"I tried," Drachus said, "several times. But I decided not to risk it anymore since I almost lost my hand."

He showed them a disfigured hand that was missing two fingers—the ring finger and the little finger.

"Monsters or mutants?" Rick enquired.

"No. Humans."

"What are they like?" Maya asked with interest.

"Those that live above? I... I don't know. I never even saw them. The thing is that they have closed off the shell of the first aeon with a security system. That system destroys anything that comes near and shows any signs of life. They have established an unassailable citadel up there and I have no idea what goes on inside."

"What a mess!" Rick frowned, thinking over what he just heard.

"You gave us really good advice, respected Warden," Maya said. "Your help has been priceless."

"It is a shame that I cannot help you on your journey, as I am too old," Drachus spread his hands. "It's a shame that your chances of success are so incredibly small, as nothing works in the sectors apart from the emergency systems. The automated systems refuse me access when I try to activate the central terminals. Thermopolis was conceived as a unified system, as a living organism in which every aeon and sector are interconnected and perform a particular function. And on their own, the sectors are worthless. The ancients knew how to control them, but the knowledge was lost. This is why the Expanse is a giant tomb now. A dead place, that had remained abandoned for many years. This is why my words are not that useful. How will you go around the security system? You can't. The knowledge of how to break the shell is inside the shell. It's a closed circle."

"We must try," Rick stated decisively. "We can't retreat just like that."

"Your motivation deserves praise," Drachus agreed. "But determination is not enough on its own. You must understand that. Or," and he narrowed his eyes, "you have something with you as well as the diagram? Something special? Some sort of password, or key, something that can overcome the security system?"

"No," Maya replied. "Apart from the prole,

the weapons and the papers, we have nothing of value."

Drachus was looking at them so attentively that it seemed that he noticed something that only he could see, and that is why he asked those leading questions. He was looking for something, staring at their faces in concentration. He was thinking, and his thoughts feverishly reflected in his large, intelligent eyes. However, he was also obviously tortured by doubt, as if he knew the truth but was also wrong in his conclusions. Finally, Drachus moved and walked around Maya, then Rick and looked them up and down. He did not afford Tommo even a single glance.

"Do you know anything about the Omega protocol?" Rick suddenly asked.

"Omega?" Drachus breathed out, his eyes going wide as if he had suddenly been sucker-punched in the back. "There are only a few words about that in the oath of the Warden of the Commune. But no one knows their meaning."

"Then, maybe you know something about the Chronos program or the Gaia and Uranus programs?"

Drachus started to look increasingly restless. He was almost running around the room now.

"I don't know anything about that. No! What about it?"

Rick watched he former Warden carefully, increasingly coming to understand that this exceptional man, who had once been the head of the Commune was simply overcome with fear. Drachus was afraid. But of what? Or perhaps, of whom?

"You say that you did not take anything with you," Drachus pronounced. "But then, how did you manage to launch the particle accelerator and make the Chorda come alive? How? Or is it a coincidence?"

Rick explained that he simply put his hand on the screen, and the machine obeyed his instructions.

"Without and access code?"

"No, there was an access code," Maya replied. "The machine called it a genetic code."

"A genetic code? What is that?"

Maya explained the main features of that ancient science to him as well as she could.

"But of course..." Drachus whispered, forcefully descending into a chair. "But why..."

He stared at Rick.

"You. Wait. Let me try and remember you."

"What exactly are you trying to remember?" Rick wanted to help find the answer with all his heart.

"Don't hurry," Drachus ordered. "Let me just sit awhile and look at you. The answer is close. I just need to distract myself."

"Then tell us everything you know," Maya offered. "Everything that might help us, and maybe you will find the answer."

"That's right."

The old Warden calmed down a little and made them another mug of hot tea each to finally gather his thoughts. Eyes fixed on the corner of the table, he started to tell them the story of his life—all that remained in his aging memory.

Drachus' life did not stand out with any particularly notable events, apart from one. It was him that managed to find several packages of seeds when he was moving onto a new life level, during a hunt in the external Expanse. When the seeds germinated and grew, they turned out to be beans—an undemanding and nutritious plant, which was a great addition to the ration. The room in which Drachus had found the seeds almost became his grave—an ancient machine was trying to kill him with a red hot beam, for some reason. The future Warden was saved by his innate sense of self-preservation, as he managed to find a safe place that the beam could not reach and escape the deadly trap. This is how he moved onto a new level into better living conditions.

Drachus was always concerned with the issue of finding sustenance. He was always thinking of how to increase the life cycle of crops and harvest them not once, but twice. He experimented with potatoes, wheat, carrots and other vegetables. He understood that plants did not just need good soil but also special fertilizers that he decided to extract from phosphorescent mushrooms. Even though these mushrooms were poisonous by themselves, they were great at being absorbed by root systems once dried and ground.

During a test to pass into another Circle of Life, they needed to collect as much water as possible. Drachus led the team and offered the most effective collection method—the evaporation of molds, mushrooms and slime. No one wanted to touch such disgusting, poisonous things, but Drachus bravely gathered pieces of it and put them into bags, so that he could condense water on a film that he put over a fire. The water was then filtered and poured into containers.

The Commune had a new method for getting water. Drachus was noticed by the aging Warden. He invited to visit him as one of the most exceptional of the adult Brothers of the Commune and without further ado, offered him his own position. Had Drachus known what accepting the position entailed he would never have agreed.

He was inducted into the secrets of the

Commune Committee.

"There is no Machine God," he uttered, stressing every word.

Maya and Rick kept listening.

"He does not exist," Drachus repeated.

"I already know," Rick smiled sadly. "Maya helped me understand and explained everything."

"Hmm, well then," the former Warden shrugged and continued his tale, "But this was not all. I found out that the Expanse was not infinite, but bound by walls that separate us from the external environment. And that it is not black emptiness beyond the borders of the world, but another world which is unlike ours. My predecessor also told me that our world is actually a gigantic tower that has different peoples living on different levels, but they are separated for safety reasons, and it is for this safety that the people of the Commune cannot be told this truth, otherwise there will be panic, disturbances and rebellions. At first, I did not understand the ideas of the Committee, but after many years passed I gradually almost accepted their dogma. And so, I gave my oath and became the new Warden. According to custom, the previous one had to go away into the Expanse, and he did it with dignity. That man believed in the ideals of the Commune and the existing order of things very deeply. He preferred to plunge into the chasm to banishment. Then, I occupied my position until my time had come to a close."

"That is atrocious," Maya said. "Keeping people ignorant—how much do you have to despise them?"

"Not despise them, but love and care for them," Drachus corrected her.

"We care for the pigs too," Maya countered, "but for very different reasons."

"Have you finished your story?" Rick enquired.

"No, that isn't all." Drachus grunted as he adjusted himself on the chair. "Apart from the Committee, there is also the Warden's Council that consists of three priests—small and inconspicuous people. This is who rules the commune. These people almost made me truly believe in their damn God."

He lowered his voice, as if they could be overheard.

"They took me to their temple—you know where it is, Rick—and showed me its internal workings. All of these little screens and buttons, which they called the greater and lesser altars of the Machine God. They taught me to read and count—not immediately, but they did teach me. The greatest shock for me was my first visit to the temple. One of the priests came up to the control panel, pressed some sort of button, and the screen in front of me came alight. Then, a face appeared on the screen. At first, I did not understand what was going on. But then the head of the man on the screen said, "Glad to meet you, Warden Drachus!" A human head talked to me out of a machine! I almost fainted, I could never imagine such a thing. Then they explained it to me that this was the way to communicate with those who truly rule Thermopolis."

"Wait," Maya interrupted, "You talked to them?"

"I regularly reported to them about what was happening in the Commune."

"What did they look like?" Rick asked.

"Like normal people. They were always surrounded by light."

Rick and Maya looked at each other.

"There was always a priest by my side, watching me," Drachus continued. "At first I nearly lost my mind, but I then I got used to it and went along with it." He was quiet for a moment, as if thinking is he should share something important, but then made up his mind. "The most unpleasant part was managing the population of the Commune. The sector had limited resources, so they had to be distributed evenly. The number of people had to stay stable. If too many children were born, more old people had to be removed, so that there was enough food and water for everyone, otherwise starvation would set in."

Maya jumped up from the chair, consumed with rage.

"And then you talk about love and care? I just can't believe it!"

"I understand you, but we had no other choice."

"That's rich!" Rick was surprised. "There is so much free space around, and you had no choice!"

"We didn't!" Drachus slammed his fist on the table. "They forbid it. They said that if a new generation of the Commune grows and starts to take over neighboring sectors, it will cause chaos and endless wars that will ruin the architecture of the Expanse and all of Thermopolis will be threatened. This is what they said and I believed them. Sometimes, they allowed us to send out small units and attack the disunited tribes outside, but it was more as a way of letting off steam, as opposed to real need."

"I think I understand why they organize all these games to reach a new level now," Rick said.

"Yes. And then, my time had come. I could not step into the chasm, I was too afraid. I chose banishment instead, where I should have died from the poisonous beasts or starvation, but fate decreed otherwise. Then, I went up here and have been living on this level since those times."

Drachus went silent and greedily drank some water from a large bottle. Tommo whistled quietly.

"The communication system works," Maya pointed out the main thing.

"And the one who controls it knows the whole truth," Rick summarized

"Could you set up a new conversation using the local terminal?" Maya asked with interest.

Drachus laughed sadly in reply.

"Everything was controlled by those damn priests!" he said. "I never touched a single button over those years."

"But surely you must have remembered the combinations and other details?"

"Of course I did! I even tried to start up the terminal by myself when I was Warden and had the opportunity. But a priest suddenly appeared by my side and warned me not to do that under pain of death. They were somehow always one step ahead of me. It was almost like they were reading my mind, the demons."

"All right, but they are not nearby now," Maya smiled.

Drachus froze—his face twisted and an unhealthy glint appeared in his eyes.

"Are you entirely sure of that?" he asked.

"I'm not."

Rick felt uneasy. His feeling were being confirmed and his fears became flesh and blood. It looked like the old Warden was gradually losing his mind after being imprisoned by loneliness for many years. But maybe there was some truth in his words? He also sometimes felt that there was someone watching them all the time.

"That sounds like..." Rick began.

"Like what?" Drachus exclaimed, and then continued, "You must understand, boy, anything is possible in this world and in these walls. I understood this a long time ago when I realized that I don't know even a hundredth part of all the wonders that fill this giant labyrinth of floors and stairways. There are safe places like my lair, but the rest is a hungry abyss, ready to consume you at any moment."

A depressing silence hung over the room. The Warden suddenly stood up.

"Let's go," he picked up his weapon from the chair by his side, "I will show you something interesting."

The followed him through the zigzagging passageways and stairways and finally came out in a spacious corridor. This sector was not particularly symmetrical or similar to the ones below—the whole sector was like a jumble of glass balls and tubes randomly connected together. Rick quickly lost his bearings. The rats ran from the Warden, squeaking loudly. It looked like they knew who was coming, Drachus probably killed many of their kin.

Then, they passed through a chain of upward and downward slopes, galleries and rooms of all sorts of shapes and sizes. Unremarkable halls alternated with multicolored rooms chock full of brightly colored machines, tables covered with green cloth, long tables connected together, tables with holes, balls and other figures in the middle as well as tables divided into squares with numbers. They passed cabins separated from the world outside by curtains with pictures of laughing men and women, as well as some sort of multicolored creatures. They passed miniature buildings and figures of people that were put together in one large horizontal space—such models filled one of the large halls. They passed halls with long paths that had large balls with holes in them nearby, with bottle-shaped statuettes lying around.

When Drachus led them into yet another hall, Rick and Maya stopped, almost unable to breathe—the hall was full of people. But after they took a closer look, they understood that these were simplified copies of human figures that were draped in desiccated rags. The companions passed by display windows with jewelry, ancient footwear and bags, clothing and headwear behind them, whole squadrons of bottles and flasks, little boxes and tins, with contents that had long spoiled or dried out.

They negotiated rows of tables, pools, sculptures and signs that seemed to go on forever and in every kind of combination. Rick's head was completely mixed up because of the plethora of items in this sector. He saw pictures, figurines and even skeletons of unknown beasts that had once live in the Expanse. He saw whole plots of land and rock surrounded by low fences that seemed to present some sort of arrangements— dips and hills, gray rocks, red rocks, black pieces of slate, whole piles of little stones and pieces of something that looked like red syrup with white veins.

Once, they saw an effigy behind glass—it was a man, bearing a spear and dressed in the furs of some unknown beast, all tanned and half-naked, with a large jaw and a slanting forehead. His eyes were the most striking feature, as his unknown creator managed to make them show both an animal and a sentient nature. There were more figures like this further along the corridor— most of them had partially decayed and fallen apart, but sometimes there were very well preserved works of stone that portrayed humans, animals and their hybrids in horrific combinations against incredible backgrounds, which invited a closer and more careful look at all the details. There were figures of humans in metallic clothing or in fish scales, those holding enormous, long knifes, figures bearing ancient versions of the blaster, wearing wide brimmed hats, conical and round helmets, figures with banners, in four wheeled machines, astride four legged animals with tails, those wearing long-skirted clothing, men bearing canes and wearing pieces of glass on their eyes and people with mysterious little boxes in their hands. There were women wearing clothing of every kind of length and style and there were children and their pet animals.

Then they entered rows of ancient technology, moving from simple tools to complex mechanisms of unknown origin that had strange shapes.

For instance, there was a double tube with glass on the end. Or a ball on a stand. There was a whole box full of little objects, like windows, signs and arrows. There were small items that looked like needles and large ones that looked like clock faces, short and long, the use of some being obvious from their appearance and others that were complex and composed of many parts. Rick was amazed by a small machine that looked like a box, but which was composed of a hundred small parts that were visible outside and ended in a small pad, probably so that it could be touched with fingers. The insides of this device were like the skeleton of the boniest fish in the world: rods, springs, cogs and wheels were connected inside like an arcane puzzle. Another device was just a ball hanging on a string above a circle. The ball was still.

"We are walking through the museum zone," Drachus explained. "Museums are something like a storeroom for objects from the past."

"What's the point of storing them?"

"To remember," Maya said. "It is very important."

"That's correct," the Warden said and gave the girl an approving glass. The ancients came to the museums and remembered how their even more ancient ancestors looked.

"It never crossed my mind that someone could have existed before them," Rick admitted.

"Us humans have a long history."

Their journey came to an end at last. Drachus brought them to yet another platform that had a door with a familiar sigil nearby.

"A terminal," Maya guessed. "There's one of these in every sector."

"Yes, but that is not what I wanted to show you." The Warden made a sharp turn on his heels and took around ten steps to the side, so she stood by a bulge in the wall that looked like wider version of a ventilation shaft.

"While those scumbags were watching me, I unobtrusively watched them too. And you know what I found out? Every time that a priest entered a room like this, they disappeared without a trace. This is how I concluded that they somehow get to the place where the people on the machine screens are. Have a look. Maybe you know something about this?

"It's an elevator, Warden," Maya says. "It takes things up."

Drachus understood, just not immediately.

"Oh, a machine that moves up and down?"

"That very thing." Rick confirmed. "The priests used the elevator and there is nothing amazing about that. There is a different question here. If the elevators in the Omicron sector had been blocked long ago, how did their elevator work?"

"The same way as the communicator," Maya replied. "They handle technology as easily as you handle a knife."

"Yes." The Warden licked his lips. "This is what I thought about when you told me about the genetic code. Maybe it will work? Try it."

"No problem," Rick answered. "But first, I want to know why this will work with me and not with you. You're the Warden."

"I am a person from Omicron, and you're not!" the Warden breathed out.

"What does that mean? I was born and I grew up in the Commune..." Rick began, but then remembered Kyoto's words.

Drachus guessed what he was thinking.

"Whatever you though right now, you already understood that you're wrong."

"What do you know? Tell me." Rick stepped towards Drachus, piercing him with a demanding glare. "Come on!"

"Relax." Drachus frowned. "It is related to your mother."

"She was born outside the sector. And what does that mean?"

"That she was biologically different to the people of Omicron. She was an outsider, and she was already pregnant when they brought her here. Pregnant with you!"

"Which sector was she taken from?"

"Only Croesus knows. He was leading the retaliation force. He said that he personally chose her among the other barbarian women and..." Drachus faltered.

"Speak!" Rick grabbed him by the collar.

"Let me go, boy! Calm down!"

"Tell me what you wanted to say! Come on! Tell me, or I will gut you right here!" Rick put a blade to the stomach of the old man with a quick movement.

"She was Croesus' concubine!" Drachus exclaimed.

Rick stepped back. His face paled. He turned away and walked over to the edge of the platform. Maya started to talk to the old man about genetics, trying to defuse the situation. Tommo calmly stood nearby and looked around without a care. Rick gathered his thoughts and came back to the elevator. He approached, as Drachus was trying to explain his ideas to Maya.

"From the conversations of the priests, I generally managed to establish that humans have different types of this code. Simple technology requires standard passwords or combinations that even a child could enter. Machines that are too complicated or dangerous work by reading the code from the hand. I saw the priests lay their hands upon panels and the machine only obeyed them because they had that code. If the machine obeyed him," the patriarch nodded at Rick, "it means that his mother was born in one of the upper sectors. Maybe they are people of a higher caste that are the direct descendants of the ancients? Who knows."

"Enough talk," Rick interrupted and approached the elevator panel.

The black square looked like it was drawn on the wall. Rick pressed his head on the panel.

There was no effect.

"That's that," he said. We can go back now.

"Wait," Maya pulled on his sleeve. "You are always too hasty."

"What is there to wait for? The machine does not react."

"Because it needs to be turned on."

She flicked the switch on the elevator control panel from the bottom to the top position.

A second later, the panel hummed quietly. Rick repeated the attempt. This time, a green light started to blink against the black background. They waited with bated breath. Numbers appeared, counting down from floor seven hundred and forty.

"Our floor is six hundred and forty," Maya reminded, and they started to watch the countdown on the panel. To their surprise, the elevator arrived very quickly.

"We can run away before it's too late," Maya said.

"Never," Rick cut her off. "Prepare to shoot."

But there was no need for shooting. The elevator opened and the brightly lit and clean cabin was empty. A pleasant breath of fresh air came out of it. It was a new and unfamiliar smell.

"It seems that this is where we part our ways," Drachus said, as he handed Rick his heavy and cumbersome weapon. "Be careful with this thing, it's quite powerful. It has enough charge for a couple of hundred shots."

"Thank you, Warden. And what about you?"

"I can do without. There are rooms full of this stuff around here."

Maya and Tommo stepped into the cabin. Rick stopped for a second to talk to Drachus.

"I am sorry for being so hot tempered and... my suspicions about you."

"You shouldn't be. I would be the same if I was in your place. You didn't just grow up without a father, you also had this happen to your mother. Be careful. Good luck!"

A moment later, the panels of the elevator slid shut, cutting the three of them off from the old man, and the cabin headed upwards so quickly that they had to grab onto the railings on the walls.

"We are coming up to floor seven hundred and forty!" Maya exclaimed.

"Why not higher?" Rick enquired.

"It's simply not possible. This elevator is made for one aeon. It's written right here," she pointed to a sign under the buttons.

The walls were translucent and they could see the lamp lights rush downwards through a matte-gray haze. After a few seconds, they heard a melodic peal. The display on the side lit up with a message—"Floor 740". The elevator reached its destination and the panels slid open. They entered a corridor, holding their weapons at the ready.

Rick had already learned to orient himself using the signs on the walls and said, "Lambda sector."

Maya, who had spent many hours studying the diagram, added as she walked along, "It's a residential sector. The whole aeon is residential. This is the core of Thermopolis."

"An empty core," Rick added, as he looked around.

Everything was just as abandoned and ruined as below. The only difference was probably the chain of emergency lamps flickering under the ceiling, as well as relative cleanliness. There was almost no mold to be seen and the dark streaks were only in the places where the air ducts had been pierced. Tommo smelled the air and moved as if he wanted to touch it. His black fingers slowly moved in the air. And then he put them together into the "Quiet!" sign.

They had already learned to understand the prole and obediently quietened down. Tommo moved on ahead, completely soundlessly—a ghost in an orange jumpsuit. They approached a junction with a large circular corridor and glanced around the corner. A stranger in a white jumpsuit and a helmet with a dark glass visor was standing on a small platform that led to an incline, a place where there was usually a view of the gap between segments. He was holding a lit datapad in his hands, which he was obviously consulting as he bent towards an electronic panel which was built into the wall and read the messages which appeared on it. The stranger was quietly and singing something incomprehensible to himself. Having finished with the datapad, he pressed a button on the panel and the doors of an elevator opened in the wall. One step, and the stranger was gone.

Tommo signed that everything was fine. The companions left their hiding place. It turned out that there were entrances to several different elevators on the platform. Rick walked up to the panel to examine it more closely. Maya was reading the signs by every elevator. Suddenly, the panel in front of Rick lit up and an unfamiliar face appeared on the screen.

"Johnson?" a slightly distorted voice came right out of the panel.

Rick threw himself to the floor and crawled over to the wall.

"Hey Johnson, stop messing around!" the panel spoke again.

Maya and Tommo also crouched down and flattened themselves against the wall by his side.

"Rushdie? Romanov? Damn you!"

And the screen went black.

Rick breathed out loudly.

"It's getting more and more fun," Maya piped up.

"What're we going to do?"

"If Ahmed was here, he would have helped us make sense of all these communications."

"But he is not here," Rick noted with regret, "which is why we mus decide what to do. What does it say on the signs?"

"One elevator only works in this sector, the other is for transportation through the aeon, and that wide one," Maya pointed ahead, "moves between aeons."

"Excellent. I'll go and lay my hand on it."

Rick wanted to get up, but Maya pulled him back.

"Wait! You're hurrying too much again, instead of thinking properly."

Rick sniffed with impatience.

"If they control the technology, they are sure to notice that someone has used the elevator," Maya continued her argument. "Someone that they don't know."

Tommo nodded quickly.

"You're right," Rick admitted. "I never thought of that."

"Apologies accepted. Let's consider this me saving your life." She winked at him happily.

"Even now, there's a risk that they can see us, I just don't know how."

Those words made everyone uneasy. But there was nothing they could do.

"What now, then? Why don't we go to the center and then go up the stairs to the top of aeon?" Rick offered.

"I don't like this idea. There could be traps there."

"And also your pals from Kappa." Rick scratched his head quizzically. "They have probably decided that your unit has died and sent out another."

"That, too." Maya agreed.

Time passed while they decided what to do. And then, a panel lit up with messages on one of the elevators and the countdown began. Tommo jumped up with amazing agility to a great height, sticking to the ceiling and hiding there like a huge spider. Rick quickly thought of what to do, whispered his plan to Maya and moved behind the projecting part of the wall by the elevator door panels. When everything was ready and the panels slid open, the unknown new arrival was met by Maya with her hands raised. Their plan hung by a hair. All Rick could see from his hiding place was the face of his female companion.

"Who are you?" a scared voice rang out from the cabin.

"I'm lost," Maya replied, almost in tears. "Please take me with you."

"What are you doing here? How did you get here?" the questioning continued.

"It's hard to tell..." she let a tear drop naturally down her face and started to sob. "Please, I beg you..."

A man in white came out of the elevator and Rick smashed the massive stock of the weapon that Drachus gave him onto his head. In a moment, all three of them were bent over the body, examining the stranger curiously—he wore a jumpsuit of thick white cloth which looked like it was inflated as well as a breathing mask and goggles that were a lot like a prole's ocular lenses on his head.

"So what do we do now?" Maya asked. "Should we throw him into the chasm?"

"We could wait for him to come to and interrogate him properly," Rick stood up straight, "but we don't have much time. Look!"

He pointed at the elevator—the panels would definitely have slid shut, but Tommo stepped into the opening and managed to hold them. Maya and Rick slid into the cabin and rushed to examine the control panel.

"That's that!" Rick said. "The way back has been cut off. As soon as that white one wakes up, he will raise the alarm. Hurry and press the button!"

"Which floor?" Maya looked up at him in confusion. "I can dial anything I want here!"

The big screen flashed a message offering a trip to floors from one to one thousand two hundred and fifty. The companions stood still for a moment, realizing all the possibilities open to them. They could go to the very first floor or go on a trip to the roof of the world. They could see the floors of any aeon of Thermopolis. Which one should they choose?

"We could go straight to the Control Center," Maya said at last.

"No," Rick shook his head. "Delta sector. Dial it in!"

And Maya pressed the required combination of buttons.

15

THE FLOORS FLASHED BY behind the glass so quickly that it was impossible to count them. Pushed down by the gravitational force of their velocity, the companions sped upwards, holding on tight to the railings. Dozens of floors were below them but none of that mattered. Rick and Maya were only concerned with one question:

how would they overcome the defenses of the first aeon?

It took them but a minute to fly past the sectors of the third aeon and arrive in an uninhabited section, which glowed green for some reason. Rick tried to make out any special detail they could find, but the cabin had already crossed another border between segments and the Kappa sector surrounded them with a sea of lights that blazed past them like a single, incandescently hot gas cloud. And then, the light was instantly replaced by darkness—the Iota sector displayed its cold, lifeless space before their eyes.

Rick and Maya exchanged worried looks and stared back out of the window, where the segments of the Theta sector rushed on by. Impenetrable darkness surrounded them again. Even the perpetually calm Tommo moved his head around tensely. Rick was about to say something when the light suddenly appeared outside—the Eta sector met them with cavernous halls filled with people and unusual machines. Then the cabin crossed the Zeta sector, where the only signs of life were on the last few floors. Only Rick could not understand who it was that lived there—humans, or a pale imitation of sentient humanoids. Anyway, a vicious battle between the denizens of the sector flashed by behind the glass. Dozens of people were mercilessly slaughtering each other...

Maya turned away. Rick followed her example, and both froze as they tensely watched the huge gap on the other side of the cabin. The levels of the new, faraway section were practically dead. There were lights shining or blinking here and there, like lighthouses in the night of the Expanse, lighting a long and steep overhang.

Rick stepped forward when the cabin rose over the overhang. It looked like a man was standing on the edge. Rick never had the chance to figure out what he was planning—the cabin careered away from him.

They sped upwards, piercing space like a blaster charge. The elevator was already sliding between the first and second aeons, with the white hot rod of the Chorda in the distance. The ceiling of the first aeon was falling towards them like the hammer of a huge press falling upon an anvil. Rick forced himself to stand up straight with an effort of will. The ceiling kept approaching and bulging metallic segments as well as wide ventilation grilles and manholes could now be made out. When the cabin flew into a dark opening that continued into a shaft, Rick's head cleared of all conscious thought.

He shut his eyes. Then he opened them.

The elevator kept moving. The security

system had let them through!

The Expanse bathed in streams of light that seemed to be pouring in from all sides.

"Epsilon sector!" Maya exclaimed excitedly.

They passed the thousandth floor and flew upwards past levels that were swimming with people. And this was when the cabin started to noticeably slow down. Floors glittering with multicolored lights slid on by. Rick and Maya were stuck to the glass—the hall through which they were passing was full of people. Brightly clothed men and women danced, ate and drunk to the sounds of groovy beats that came through the thick glass of the cabin. Rick had never seen faces so full of joy. The eyes of every resident, young and old radiated satisfaction, comfort and fulfillment, their cheeks had a healthy glow and everyone without exception looked strong, robust and healthy! People were sitting or lying down on soft and comfortable looking chairs and sofas, the tables were heavy with delicious foods and long shelves full of various objects lined the walls...

After the hall, there was another level where around twenty residents were carousing around a long table and moving tall glasses full of a golden liquid around in front of themselves. One man was rapturously saying something while they did that...

The cabin kept smoothly moving on. On

another level, a heavy-set old man in a colorful jacket was delivering a speech from a raised pulpit to a hall of listeners. The audience sat behind separate tables of four or five people each. They were eating and drinking well here, the same as in previous halls. Many happily applauded the old man and raised their glasses in greeting...

On the third level, small, separate groups of people were obviously having fun with various games, laughing and arguing amongst themselves.

The next level was full of those who danced in a dark space that was suddenly lit by flashes of multicolored light.

The following hall was full of blue light and people swimming around in a big aquarium and lying under bright lamps. Their bodies, weary from the heat and pleasure were occasionally making slight, lazy movements in the steamy mist.

Further on, there was a hall where people sat behind tables lit by the soft light of spherical lamps and attentively studied something, some of them conversing among themselves, writing things down and making drawings.

There was a room where a little boy was assembling a tower from different colored cubes. The boy got distracted and curiously glanced in the direction of the elevator cabin.

There were rooms where some men and women got washed, clothed and had their hair dressed by other men and women and other rooms where they battled humanoid machines, shooting them with blasters, probably so that they could train their reactions and stamina. And yet more rooms where they watched moving pictures and entire shows...

All of these levels and rooms glided by Rick and Maya, making their hearts beat at a breakneck speed, promising an encounter with something even more unusual and undiscovered. The young travelers were so entranced by what they had seen that they did not immediately understand that the elevator had stopped. A soulless metallic voice declared, "You are about to be disinfected." The cabin was filled with steam that had a caustic and unpleasant smell, but Rick and Maya did not have the time to get scared as the gas was quickly pumped away and the panels of the elevator slid apart.

Rick waited, looking at Maya. They both turned around—Tommo had completely disappeared. They did not try to find out where the prole had gone, but hurried to exit onto a spacious balcony. Rick could not resist and glanced at the cabin, noticing how the hatch in the roof of the cabin moved and then got closed tight. It seemed that Tommo decided to leave their company for some sort of reasons of his own. But why?

"Rick, come on, where are you?" Maya was waving him over while standing by the barrier.

Entrances to circular corridors could be seen on both sides and an enormous hall filled with several hundred people lay ahead. Some were conversing, lolling around in large armchairs, others were strolling around, drinks in hand and others were looking at stone idols on podiums or pictures on the walls. Music was playing, its subtle melodic patterns like nothing that Rick had heard before. It was warm here, but not hot, with the touch of gentle currents of air which were cool but never cold. This was the kingdom of beauty, harmony and peacefulness.

Rick and Maya stood completely still with inane smiles plastered across their faces until their attention was attracted with the sound of footsteps coming from one side. A group of people dressed in white and gold clothing appeared in one of the circular corridors. The group was accompanied by armed guards dressed in red. When they came out onto the balcony, a tall, bald man with a long face and large gray eyes stepped forward.

"Welcome," he said.

Everything looked like they had been waiting

for Rick and Maya and knew about their arrival in advance. Maybe Drachus was right and had kept quiet about something? Rick swallowed nervously. He was worried by Tommo's disappearance, he did not like the armed guards dressed in red and he did not know what to expect from these strangers, how they would welcome them or what he should say...

Recovering a little from the unexpected greeting, he suddenly understood what he looked like in the eyes of these people at that moment: wearing a dirty jumpsuit permeated with the smell of slime and sewage, uncombed and unshaven, his eyes looking wild and trapped, like those of an animal. And of course, he had that terrifying blaster at the ready...

"We..." Rick started and then stopped, pretending to cough.

"You have been on a hard journey," the bald man said respectfully. "Which is why you need to rest and get yourselves in order." Then, in a tone that brooked no objections, he added, "Please, follow me."

They were taken straight into the hall. They walked along, looking around while all of these shining people in their golden clothing were curiously examining them. Rick felt uncomfortable. It was not because these people looked at them like they were uncouth savages or barbarians, the problem was that he could see that the compassion in their eyes. They genuinely felt sorry for them, which angered and irritated him for some reason.

They left the hall and walked on through a gallery decorated with frescoes of beautiful everyday scenes until they reached a room filled with round tables covered in pristine white tablecloths, occupied by other people with compassionate eyes.

"Have a seat," the bald man said and signaled the waiters that immediately brought bowls full of steaming, delicious smelling soup.

To add to this, unfamiliar but appetizing looking fruit was placed on plates in front of them. Rick was looking at it and barely stopping himself from attacking the food. Judging by Maya's face, she had the same feelings.

"What are you waiting for?" the bald man asked in confusion. "Please, help yourself. We are not going to interrupt you."

And everyone quietly left, leaving them along in the large room.

"By the Great Axis," Maya exclaimed as her hands darted out towards a juicy red fruit and her teeth pierced its sweet flesh, releasing the juice.

Rick did not waste time and attacked the soup, also trying every single fruit that was on the side plate. They drank and ate, smiling at each other and forgetting about everything. The soup and the fruit were simply exquisite. Finally, once they had cleaned out all of the plates, they blissfully sat back in the chairs and laughed.

"I can't get up," Maya groaned, rolling her eyes with pleasure. "And I don't want to..."

They began to feel sleepy. The serving staff quietly appeared nearby to replace the empty plates on the table with hot drinks and sweets. Without pause, Rick and Maya both consumed their portions, after which they were invited into neighboring rooms that had soft and clean beds laid out for them. They were informed that these were now their personal apartments. Rick thanked the serving staff and started by looking around the room. He found a clean towel and a piece of soap on the bedside table, as well as a curtained alcove containing a basin and a shower cabin. New clothing hung on a chair nearby.

A pleasant looking woman came into the room, after knocking and asking for permission to enter. She asked Rick to give her his filthy jumpsuit so she could wash it. A short man came in next and asked him to try on the clothing, taking Rick's measures and promising him to adjust the clothes to his size.

"This is only temporary," the man said. "We will tailor you a decent suit later."

Rick looked at himself in the mirror. His new, white suit was comprised of a pair of trousers, a shirt and a cloak which was cleverly held by a pin at the shoulder. Noticing the reflection of the blaster he had left by the bed, Rick glanced back at it. The blaster seemed to be an ugly black piece of wreckage, a savage's club which had no place withing these walls. He did not want to part with the weapon and no one seemed to ask him to, so Rick moved the blaster under the bed.

Then, a man with a pair of scissors and a comb came in, introduced himself as a hairdresser and cut Rick's hair exactly the way he wanted. Afterwards, the hairdresser beautifully and neatly combed it and sprayed it with some pleasant smelling liquid.

Rick could not resist and decided to visit Maya in the neighboring room. She did not waste her time either—it turned out that the servants looked after her as well. Rick did not recognize his companion when he entered Maya's room—a white dress outlined her figure, her golden red hair was gathered in a bunch, a golden necklace glittered around her neck and her wrists bore bracelets decorated with smoky blue stones.

The pair were looking at each other in surprise, unable to say anything.

"You look... Very beautiful," Rick managed to

squeeze out.

And then he blushed in embarrassment.

"Thank you. You too." Maya looked at him with interest. Her eyes shone with happiness and delight. "It suits you."

"Is everything all right?"

"I think so."

They went quiet. The serving man that Rick had already met appeared in the doorway and asked, "Are you ready?"

They both nodded, and the man continued, "Then follow me to meet the Chairman."

Rick tried to ask their escort about the Chairman and what he would talk to them about, but always received a standard answer: "In time, everything will be explained to you."

Their escort brought them to a balcony over the sector segment gap, where they were awaited by the bald man with a long face who had met them by the elevator. This time he was alone and unguarded.

"So there you are, my friends," he began. "I am happy to see you again. My name is Paris."

Rick and Maya introduced themselves in turn.

"Pleased to meet you," Paris replied. "I immediately took a liking to you at first sight. I can feel the power in you. Although, only people of that kind could ever get here."

"We didn't just go for a walk," Rick replied. "And you know that very well. Thank you for the food and rest and for all this beauty," he flicked the cuff of his shirt, "but we really need to solve an important problem."

"You are right, of course, Rick from Omicron. Or, perhaps, Rick Omicron? It would be more convenient for me to address you in that fashion. And you, my dear girl, would be Maya Kappa, of course."

Rick nodded.

"As you like," Maya shrugged. "I don't mind."

"Excellent," Paris continued. "I am prepared to offer you any assistance you require."

He spread his arms, demonstrating his good intentions.

"We need to visit the archive," Rick demanded. "Right now."

"All right. As you wish." Paris smiled and led them towards the Chorda along the balcony.

Rick was bewildered—everything was too easy. He never took his eyes off Paris, who began telling them about the structure of the first aeon and the Epsilon sector.

Like the other four, the first aeon consisted of five sectors: Alpha, Beta, Gamma, Delta and Epsilon. There was a hangar and landing pads for flying machines at the very top, as well as equipment for communicating with the outside world which was not working at the moment. The ancient architects had installed power generators to collect solar and wind energy in sector Beta. These generator complexes were so powerful that they supplied the whole aeon with energy. Moisture collectors were located there too. The third sector was the Thermopolis Control Center. This was where all the data from all aeons and other sectors arrived. The operators constantly monitored the state of the external surface, thermal networks, water supplies and other life support essentials. The fourth sector, where the Chairman was now leading Rick and Maya, contained scientific research laboratories, archives and technical databases. There was also a book and media library that contained millions of units of information created by ancient humans. The scientists of Epsilon sector had spent years working in the archives and studying every grain of information. And finally, Epsilon itself was designed for residence and recreation.

As Paris explained things to them, they reached a connecting corridor that led them to the well of the Chorda and approached a stairway where the steps moved upwards by themselves. Rick concealed his surprise and stepped onto the stairs after Paris and Maya.

"The escalator," which was the way Paris called the moving stairway, "will deliver us to the archive in a few minutes."

"Where do you get your food?" Maya asked with interest.

"Oh, we have all we need to do that!" Paris smiled at her. "It would be a pleasure for me to take you through every floor of each of the four segments and show you the life of our sector. And then, if you wish, we can rise floor by floor until we reach the roof."

Rick was looking at this bald man and did not know how to behave. Paris was genuinely happy to see them, as if he had been waiting for their visit for a long time and could not wait to show off the local attractions. As soon as they even glanced at some structure or level, Paris caught on what they were looking at and enthusiastically explained the purpose of such things to them until the attention of his guests switched to something else. Rick exchanged glances with Maya a few times, but did not manage to understand her reaction to what was going on.

The escalator snaked upwards along the inner wall of the Chorda well. Rick looked down into the chasm, which was enshrouded by darkness. A barely audible rumble came from below. The Chorda stretched out into space, a pillar of white light which it hurt to observe.

Noting Rick's interest in the Chorda, Paris

perceptively said, "It has been three days since the Axis came to life. The operators have noticed the activation of the external shell—the air intakes have closed and the outer wall has started to heat up. Do you know anything about this?"

"We'd like to know ourselves," Rick mumbled thoughtfully.

Paris nodded.

"In that case, we will address this issue as soon as we are finished with the archive. There is a lot we need to tell each other."

Rick was in full agreement with him in this matter.

The escalator took them higher and higher, and they had now gone past the residential levels of the Epsilon sector. The floors covered with flat windows were replaced by walls with oval bulges, divided into equally sized segments. The ovals blinked with multicolored lights, lighting up and going out in a complex pattern. Rick looked up— the ovals made the internal surface of the well into a living mosaic, in which the fragments constantly arranged themselves into patterns and spots of color.

"The Central Computer," Paris explained. "The brain of Thermopolis. It processes all of the information that comes in from the external and internal sensors, archives it and issues instructions. All of the automatic functions rely on it."

They heard a crackling coming from the depths of the wall. Now and again, lightning arced between adjacent ovals.

"The memory units are charged with electricity. I would not advise touching them, or you will turn into pieces of charcoal."

"And what if the machine breaks down?" asked Maya.

"It's best not to think about that," Paris replied. "There are only around ten people that know the inner workings of the computer, but even they would require half their lifetime to find and fix the fault."

"But this machine can't work forever," Rick noted. "Any machine has a finite lifetime."

"That's right." Paris gave him a strange look. "But this computer is made so that it can repair itself. It is self-sufficient—there are small machines that look like insects that work inside. The ancients made provisions for everything. By the way, I will show you the observation windows that face outwards. Would you like to see the outside world?"

"That would be really interesting!" Maya supported his idea, keeping quiet about the fact that they had already been outside once.

"So it's decided!"

The escalator delivered them to their destination. Paris led them under an arch labeled with a glyph Rick did not recognize and they found themselves in a corridor, which was walled with shelves several levels high, filled with oblong objects that looked like bricks of different shapes and colors. Paris went over to the nearest shelf and took out one of the bricks. It turned out that the brick could be opened and that it contained sheets of paper covered with tiny letters inside.

"These are books—and obsolete carrier of information," he said. "The ancients used to record their knowledge in them."

Maya stroked her fingers down some of the spines and read one of them out loud, "Ovid. The Art of Love."

They walked on, looking at the shelves which were occupied by legions of books. It seemed that there would be no end to them. The shelves extended into space on every side and it would have been easy to get lost in this monotonous labyrinth—it was enough to step in the wrong direction and lose sight of one's companions.

Finally, they came out into an open space, arriving in a hall full of tables and lamps. A deafening silence hung over the hall and Rick counted three strangers behind the tables. They were poring over books and ignoring the new arrivals. Only one of them raised his head for a moment and then returned to his reading.

Wordlessly, Paris headed towards a wide stairway that led to the highest level, plated in glass, as Rick and Maya quietly hurried after them.

Yet again, they found themselves in a labyrinth of shelves, but their structure had changed, as they became semicircular and smaller in size— they were filled with cases of discs similar to those that Rick and Maya had seen in the room where they watched the living pictures. However, Paris did not even think of stopping, as he passed through the gallery to lead his companions along a corridor that contained a chain of white doors to both sides. The doors had serial numbers and signs. On one side Rick read "Astronomy", "Solid-state Physics", "Biochemistry" and "Bacteriology". On the other side, the signs read "Sociology", "Macroeconomics", "Statistics" and "Philosophy". One of the doors was ajar and Rick stopped as he came alongside it—he saw a room filled with a row of chairs with small screens over the armrests. Paris walked on and stopped by a door with a sign that said "History".

"So what do you want to find out?" he asked.

Rick and Maya exchanged glances and chorused, "Everything!"

Paris smiled.

"That is about the answer I expected. However, you will not manage to find out "everything" today."

"We understand," Rick said. "We want to know what Thermopolis is. The whole truth."

"All right."

They entered the room. Paris sat them down in the chairs. For some reason, Rick thought that they were completely in this man's power, but he did not show his feelings and did not object to anything. Paris let them both swallow a purple pill and explained, "This improves brain activity. It will help you understand and remember everything well. I will now connect electrodes to your foreheads and temples and you will need to put helmets with glasses on your heads so that you can see a colored living picture. It's not painful. The only thing you might experience afterwards is some slight dizziness. Watch. I dial "Thermopolis" in on the panel. The machine gives a list of results: "Thermopolis. Technical Data.", "Thermopolis. Demographics", "History of Thermopolis" and many others. We are interested in history. So we select it. The film is going to load now. It might seem long to you, but that will because of the stimulant, that pill I gave you. I will be close by. Enjoy watching."

Paris left. Rick glanced at Maya. She was

biting her lip, blushing with excitement. The large screen on the wall displayed a message: "Film loaded. Put on your helmet."

And Rick obeyed the instruction.

16

MAN WAS MIGHTY in his power. He transformed the world in which he lived, building cities, redirecting rivers, constructing dams, eroding mountains to their very bottom, raising islands among the seas and draining huge bodies of water. He flooded the deserts with oases and turned whole continents of ice into oceans.

Man was great, and all he touched bore his mark. Especially the cities, some of which stood for thousands of years until being abandoned.

When humanity became a global civilization and populated the whole planet, the creations of human hands reached an unbelievable scale. Man had climbed the highest mountains, descended into the deepest trenches of the world ocean, had visited the Earth's satellite and its neighboring red planet and finally left the confines of the Solar System.

One of the greatest architects lived in those times. His greatest creation rivaled the ancient pyramids of Cheops.

His name was Archimedes Spanidis.

Archimedes was a true master of his art, because he could construct buildings to any order, anywhere in the world. All of his creations stood out with their originality and durability, and it was impossible to mistake them for any other buildings. He approached construction as if it was a divine creation, giving all of himself to the process.

Since the time of his youth, when he walked amid the ruins of the Parthenon of Athens in his homeland of Greece, he decided to issue a challenge to eternity, surpassing all of the existing achievements of world architecture by constructing a building that would remain standing even after the fall of humanity.

The years passed. The young man grew and learned the intricacies of the art of architecture. As he gradually acquired knowledge and experience, his plan became increasingly clear. This was no longer a dream, but a project, that started to combine a plethora of sketches and calculations into a concrete diagram.

Archimedes Spanidis spent his whole life moving towards his goal. His project was named Thermopolis. Inspired by the ancient Greek legends of Olympic gods and the cultural life of the polises, Archimedes decided to create a hand-wrought Olympus—a gigantic, autonomous city-building, that was perfect in its engineering. It was a hollow mountain, filled with all that is necessary for a man to lead a fulfilling existence. Archimedes personally worked on the blueprints, contemplating and calculating every detail and element of the future construction, from its foundation to the top of the tower.

Once he completed his work on the blueprints, he sent an application to all of the architectural contests that took place in different countries around the world. He traveled to conferences, symposia and round tables, presenting his grandiose project to the public every time and fervently trying to prove that it was both possible and feasible.

But no one believed the architect.

At best, they attentively listened to him, nodded and then politely refused. At worst, they laughed. The project was unsuccessful over and over again. Meanwhile, the years passed and Archimedes lost the valuable time that nature had provided him, fully understanding that no other could ever implement his life's work.

Then one day, when he was sitting at home on his verandah and miserably looking out at the Aegean sea, his phone rang. The voice at the other end of the line uttered, "I will give you money to build Thermopolis."

At first, Archimedes thought that this was a prank call and was about to put the phone down, but then that same voice added, "This is my first and last offer."

The caller turned out to be a young Arab billionaire, the grandson of Sheikh Mahmoud ibn Al-Saadi—Madah Mahsood. The young man had inherited a gigantic fortune from his wealthy grandfather but decided that he wanted to use the money in another way, instead of growing it. When the architect and the billionaire met, Archimedes could not resist asking, "Why?"

Mahsood smiled.

"Money and wealth are worthless by themselves, and nothing is left of them in the end. A man must leave something more significant than bank accounts after he passes from this world."

"I understand."

Once the partners had discussed the cost of construction and the most important issues, Mahsood said, "You will have your financing. But under one condition."

Archimedes was ready for this to happen. He knew that the young man will make some demand, but the achievement of his goal had blinded him so much that he would have agreed to commit any crime and offer any sacrifice for his great project. Mahsood told him his condition, and added, "This must be done. You must give your oath!"

Archimedes was surprised, but he swore to fulfill the condition. And he did so.

The construction soon began. Archimedes hired a huge number of builders, contracted hundreds of companies, negotiated with a whole army of experts, carefully selected a construction site and built an entire city around it to house all of the workers. He obviously wanted to keep the project a secret until the very end, but it was very difficult no to notice a construction project on such a great scale. The news of the great construction traveled around the world, and journalists, investors, adventurers, religious fanatics, politicians, fraudsters and con men of all kinds made their way to the Thermopolis construction site. Even though the prudent Mahsood had purchased a huge piece of land which was treated as private property and surrounded with a whole regiment of guards, someone always managed to make it through the barrier. However, this did not prevent the builders from working on the project.

Archimedes was ecstatic.

His lifelong dream was becoming reality. His moments of joy did quickly change into hours of thinking about various issues, however. Difficulties arose from the first days of construction. As soon as the architect solved one problem, two new ones would appear.

Everything started when the foundation was being laid. Archimedes understood that even the most durable foundation would be unable to cope with this degree of stress. Something entirely new was required. However, there was no time for research, which was why he brought the best engineers in the world and set them this task, which they started to solve on-site. Through trial an error, the group of architects gradually managed to solve the complex problem. They designed four wings which would use each other for support and solve the issue of weight distribution and the pressure on supporting structures. To prevent the building from collapsing, thousands of especially modified liquid piles, that would increase in volume and penetrate the soil like the roots of a tree.

It was only then, as he watched the piles being poured in from a helicopter, that Archimedes was confirmed in something he had guessed at a long time ago, and which now became entirely clear to him—the Thermopolis had to be *grown*, not built. Like a sapling in the garden.

The first stone was laid by Mahsood.

A year later, he fell terminally ill. Following another half a year of battling the disease he still left this world. There were rumors that Mahsood had left some sort of secret message just before he died, but no one ever managed to find it. Archimedes inherited all of the Sheikh's fortune from his will. The relatives immediately initiated lawsuits against him. A scandal which threatened to grow into an international political conflict arose. Influential Arabs were threatening sanctions against the country which had allowed the construction of the gigantic complex in its territory. Pieces about the construction and its architect never left the latest news reports. Journalists never left Archimedes alone. In the end, he was forced to break all contact with the outside world and entirely concentrate on the construction project. His brother who was a Greek lawyer dealt with all connections with the outside world.

The lawsuit brought against Spanidis to the International Court should have been considered over the course of a year. An entire battalion of lawyers was working for the Arabs, who intended to not only claim the inheritance and all their expenses, but also to make the architect liable for apparently blackmailing the young Sheikh. Archimedes' brother brilliantly parried every attack using documents that proved that the agreement was signed in good faith. However, the hosting state recalled the protectorate status of the site under pressure and demanded that Archimedes must stop the construction.

The situation was growing dangerous. Archimedes had not even started the construction of the first floor yet. And then, his brother thought of an interesting idea.

"What is we make your building recognized as an independent state?"

"How will it solve our problems?" Archimedes did not understand.

"No state may limit the sovereignty of another. That means that any claims against us will be void, as you will turn from a private landowner into the head of a small but independent country called Thermopolis."

"But I can't be the only citizen of this country!"

"You won't be. It's time to invent a mission for your project, brother mine."

So while they were connecting the communication lines and digging pits to build level zero, which would be located underground, Archimedes began to think of a purpose for his brainchild. He held a large press conference on the following day, where he made a report that became history.

Archimedes spoke of the rapid development of human science, about progress and about the improvement of technology. The architect described the main issues of the century—environmental disasters, military conflicts, the economic crisis and planetary overpopulation. Archimedes warned that the growth of humanity would lead to mass starvation and a new world war. However, there was a solution, and it was much simpler than it seemed.

Thermopolis.

A city-building. A gigantic, autonomous complex that could hold up to two million people, the population of a small metropolitan area. A complex which included all that someone might need to lead a fulfilling life. Without going into technical details, Thermopolis would help solve the issue of housing, employment, food production, provision of clothing and entertainment and many other requirements without outside assistance. Archimedes turned on an interactive presentation of his project, describing every sector and every level of this gigantic building in detail. And then he made his clothing statement.

"I would like to invite all those that would like to a cheap home that includes every convenience that they might require to purchase it in Thermopolis at a bargain price which will only grow with time. Moreover, those that will want to purchase a place of their own in Thermopolis will become the citizens of this small state, with every right, guarantee and responsibility. You will want for nothing."

No one expressed any particular interest. Individual eccentric wealthy individuals applied and that was the end of it.

Archimedes was not taken aback—this was the reaction he expected. While the legal deliberations, issues with documents and endless negotiations went on, he could focus on his work.

The construction of Thermopolis took forty years.

The most technically complex and difficult works were carried out in the first five years. Having finished the construction of level zero, they laid the foundation layer on top of it and started to outline the shape of the future building. The wider the area the less pressure there would be at the bottom—this simple law was used in this case as well. According to the master blueprint, Thermopolis was shaped like a stepped cone that consisted of five segments called aeons, which would then be divided into five sectors each. There would be twenty five sectors, each containing fifty floors, making a total of one thousand two hundred and fifty floors at a height of just over five kilometers

A hand-wrought Mount Elbrus.

Every sector had its own purpose, which was inextricably linked to the other sectors and made one whole together with them—a gigantic residential complex. The sectors were designed with a dual purpose—both as elements of the whole building system and as mini-autonomous systems able to survive in isolation for a while.

The second five years was spent on building the fifth aeon—it was decided to count them from the top as that was what Archimedes wanted. At his stage, the architect hired the leading energy, communication and construction specialists, as well as many others, generously compensating them for their labor. Whole caravans of raw materials were brought to the building site, because transporting ready made objects was difficult, expensive and dangerous. The city around the construction site was overgrown with plants and factories and now had its own administration, taxation system and security forces.

Archimedes spent the next ten years on the erection of the fourth aeon. This was an incredibly complex stage, because the four wings and the main body of the building had to be connected into an impervious frame that would not collapse if there was an earthquake and which could resist floods. By this time, the tower was around a kilometer in height and already drew attention from afar, like a mountain in the middle of the plain. The laughter and mockery of

Archimedes gradually and inconspicuously quietened down. The populations of every country wanted to know what was going on at the building site. But Archimedes turned away from the people and did not want to comment on anything outside of official press conferences which were planned for the end of the construction of the latest aeon.

When the fifty-year-old Spanidis held his second conference, the world finally understood that he was not joking. An avalanche of Thermopolis citizenship applications was sent to Archimedes' construction company. However, the limit was very quickly reached. The number of application surpassed the capacity of the complex one hundred and twenty times over—two hundred and forty million people wanted to become citizens of Thermopolis. In the end, a general database was created. An especially selected team chose applicants based on secret criteria that were known only to a small circle of people. Spanidis did not just need people, he needed people of particular backgrounds, races, mental acuities, genders, ages, levels of education and natures of employment. An offer to become a citizen of the city-building could come to anyone that lived on planet Earth if Archimedes' team deemed them appropriate. Any person could become a citizen of Thermopolis—the poor of the slums of India and the wealthy residents of Swiss mansions had an equal chance of acceptance.

The construction of Thermopolis stimulated the development of the science of engineering. It was at the construction site that a huge number of innovative methods for joining frames were invented, as well as a new building material called plasteel. Technologies of building growth were used, where the frame was not made up of connected elements but grown through a process of cold melting that ensured the integrity of the structure. Special block models were developed for the internal walls—universal blocks and blocks with brackets, railing, and openings, just like a child's construction set. This allowed for the blocks to be assembled in any order according to the current building plans. The plates for the external lining were modeled according to similar principles. All of the building elements met the standard specifications developed by Archimedes' companies and were identified by a specific symbolic mark. It could be a circle or a triangle, a cross or a square— whatever the company decided was appropriate.

The chemical composition of the central core rod of the building was kept a secret. Some structures that were under construction were under restricted access, and the security service carefully checked everyone that worked there.

The third aeon was erected faster than the fourth, over six years. The sectors were assembled piece by piece, from four segments that were pulled towards the central supporting rod and linked to each other with resilient beams, making a giant internal ring around the two hundred meter thick rod. The sectors were laid one on top of another and attached to the rod, as well as around their perimeter, looking like a pyramid. While one army of builders grew the levels, the other was covering the lower aeons with three external shell layers, ensuring the complete isolation of the internal space from environmental effects. Helicopters, cranes, winches, internal elevators and massive anthropomorphic construction machines called exoskeletons operated by a single crewman from a cabin were used for the construction.

The second aeon was constructed over four years.

And the first, upper aeon, which was the smallest in volume took five years to build.

Thermopolis now had its shape and became noticeable dozens of kilometers away, looking like a gigantic stalagmite from afar. Some compared it to ancient Egyptian tombs where thousands of people would be buried alive, some called it a human termite mound and other's called it the Noah's Ark. Every observer found something of their own in Thermopolis. No one considered the building a flight of fancy anymore. Everyone agreed that this was a new wonder of the third millennium

The final five years were spent on interior decoration, the installation of utilities, elevators, communications and the placement of complex machinery. The builders were replaced by engineers and fitters, who were replaced by specialists in even more complex disciplines in turn. Thermopolis was like a sponge which absorbed particles of human culture, striving to summarize them and make a smaller copy of them. Books, artworks, ancient relics, unique objects, examples of different machinery, geological samples, soils and various plant and animal species were all brought to Thermopolis— everything that the planet and humanity could muster.

By the time construction was complete, Archimedes was seventy two years old. His eyesight was failing and he suffered from arthritis and hypertension. He felt the end approaching, but he could not yet rest as he had not finished the last of his work on Thermopolis. When all of the fireworks had thundered in honor of the grand opening of the building and when all the parties and other official ceremonies had passed, the state of Thermopolis declared itself complete and entirely independent of the outside world. The candidates chosen to be citizens were traveling to the tower from every corner of the planet.

But the construction works continued. Workers still toiled in the final levels and the final sets of machinery were still being supplied to the hangars. Thermopolis came to life—the generators that were its heart had been turned on, the ventilation system that formed its lungs was passing air through the pipelines and the automated systems which were its eyes, nose and ears were collecting and processing incoming data. However, the main thing was its lifeblood—its residents.

The date when Archimedes Spanidis died is unknown. A year after the Commissioning of his brainchild, he vanished without trace. The great architect's son said that his father was deep in thought in his last days and often sat on the balcony looking up at the starry sky.

The architect had made his dream come true.

His dream became reality not only for him, but also for over two million people that got a new chance in life. The Great Thermopolis still stands, its visage a testament to the power of humanity.

17

ONCE THE FILM was over, Paris returned to the room and led his guests further along.

He was graciously explaining everything that he knew about and answered the questions he was asked, but Rick's thoughts kept coming back to the archive and that first moment after watching the film when he could not understand where he was, and then how he saw Maya's bewildered face and stretched out towards her like a child towards its mother when it wakes up. The girl also stretched her hands out towards Rick and they embraced each other clumsily, almost falling out of their seats. It was a funny and pleasant moment, and Rick was smiling at the memory as he followed Paris down the corridor.

They soon approached the observation post in the Thermopolis Control Center.

A large section of the hall where the post was located turned out to be abandoned. The people of the Epsilon sector did not have enough specialists to watch all of the monitors and terminals. The operators took up barely a quarter of the places in the main hall, which was entirely filled with screens and control panels.

A three dimensional holographic model of

Thermopolis flickered in the middle of the hall, projected from the center of a round table. The model flickered in blue now. Paris explained that if an accident were to happen, that area would be colored in red. Blue meant that the complex was in hibernation mode. But now, the diagram started to show green lines around the Chorda and the outline of the well. This happened as the results of the actions of someone in the lower sectors—that was where they launched the Uranus program.

"What is that?" Rick asked about the program.

"We don't know. That information is secret and none of our citizens is able to gain access."

"Chairman, could you tell me why Thermopolis became the way that it is if it was planned as a fortress city?" Maya said. "Whole sectors are dark and abandoned. How did this happen?"

"It all happened because of the plague. The epidemic came in here from the outside world, and the sectors were automatically isolated to prevent its spread. And then somebody turned off the generators."

"What sort of plague was it?" Rick exchanged a meaningful look with Maya, who had once told him about the illness that had stricken the residents of Thermopolis.

An assistant approached Paris and quickly whispered something into his ear. A shadow passed over the face of the Chairman for a split second, but he quickly pulled himself together and nodded.

"We don't know what happened for sure, because the whole world was in chaos after the plague. No one recorded what was going on. Our historians know that no one paid much attention to the epidemic until the disease engulfed all of humanity like wildfire. As soon as they understood the gravity of the situation, it was too late. The infection attacked the human brain and destroyed the neurons—the brain cells, turning humans into dumb animals. Some died immediately, while others suffered from unbearable pain. The disease was considered to be infectious, but they could not work out the way the virus was spread. A quarantine was introduced around the world, but it did not help. The research required time, and there was none left. Soon, people started to get infected here as well. There were more of them every day, until the disease started to spread through the sectors. The President of Thermopolis then decided to seal the tower and introduce a strict quarantine in every sector. The epidemic seemed to stop, but then reignited with a newfound power. It was a terrible time. The crazed patients were running through the corridor, not knowing how to numb the pain. They attacked healthy people and destroyed anything they could lay their hands on. They were animals—wild, angry, rabid beasts.

The Government of Thermopolis decided on a desperate measure—sector isolation. All transport links were closed off. People spoke to each other using internal communication networks. This could not continue for long. Then, the revolts started. The sectors were going out of control. Some decided that it was time to get out, while others cut all interactions and switched off communications. There was also the third kind that declared independence and blamed their neighbors for all their ills."

Paris said all of this while looking at the hologram of the tower over the table. He turned back to them and finished his story, "The society of Thermopolis fell apart into factions. Fear of the plague ruled over all. The survivors were afraid to come outside for a long time. Every sector survived the way it could. We were a little luckier—we have energy installations and an autonomous life support system. This is what probably saved our lives."

"Did the plague recede?" Maya asked tensely.

"It vanished. The last person who was sick died many centuries ago. And we are praying for it never to repeat." Paris glanced at Rick. "You wanted to have a look at the Control Center. Here it is. I will be happy to answer any of your questions."

Rick was looking into the hall, glittering with the lights of control panels and monitors. They journey was over, here and now. Only one step remained.

"They told us that it is impossible to get in here. That the aeon's security was reliable."

"That is so."

"What for?" Rick asked. "What I mean is, what is the point in fencing yourself off from the rest of the world if the plague is long gone?"

"Maybe so that the remains of a sentient human race can be protected," Paris said. "The system is in place and it is stable."

"But people live below as well, and not all of them are monsters."

"Exactly. And they are also part of the system."

"I don't understand..."

"By the gods!" Maya covered her mouth with her hand.

"It seems that our sweet Maya Kappa has worked it out before you did," Paris said with a sad smile. "She is an intelligent young lady."

There was a pause, and one of the operators clearly stated, "Theta sector. Threat of main pipeline breach. Automated systems in standard mode. I would like to request the technicians to take charge of the situation and report."

"Let's not interrupt them," Paris offered, and set off towards the elevator.

"Chairman, I don't..." Rick tried to say.

"Dearest Rick Omicron," Paris made a sharp turn and raised his voice for the first time. "Over the last twenty four hours of your presence here you never expressed any interest in something that any normal person would have thought of in your place. Lovely Maya is polite, because she gives you the leading role, otherwise she would have asked how I know your name, why they call me Chairman and what is it I chair here a long time ago."

They entered the elevator, Paris pressed a button and continued, "This question is directly connected to another that keeps tormenting you. If it is difficult for you to connect all of the facts, then a practical demonstration should definitely help. While we descend to the Meeting Hall, I will answer the question that you didn't ask. I am the Chairman of the Government of Thermopolis, probably the last state left on Earth. Our small society has managed to not only survive in the chaos of oblivion, but managed to preserve its knowledge and the culture of its ancestors to take them through the dark present into a bright future. And this has all been achieved by the Government, that created a new control system on the ruins of the past that has let us keep the remains of humanity," and here he clenched his hand into a fist, "together."

The elevator quickly delivered them to the entrance into a spacious room, a lobby before a round hall with a mirrored ceiling and walls as well as a large oval table with people sitting behind it. Paris did not take Rick and Maya there—they walked along the corridor around the hall and walked up a small raised platform that led to the balcony. It was a good place to observe everyone that sat behind the table.

"Rick, Maya," Paris said loudly and clearly, "those present in the hall cannot hear or see us."

Rick glanced at the faces below and grabbed the barrier railings tight.

Seven sat behind the table. One sat at the head, as if underlining his importance among those present, who were exchanging short pleasantries. He was dressed in white, and it seemed to Rick that he had already seen him in Paris' retinue. The other participants in the meeting were obviously waiting for someone, passing the time in idle conversation. One of those present was a very squat far man, with bulging eyes and stooped shoulders. A man with faded hair who wore a formless gray robe sat to his right with an expression of concern on his face, which was as long as that of Paris. The next was a slender old man with a long mane of gray hair, who wore baggy green clothing and gesticulated wildly as he rocked in his chair. The next was a woman dressed in a tight, form fitting suit. She took almost no part in the conversation. And then there were people that Rick could never fail to recognize—Warden Croesus slouched in a chair, chatting to Mentor Arcadius without a care in the world.

Maya gasped by his side. It looked like she also saw a familiar face.

"Keeper Victoria," the girl said in a small voice. "She is the head of the Order."

"A wonderful lady," Paris reported. "Intelligent, tactful and careful. It is a pleasure to work with her."

Rick and Maya looked at him, waiting for an explanation.

"There were ten of them before," Paris continued. "Not counting the Chairman or our Secretary. However, the Council became smaller with time. Lambda died out. Iota got assimilated by Zeta, Nu and Xi exterminated each other through raiding—we did not manage to solve the issue in time, and it was too late to interfere later."

Rick and Maya could not think of what to

say, so all they could do is keep listening.

"The Council gathers when the Government demands it every time when we find a situation to be sufficiently serious. I admit, that there were few situations of this kind over the last few years. In the past, the Council was not called together for decades, but it has been several days of Thermopolis buzzing like a disturbed wasp's nest. Today, we will speak of Cornelius' rebellion in sectors Sigma and Tau. Do you know anything about that?"

"We actually ran away from there right at the time of the mutant attack from the space between the aeons," Maya replied.

"You were lucky. They say that men are being thrown right into the smelting ovens down there. Cornelius has many followers. That man is out of control. Possibly it was his fault that the Particle Accelerator has been turned on. We need him alive." Paris was rubbing the wide, white palms of his hands. "Rick Omicron, do you understand that we are all united now?"

"Strange that we had to travel through half of the Expanse and hear this from you personally."

Paris grimaced with displeasure, but admitted, "You are right. But there is no other way."

"Why not?"

"That's a naive question. You are still too young, which is why it is difficult for you to understand certain things."

"What things?" Rick started to get angry. "That people must be kept in sectors like pigs in a pen?"

He wanted to smash his fist into the narrow face of the Chairman.

"That is too much of a crude comparison, my friend," Paris answered with his usual smile. "People are stupid and aggressive. They need to be controlled, or there will be chaos. To control a man, you need to be in charge of their thoughts. We have formed a system of order. If it was not for this system, you would have killed each other, torn each others throats out and fought for the last chunks of meat. You would have also ruined the space that we all share in our common home and turned Thermopolis into a real tomb. You have grown too savage in your sectors and you are not ready for freedom yet. In time, the people of Thermopolis will truly unite into one society and we will live as we did before. But we cannot be hasty. We must be careful. In this situation, any risk is the same as death. We all need to have patience and great wisdom."

"Beautiful words," Rick clapped his hands a couple of times, and the stabbed his hand out pointing at the man sitting at the table. "It's the same song sung to me by that scumbag Croesus, as he sat in his warm office while the children and the elderly were freezing on the lower levels! What will you say to that?"

"I agree," Paris nodded. "Croesus must be removed. Your traditions require certain reforms, anyway. What if I offer you the position of Warden of the Omicron Commune?"

"What?" Rick was taken aback.

"Yes, yes," Paris replied with a wave of his hand. "I must go, they are tired of waiting. Think about my offer, Rick Omicron. You can stay here and listen, and then I will return and we will go and have lunch together. Is that all right? Excellent!"

Paris descended into the corridor with a self-satisfied expression, entered the lobby and quickly went into the hall, where everybody rose from their seats in greeting.

Rick turned to Maya, finding is hard to think and asked, "Did I hear him right?"

"No," she shook her head. "That's exactly what happened. He offered you one of the seats down there."

"I can't believe it," Rick muttered. "I can't get it through my head."

"Yes, all of this is..." she cut herself short and offered, "I think we had better listen to them.

And they stood still by the barrier, holding

hands. The representatives of the sectors were obviously hesitant in Paris' presence. They started off with a short report of the state of each of the sector. The fat man turned out to be the representative of sector Xi, the lowest one that was still inhabited and answered to the title of Commander. The man in gray represented sector Mu, which was still closed to the outside world and was addressed as Abbot. The gray haired old man was the King of sector Zeta. They all talked about the limited fuel supplies for their sector generators. The Church of Mu was in the best situation—they still had a whole fifteen percent of charge left. The Omicron Commune was the worst off. Croesus fidgeted in his seat and looked more nervous than the others, even though it was Arcadius who should have been worried because his sector was engulfed by a revolt. He had closed his eyes and seemed to be having a nap. And then, it was his turn to speak.

Arcadius gave a short account of the situation, describing the fight between Rick and Cornelius and the ensuing events. Paris listened, and his beatific smile never left his face. Rick understood that Paris smiled all the time he saw him, and the smile was either wide or only touching the corners of his mouth. He also understood that it was not really a smile.

Arcadius switched to the incident with the

particle accelerator, but Paris raised his hand.

"Let's put that subject aside for now," he said. "When will the revolt be suppressed?"

"The rebels have united with the mutants. They have taken over half of Sigma and the bottom levels of Tau, squeezing us like a vice..." Arcadius stopped, looking for the right words.

"That does not concern me," Paris cut him off.

Everyone went still, not daring to move a muscle. It was as if the air had been pumped out of the hall.

"We," Arcadius managed to rally his self-control, "take back the levels from them and throw them back out above. In two days."

Paris was sitting very straight. His hand slowly rose from the table, as if overcome by laziness, and his finger aimed straight at the head of the rebellious sector.

"If the revolt will not be suppressed within two days, you shall leave your position and go straight to the ovens and fed as fuel into your reactor. Do you understand?"

Arcadius nodded.

"What did you want to say about the accelerator?"

Arcadius hurriedly related everything that happened after the ritual combat up to the scene in the office when Maya threatened them with a weapon. Paris leaned forward slightly.

"That is all, honored Chairman."

Paris made Arcadius repeat everything about the part of the story with the chair in the technical room behind the control post, carefully asking about every small detail. It was like an interrogation. The Secretary impassively documented the proceedings in the corner. Finally, Paris leaned back in his chair and started to think. The members of the Council waited respectfully.

"Young Rick Omicron has launched the Uranus program. We will find out why he did this. The supporting rod of Thermopolis has been activated. The external shell of Thermopolis has been activated. Rick Omicron did all of this and it is all part of the Uranus program." He looked at each Council member in turn. "But nothing terrible has happened. If it wasn't for the revolt, we would have sent down a technician with grade four access long ago and put things back to their initial state. The situation is under control. All we need to do is suppress Cornelius' revolt and stop the Uranus program."

"Honored Chairman," the fat man from sector Xi stated, as his chair creaked, "we are prepared to send out combat units to help Sigma and Tau. If the problem must be solved, we cannot accept defeat."

"So how do you propose explaining the existence of neighbors above you to your people?"

"We have a couple of things prepared for that eventuality," the far man grinned ferally.

"Thank you, Commander Gerard. We will avail ourselves of your help, depending on the situation. Be prepared."

"Always!"

Everyone started to move to get up.

"We have not finished yet." Paris stopped everyone with a wave of his hand. "I will take up your time for but another two minutes. This concerns the young Rick Omicron." He settled his icy gaze on Croesus. "Could you please give us a hint as to how a person from the third aeon has grade four access to the machinery of the bottom aeon?"

The way that Croesus' bottom lip trembled could even be seen from above.

"He is the son of a woman from the upper levels. She was brought back from a raid on Lambda together with other women. I did that for the good of the Commune." Croesus thought for a moment and added, "She was already pregnant, as it turned out later. I don't know from whom. She died of illness several years ago."

"Lambda is also part of the third aeon," Paris said. "That means that the woman was not born there but somehow came into the sector from outside. When did she arrive in Omicron?"

"Twenty years ago."

"Thank you, Warden. If you remember anything about her, no matter what, please report to me. This is in your interest."

"Of course, honored Chairman!" Croesus blurted out and then followed up by quietly, "Why d'you even care about that pup?"

Paris remained unperturbed and declared, "You are now free to go."

The Council members hurriedly left the meeting hall. Paris turned to the Secretary. He was looking for something in his tabletop computer.

"Nothing, Chairman. No incidents, no perimeter violations. The number of citizens remained stable. All of the deaths and births are documented. Nobody left the aeon in the space of a year."

"Are you sure?"

"Absolutely."

Paris' face reflected serious concern for the first time. Wrinkles appeared on his usually smooth forehead.

"I will need to talk to Rick Omicron himself. Maybe he remembers something." With these words, he looked up, right at the spot where the two young people were standing.

Rick could not help recoiling from the

barrier and exchanging glances with Maya.

"What is he trying to achieve?"

"Don't you understand?" Maya exclaimed. He needs to make you safe so you no one could ever start up the Uranus program again, whatever it may be."

"We need to get out of here." Rick looked around, looking for an exit. "Now I understand why he is so worried—he wants to hold on to his power. Why are you just standing there?"

"He is coming here!" Maya freed her hand from Rick's. "Wait. Let me think. Maybe he really does not want to harm us?"

"That doesn't depend on us. He is nice right now, but what will he be like tomorrow? Did you see his guards?"

Maya nodded.

"There you are."

"He would not be so gentle with us and he would never let us listen in if we could run away from here. We would have guards following us every step of the way. Something tells me that running away is pointless."

"Maybe you are right, but what are we to do? Wait until they start torturing us?"

"He's not going to torture us, he's not that kind of person..."

"Damn it!" Rick smashed his fist into the railings. "We missed our chance."

"Missed your chance?" asked Paris from the doorway. "To do what? To run away? And why would you run, my friends?"

"Dear Rick and Maya," Paris spread his hands, "I swear that no one will ever harm you, and you will live a happy and carefree life here. No one will lay a finger on you. You have already proven that you have the right to remain in the first aeon. We do not have slavery or dictatorship and everyone is free and equal, within the limits of the space we reside in. You can go anywhere you like in the aeon and choose any place you like for yourselves. You can be together and found a family line here. This is a golden opportunity for people from below to start afresh. Look at yourselves, you both young, strong and beautiful. Do not throw your future away."

"It all sounds too good to be true," Rick said. "I don't believe you.

"Then I have no idea how else I can demonstrate you my good intentions." Paris seemed to be genuinely upset. "You have been lied to for too long, or this world has turned out to be too good, so good that you still can't accept it?"

Rick felt Maya's gaze upon him—it was seeking and questioning. It was full of doubt.

"I think I know what the problem is, Rick Omicron," Paris said cheerfully. "But this issue was resolved as soon as you arrived here, while you were getting yourselves in order."

"What are you talking about?"

"Follow me."

"I am sick of following your every step!"

"We are just going to have lunch. You would be an idiot to deny yourself a meal. This is something that you need more than anyone. But if you decide to find out what it is, got to the west wing of floor 1045."

Paris turned around and left. The blood was hammering in Rick's temples. He wanted to act immediately, but he did not know how.

"Rick, maybe we really are too suspicious..." Maya began and then fell silent.

e looked at her as if she had slapped him.

"What are you on about?" Rick swallowed. "We shouldn't even turn our backs to him!"

"He had a thousand opportunities to kill us, but he didn't do it."

"Because he is in no hurry. When will you understand that he needs us?" Rick sliced through the air with his hand. "We are only alive because he thinks I know something!"

Maya narrowed her eyes into two thin slits.

"Oh mighty savior I believe I am interrupting you in your mission."

"What are you talking about?"

He tried to take her by the hand, but Maya

did not allow him and stepped back.

"Nothing." She turned around and started walking away. "Leave me alone."

"Where are you going? To him? Can't you understand that he wants us to argue? He wants to make us his pets, so that we obey him and the local customs. Maya!"

She did not reply and she did not stop. Rick swore incoherently in her direction and got into a fit of rage. He circled the balcony like a cornered beast and smashed his fist and leg into the barrier several times. Then he leaned on the railing, breathing heavily, and tried to calm down. He was fooled and tricked like a little kid. That Paris knew everything about him and he knew nothing about the Chairman.

Lick stood around leaning on the barrier for a little while and considering the facts of the matter. He let out a sigh and ambled towards the elevator. Having entered the cabin, he dialed in the floor he needed and descended. A familiar escort already waited for him in the corridor and took him to the big dining hall, and invited him to join the people at the table. There were three of them. It was not hard to recognize Paris and Maya, but the third was still hidden from sight behind the back of the Chairman. Paris turned his head and said, "Rick Omicron, at last! Join us, before the cake had gone completely cold."

Rick approached the table, pulled out a chair, sat down and looked at Aurora.

"Hi," his sister smiled. "I really missed you!"

18

RICK'S SENSE of alarm changed into wary anticipation. A day had passed since the meeting of the Government Council. It was late evening. Rick sat in his room, while Maya, Aurora and Paris were walking around the different floors and levels and entertaining themselves. They even tried to bring Rick along, but he was stubborn and refused to join them.

It was all the fault of Chairman Paris. He behaved as if he did not notice anything. Paris even tried to talk to him. Rick understood that the tactics the Chairman used were far more skillful and subtle than the direct threats of someone like Croesus. He often acted directly, but in this case, however you considered it, Paris had found his most vulnerable spot—Aurora. Rick understood that Paris was not openly threatening him and his sister, but should he go against him, his sister would become a hostage. It was not possible to act openly in such situations, he needed to think. Think. And think some more!

But the minutes passed, turning into hours, and Rick became increasingly sure that he had nothing to oppose Paris with. The Chairman only needed a reason to involve his armed guards in the situation and he had no chance against them. He should run! But where? Even if he managed to somehow quietly steal his sister away, they would immediately track them down, stop the elevators and that would be all, they would get caught. Running away was not a solution.

Rick gradually started to hate himself for having increasingly frequent thought of surrendering to his fate and somehow arrange things for the future, basically, to go to Paris and give himself up to his mercy. And all for his sister, that was his main justification.

If his mother was by his side, she would probably have found the right words and calmed him down. Rick took the talisman from his neck—a cross-shaped, black piece of metal, which was the only thing that reminded him of his mother.

As he sat on the floor in the middle of the room, he turned the talisman around in his hands. The light cast beautiful reflections from its sharp edges. They had not even taken the weapons away from him and Maya! The massive blaster he was given by Drachus was still lying around under the bed and a knife still hung from his belt. It turned out that Paris was sure that Rick was wise enough not to use it.

The most upsetting thing was that him and Maya had reached the final destination of their journey. Yes, they had got into the Control Center, but it somehow imperceptibly turned out that there was no point in going there. However...

Turning on the generators. They desperately wanted to turn on the generators. That was their goal—turning on the generators. But for whom? For all the people of Thermopolis. Rick remembered who he came across over the last few days—a collection of filthy and often truly ugly people. No, it was not for them that he overcame all of these steps and corridors.

It was for his sister.

Who was now by his side.

But what about Kyoto? What about Ahmed? Paris could probably free them to, if only he asked...

Rick froze for a second. But that would mean that they would break him. That would mean that he admits defeat and submits to the will of another.

He furiously spun the talisman on his palm, staring blindly at the wall. Paris wants to find out why some ratling from a dying lower sector managed to run the mysterious Uranus program. If only he knew himself! His mother had never talked openly about such subjects. She always gave evasive answers to questions about his father, and was more likely to turn away, hiding her tears.

Rick hissed with pain, as he dropped the talisman which had suddenly broken into two halves. One remained hanging on the chain, and Rick automatically put one on the bedside table as he looked at his finger and the blood coming out of the cut.

This was how Maya found him—with his finger in his mouth. She had looked happy only a second ago.

"What happened?"

"Nothing." Rick got up on his feet. "I just cut myself."

"Let me have a look."

"It's nothing..."

Maya grabbed him by the hand and led him to the basin to wash out the wound.

"So, how was your day?"

"Great."

"Any news?"

"Paris sends his greetings. He was sorry that you did not come to the aquatorium with us. He wanted to show us the museum of ancient art and sculpture, but Aurora got tired and I took her to sleep."

"How is she?"

"Everything is fine. She is so sweet, unlike her brother."

Rick did not bat an eyelid. Maya started to tell him about the aquatorium, the recreation halls for young people and children, who turned out to be lucky former residents of the lower sectors—some had ended up in this place by accident and some as a result of their abilities. It turned out that there were special people that tracked prospective candidates to become citizens of Epsilon. Maya even found an old friend from her own sector who had apparently vanished without trace. They thought he had fallen down a garbage chute. The girl kept telling him about her experienced, while Rick grimly listened.

Epsilon society was organized very democratically. Everyone had the right to use their abilities in the way they saw fit. Because they had no problems with food, heat and lighting, the people of the sector were not engaged in survival but in more highbrow activities that let them continue the development of culture. The history of humanity was greatly valued in the Epsilon sector. This was why the Council had come up with a way to keep these memories alive in the case of a global disaster, if the Main Computer was to break down and the library and archives were to be destroyed. The hundred most intelligent people in the sector were selected for this, and they took the names of the cities of the earth for themselves. They were united into a sort of Fund—a community of living memory, that included Paris himself and people such as London, New York, Moscow and Hong Kong.

"Can you imagine that?" Maya's admiration was limitless. "But that isn't all."

She told him that the sector was divided into virtual ancient states that had once existed on planet Earth. There were many of them, and they were all different, with their own cultures and systems of values. The scientists from each of these areas of the sector studied the history of the country assigned to them. There were also universal scientists that tried to understand the way the world worked and came up with various theories. There were artists, poets and musicians.

Maya was especially impressed with how cultured everyone was in the Epsilon sector—the people were polite and friendly, and it was possible to speak about a whole range of subjects to any of them for hours. However, they were not particularly interested in outside space. It seemed that they were completely content with everything and they were entirely at ease in this comfortable world.

"Yes," Maya said, "it is as if they are running in place. There aren't that many scientists compared to the majority. Everyone likes to play and enjoy themselves."

Maya looked happy. Her eyes shone as she laughed about some amusing detail or talked ceaselessly as if she was afraid to forget the details of this eventful day. Rick could feel the smell of spices coming from her.

Suddenly, Maya fell onto the bed, stretched and yawned.

"I think I'm tired as well..."

Rick sat down by the bed.

"Maya," he called out.

"What?" She was almost asleep and closing her eyes. "I hope you don't mind if I stay with you?"

"Of course not."

"Thank you. I almost forgot, Paris was saying something about the rebels. That they had fought back against the mutant attack and they are now... pushing Cornelius back down towards the reactor... Paris was very satisfied. He promised that Ahmed would not be harmed."

Rick sat down on the floor with his back to the bed. Then he felt her hand on his shoulder.

"Rick," she paused. "I'm cold."

He took her by the hand. Her palm was burning hot. Rick sprung up in concern, bent down over her and touched her forehead. No, everything seemed to be fine. Now, he sat by her side and carefully looked at her face—her fiery red hair was strewn across the pillow. Maya opened her eyes wide, and her sleep seemed to be gone in an instant. The girl's palm gripped his hand tight.

"Promise me," Maya whispered.

"What?"

"Promise that you won't leave me."

Rick spent a long time looking into her big, bright eyes.

"Why are you asking me to do this?"

"I'm afraid," she said. "I have had a headache all day today. I tried to read the sign above the recreation hall, but the letters turned into spots. Paris was telling me something for a while, but I did not remember a word. He said things to us, and I nodded without understanding what he was talking about."

"You just got tired by the end of the day."

"I am forgetting words. What's happening?"

"I don't know. Don't be afraid, you are just very tired. You will wake up as good as new tomorrow morning."

"Promise me anyway." She gripped his hand so tight that it seemed that she was hanging above a chasm and Mother Darkness was about to accept Maya into her bosom.

"I promise," Rick breathed out quietly.

Maya spent a while looking at him and then closed her eyes. Rick sat there, not daring to move until she started to breathe deeply and evenly. Then he carefully disentangled himself and crept out into the corridor. He did not want to sleep.

The ceiling lamps had been dimmed a little, but even this soft light would have been considered a frivolous luxury in the Omicron Commune. Rick slowly walked along the corridor, without thinking of the direction. There was music playing somewhere ahead. The flowing chords brought forth mixed feeling of joy and sadness at the same time. He approached the source of the sound and soon found himself by the entrance to a small hall where the lights were out. Only the stage was lit. A man sat on a stool there and conjured up sounds using a giant box which stood on three legs. It was so unusual that Rick could not help but stop and listen.

The music poured forth, full of dignified grief and sublime pride, like a long dream. The melody seemed to be an echo of someone's life, a life lived millennia ago. This was the music of the ancients and it was full of such hidden meaning and such substantial depth even though it was devoid of words that Rick was in awe of the masterful skill of its unknown composer. The music was doing something to him, it was changing him from inside, taking over the most hidden corners of his soul, bringing forth emotion and an incredibly strange but once familiar feeling. It was as if someone spoke to him and sent their greetings from the depths of the centuries, someone he knew, "Hello! At last, we meet again!" Standing still and holding his breath, afraid of disturbing the fragile harmony of the feeling that engulfed him, Rick looked at the stage where a stranger performed an ancient melody, gently swaying in time on the stool in front of the instrument.

The stage was bathed in the soft, silvery light of lamps hidden from the eye by a drape under the ceiling, and Rick suddenly thought that this light was coming here from outside. His perception of time seemed to disappear, it seemed that it had stood still and only the sound of music could be heard. Suddenly, the stranger in front of the instrument was still. The last chords rang out like a faint echo, and the light that poured upon the stage went out. Rick left in complete silence, not daring to look back.

He was thinking about the ancients.

The corridor led him to the balcony over the gap between segments. The windows on the opposite side were dark, apart from one or two, as well as a long row that was lit below— something was happening there. Rick saw a figure walking back and forth behind a translucent curtain, but he did not look closer. He just leaned on his elbows on the railings and stared into space, deep in thought.

A light wind was howling as it flew among the air ducts between the segments. Or maybe it was Mother Darkness herself that was crying and calling out for lost souls. This quiet howl got stronger or weaker, sometimes replaced by barely audible whistling.

Suddenly, the whistling had a pattern. Rick did not immediately realize that the rhythmic sound was not made by the wind when he felt the presence of another.

He turned his head and saw Tommo sitting on the railing a mere two paces away. Dark ocular lenses with red dots stared directly at Rick, who tried to say something in greeting to his old friend, but Tommo softly shook his head and raised a finger to his chin, which meant, "Be quiet!"

The prole slid onto the ledge on the other side of the railings and called Rick over with a wave of his head. Rick approached. Tommo was stubbornly indicating that he should follow. Rick looked down and the world swam before his eyes, with an idiotic desire to jump into the black abyss as he felt weakness in his arms and legs and an unpleasant ache in his bones. The prole continued to insistently make signs at him, despite his silent protest. Rick looked around, but mostly because he wanted to get himself together and get his thoughts in order. The corridor was still silent, and this was when Rick made his decision—he breathed out and climbed over the railing. Holding on to it for dear life, he followed Tommo using small and careful steps.

They passed around ten sections this way. Rick moved his feet trying to keep his head clear and not think of anything. He knew that if he looked down, fear will overcome him and he will be unable to ever move again, gripping the railings until his muscles would cramp and he would fall into the chasm. A gust of wind suddenly blew into his back and Rick lost his balance for a split second. His palms immediately got covered with sweat. One of his hands slipped, and Rick clumsily waved it, balancing on the edge, but Tommo was quick to react and supported him, preventing him from falling. The prole pulled him after himself and then suddenly disappeared from sight in a niche, dragging Rick inside forcibly.

Ough... Rick was staring into space, unable to stop trembling.

He was alive!

Meanwhile, Tommo opened up a panel on the wall, pressed something inside and a rectangular section of wall slid aside right in front of Rick with a faint hiss. Tommo grabbed him by the sleeve a dragged him through the opening.

Bending down under the low ceiling, Rick followed the prole along a long tunnel. They turned into separate branches several times. Unlike the lower levels and the air ducts, this place smelled of something unusual and chemical. The tunnel came to an end at last. They stood in a huge space which looked like some sort of warehouse. There were boxes and box racks as high as several grown men, with removable shelves and labels. Some of the boxes had glass doors and shelves full of glass flasks could be seen inside. The flasks contained germinated seeds and were labeled in two languages. Rick walked along the racks and read the labels, choosing them at random: "Flour Corn (Zea mays amylacea)", "Apple tree (Malus domestica)", "Radish (Raphanus sativus)". The shelves full of plants ended and shelves full of thousands of flasks filled with multicolored liquids began. The boxes were shut tights and radiated cold. Rick read a couple of the labels: "Horse (Equus ferus caballus): 10 000 embryos", "European Perch (Perca fluviatilis): 100 000 eggs".

Tommo kept walking on towards a pillar of light that could be seen among the racks. Rick decided not to fall behind and think on what he had seen later. They crossed several large halls, which were connected with archways, until they arrived in a round room that had a strange diagram on the floor: uneven yellow blotches on a blue background, with a net of curving lines drawn over the top that were at an equal distance to each other. He walked over a small blotch labeled "Australia" and stepped on slightly larger one labeled "Africa". A comfortable chair with a control terminal on the side towered over the largest blotch. Tommo looked at Rick and pointed at the chair, as if he was saying "Sit down".

"How did you find this place?"

Tommo stayed silent. Rick did not hurry to sit in the chair. He carefully examined the space around him—several storage galleries led into the room from different directions, containing plants, animals and definitely some other things, but there was no time to stroll around the galleries and look at the details. The room had a high ceiling, forming an ideal semi-sphere. Mysterious drawing and diagrams were drawn on the ceiling, but without the blotches this time—instead, there were many flickering dots scattered against a black background, some of them connected by lines into odd figures that were labeled with names.

Rick looked around at the labels, greedily

memorizing the ancient names, as he knew that it was important even if he did not understand their meaning. There was one there that looked like a scoop: "Ursa Major". Or another one that looked like a worm coming out of a cup of compost: "Hydra". And that other one was called "Orion". And that twisted figure was called "Bootes". He was moving his lips, looking up as he walked around the chair and reading the same labels several times. There was a thick scattering of dots going diagonally across the middle of the semi-sphere, which looked like a dusty path.

What did it all mean?

Rick took another step and almost fell as he walked into the chair. He looked at Tommo, who was patiently waiting and pointing at the terminal. Then Rick turned around and fell with his back into the chair. He raised a cloud of dust which tickled his nose and made him have to make an effort not to sneeze. He examined the control panel and moved around, getting used to the seat and the armrests. The chair was very similar to the one that Rick had once sat in the particle accelerator control room.

His hand stretched towards the screen all by itself.

The mechanisms hidden within the terminal and chair made their familiar, steady sounds, breathing life into the ancient machine. When his fingers touched the screen, Rick felt a wave of energy that ran along his arm to his shoulder and then throughout his body. It was very pleasant.

"The future does not come instantly," a confident voice suddenly spoke.

Rick flinched—a gray-haired stranger in a gray suit was looking at him from the screen with a smile. The figure of the stranger rippled for a moment, as it if was coming from the surface of a cup of water, but then the picture became clear.

"It surreptitiously sneaks into the present," the gray-haired man added.

"Who are you?"

"I am the Architect."Rick's hands, legs and chest were suddenly fixed in place by soft bands of tape. At first, he only felt the pressure of the belts but then started to feel heat in the places where they touched his body. His head suddenly cleared, and a wave similar to the one he experienced when he touched the screen passed through Rick's body as he suddenly understood that this was the pulse of Thermopolis.

"Greetings, my distant descendant," the gray-haired man said.

"Are you still alive?"

"Of course not." The Architect smiled. "I passed away a long time ago. You are speaking to my interactive projection. There is no other way to have this conversation. I don't know how many years have passed, whether it is a hundred, a thousand or even more or if you even keep track of the years. But you are here, and this indicated two facts. The first is that you are a bearer of the unique genetic code of the descendants of the Spanidis family. Which means you are my distant great-grandson. And the second fact is that Thermopolis is ready for the Uranus program. The fruit is ripe."

Rick's mouth went dry.

"What is the Uranus program?" he whispered.

"It is the salvation of humanity." The gray-haired man waved his hand. "This is an Ark, which was created a long time before the end of the world. Do you know the Biblical legend of Noah?"

"No."

"Noah knew how to talk to God. One day, God told him that humanity will be destroyed, but he had a chance to save everything that was best. And Noah started building a great boat, an Ark that he used to gather every animal to begin afresh. The people laughed at him but when the end of the world came, they were washed from the surface of the world like dirt. And now I have become Noah for the people of my time. I predicted the epidemic long before it occurred and started to prepare a plan for salvation, preparing for it all my life. The virus that appeared attacked the brain and destroyed neurons, turning humans into mindless animals. Nature's self-preservation mechanism did its work, as it turned on at the last moment when we had used up all the resources and almost destroyed the planet's biosphere, as we got obsessed with the modification of antibiotics and thought that we had defeated all diseases. However, we forgot about natural entropy. In principle, nothing on Earth could save itself from the virus, even the population of Thermopolis. This is why I predicted the gradual deterioration of our civilization to a medieval level, to slave ownership or even to a prehistoric tribal system. I don't know how long the deterioration will continue, but it will end one day. The Earth will have a rest from humanity and will be ready for our arrival again. I predicted this development. Evolution needed hundreds of thousands of years to turn the neanderthal into homo sapiens, but I decided to speed up this process. Thermopolis is not only an Ark, but also my evolutionary machine that must drag you, the people of the future, from your animalistic non-existence, awaken your dormant intelligence and give you the keys to the future. That is the Uranus program."

The Architect looked up, thinking about something. Rick waited for him to continue.

"Because Thermopolis is an incredibly complex structure, access to some sections of it is very limited and you would have to have a very high level of intelligence and a certain degree of luck to get in here to talk to me. There can be no mistake. You did not get here by accident. This means, that you are the same as me. Not just in terms of your personal qualities, but also because of my means of control. One of them is the proles, complex human-like biological machines developed in secret from humanity and made for the observation and selection of the descendants of Archimedes Spanidis among the population of Thermopolis. The duty of the proles is not just to observe the candidates but also to note particular abilities in their behavior, as well as bringing the descendants here for a conversation. You might not be the first to come here. And perhaps, you won't be the last."

Rick tried to get his head around what was going on, but the information was so unexpected and disheartening that his head was spinning.

"I am the descendant of one of the most ancient human civilizations," the Architect continued. "My people laid down the main principles of intelligent thought and created a culture which was the foundation for the rest of humanity. I am proud of our mythology most of all. There is nothing more elegant than the myths of ancient gods that populate the ethereal heights. I firmly believe that man will one day be like the gods in his perfection. I might be mistaken, but life is made for taking risks. This is why the Uranus program does not just represent salvation—it is also my challenge to the skies. A letter means nothing by itself. It is an empty symbol, a useless sign. However, when letters are put together into an alphabet to make words, words can be made into sentences, poems and stories based on an enormous system of meanings—that is a language. And that is when every letter finds its true meaning, its own great power. Thermopolis is an alphabet, which will be the foundation for a new language of the gods. If you share my ideals and you agree with me, my descendant, then you should bravely continue executing the Uranus program and regret nothing."

The Architect vanished into thin air. Rick spent a long time staring unblinkingly at the empty screen, until a message appeared: "Continue executing the Uranus program. Yes—No?"

He did not hurry this time around. He carefully read through his options which were described under the message in a small font. One of them was called "Tutorial". Rick activated the section by tapping it with his finger. More options appeared: "Standard", "Extended" and "Quick start".

He chose the "Quick start" option. The machine offered him to select a timescale from one to twelve hours. Rick chose the minimum time without hesitation.

Another message appeared on the panel: "Relax and close your eyes. Please note: there may be negative side-effects".

There was nothing to lose anymore—he submitted to the will of the machine. The back of the chair smoothly adopted a horizontal position and the tentacles of the electrodes touched his temples and forehead. After this, his consciousness was torn away from reality and thrown into a series of rapid, image-filled visions that were accompanied by compressed masses of information. This was the same as the film about the history of the building of Thermopolis, but a hundred times faster. The knowledge of thousands of generations entered Rick's mind as a concentrated stream, dividing into modules inside: mathematics, logic, geometry, writing, physics, chemistry, biology, geography, geology, the most widespread languages that humanity spoke before the virus attacked, the foundations of poetry, philosophy and the humanities, engineering, information technology, cybernetics, psychology, general history...

Formulae, invariables, conformities, dates, events, categories, paradoxes, pictures, diagrams, tables, blueprints, graphs, binary code, singularity, even horizon, synergy, quantum mechanics, dark matter and the periodic table...

All of this was being layered, fitting tightly together inside his head, which began to spin and be in noticeable pain because of the amount of information, but more and more new packages of knowledge kept filling his consciousness like jar being filled to the brim. Soon, he became cold and feverish. His body was shaken by major tremors. His consciousness gradually slipped away, and new packages of information kept appearing before his mind's eye, but he could not perceive them or even learn them. Rick was in a semi-conscious state by the end of the session. His temperature rose, and Rick felt blood dripping from his nose and that his head was about to explode with pain. His burning mind could barely cope with the pressure.

However, Rick could now use various clever words to describe this mental torture. He smiled through his tears and suddenly understood that it was all over. The back of the chair returned to a vertical position and the restraining belts disappeared. Rick opened his eyes and fell on the floor. As soon as he managed to get himself up on all fours, he vomited all over Egypt. Oh yes, Europe was on the map behind his back, so Asia must be on the left and Africa straight ahead. He wiped his mouth a spat the bitter taste out of his mouth. Yes, it seemed like he had got off lightly. He was lucky, he could still think and even move.

Rick carefully rose, holding on to the armrest and stood around for a while, calming his breathing.

Tommo was nearby, frozen in standby mode. Rick could not help shaking his head—this was all new knowledge. A prole was just an improved android. It was funny to understand such a simple fact. He wondered, how long would it take to explain this fact to Maya?

Rick raised his head and looked at the constellations on the semi-sphere. Now he was armed with knowledge, he easily navigated the map of ancient symbols and understood what it meant.

Only the last and most important thing remained—to make a decision.

He climbed back into the chair and confidently opened the Thermopolis control interface. Now, his fingers swiftly flew over the keyboard, hitting exactly the buttons he needed. He activated the display of the particle accelerator sensor data—the bar was rising towards the eighty percent level. Acceptable. It would warm up to full power later.

"Activate generators? Yes—No. Activation is synchronized."

"And now, my friend," he addressed the prole, without taking his eyes off the screen, "comes the moment of truth."

Without looking, Rick put his hand under the seat and took a wireless communication set from the storage compartment. He put on a headphone, turned on the microphone and called the technical post of the accelerator. His fingers danced over the keyboard, making images from the Thermopolis observation cameras display on the screen one after another. First, he saw empty corridors, one of which contained a crawling and wounded-looking manlike creature, then there were a couple of flashes of impenetrable gray and it was only when he finally got the images from the Sigma and Tau sectors that he understood that the jungle was burning. Smoke billowed through the corridors and he could occasionally see rushing human figures. Another camera showed the picture of a massacre—bodies of workers and mutants strewn around the floor, surrounded by pools of blood. Then the picture switched to the observation platform and the sarcophagus of the particle accelerator, which was hidden from sight as it was boxed in by its armor. A man was sitting behind the table at the operator's post.

"Rick Omicron calling Cornelius from Sigma and Tau," Rick said loudly.

The man shuddered and fell of the table onto the floor with a terrified scream. However, he immediately got up, glanced at the camera and ran into the darkness of the hall.

Rick repeated his call loudly and clearly, but there was no reaction, so he continued to repeat himself until a group of people headed by Cornelius appeared in the picture. The burly man looked like he had been in a fight—his face was covered in fresh grazes, his arm bandaged with blood-covered rag and he was holding a massive wrench in the other.

"Cornelius!" Rick called out. "It's me, the monkey from the upper levels!"

"By the Red King!" he barked. "How did you get inside the machine?"

"It's too long to explain, but I am alive and well!"

"You haven't got the girl killed?"

"She's fine!"

"You're lucky, if anything happened to you, I would skin you alive! Is Tommo with you?"

"He's here."

"Good."

"Are you defending the Reactor?"

"Our strength is running out! Arcadius' dogs are blowing up the barricades and lots of other boys have died. But I won't let them take me alive!" he shouted, shaking his wrench.

"Where's Ahmed?"

"He's in the next room. He's armed, alive and well. He wants to fight for us."

Rick asked him to bring Ahmed so he could talk to him. Soon, a dark skinned engineer who had grown lean but seemed full of courage was happily speaking to him. After they exchanged their greetings, Rick gave a short explanation of the situation and told Ahmed what was required of him

The engineer's eyes went wide with surprised and he exclaimed, "I don't recognize you! How do you know all of these things?"

"Techno-magic." Rick smiled. "Please, do what I told you."

He waited for Ahmed to go to the neighboring room and sit at the operator's control console, and switched his camera to the technical post.

"Excellent." Rick only thought for a moment and then continued, "Let's begin the launch of the Uranus program."

"Rick, wait! Do you even understand what you're doing?" Ahmed worried. "What if you are launching a machine that will bring about everyone's judgment day?"

"It can't be worse than it is now! Are you with me, or not?"

"Yes, but..."

"Leave your doubts behind, it's time to act. Confirm the launch of the generators."

They pressed the green buttons simultaneously, each on his own control panel. A light circular shape appeared on the screen, which started to fill with color and a dark message saying "Please wait". The shape was growing into a circle incredibly slowly. Then, it disappeared to be replaced by a picture of four three dimensional rods, which started to get filled with a green color as if they were vessels. All of this was accompanied by a message: "Please wait: 1%... 2%... 5%... 18%...". Another message appeared, this time stating "Generators turned on. Timescale for reaching design capacity—12 hours. Initiate next stage?" Rick confirmed the command. The machine asked: "Hermetically seal aeons? Yes—No." Rick confirmed the selected action again. A cross section projection of Thermopolis appeared. The shapes of five aeons were outlined with thick lines, and an icon was displayed, showing the progress of the operation: "1%... 2%... 3%...". The computer answered: "Aeon hermetization will take place in 6 hours". The screen went dark and another message appeared: "Uranus program launch will be possible in 12 hours. Prepare the key to enter the last instruction. Activate by turning the key in the console simultaneously."

"A key?"

Rick re-read the message several times. Then he asked for a help file. The machine showed him a diagram of the key—a cross-shaped item marked by the number eight on its side. The three dimensional model of the key was spinning in front of him. Rick entered a new query. The machine showed him the mechanism for inserting the key into the opening in the control panel. Rick examined the controls, but could not find the familiar slot on the panel. But he was sure that he had already seen the sort of edges, angles and incisions that would fit. He tried to think on it for a minute. And then he grabbed himself by the chest.

The talisman!

He almost tore his new shirt while he took out the talisman and took the chain off his neck. The size of the key ideally matched the slot displayed on the screen. However, he did leave the second part of the key in his room on the bedside table.

"Rick? What's going on?" Ahmed asked.

"Nothing. I found the program activation key," he replied as he remembered his mothers only words about this.

She always told him, "Take care of this talisman like it was your very soul, because your father always looked after it and carried it with him, and the talisman belonged to your grandfather before him, your great-grandfather and your previous ancestors, reaching back to the most ancient one of our forefathers.". "Why?" asked little Rick. "Because this talisman is our future," his mother told him, but never explained what that actually meant.

"Ahmed, please examine your control panel and look for a slot that will now be displayed on your screen."

Rick typed on the keys, sending the message to Ahmed using the local Thermopolis network.

The engineer stayed silent for a minute. Rick painfully clenched his fists as he waited for the answer. Then, Ahmed said, "I don't have a slot like that on my control panel."

"Are you sure?"

"Yes!"

Rick desperately smashed his fist on the armrest and started to think out loud, "Then where could the correct console be located? Ahmed, please think, the answer is near, but we just need to find it. We carried synchronized the launch of the generators. But Maya was talking about launching them from... that's it! The

Control Center! It looks like I need to go there."

"And..."

"Defend the post! I'll be in touch later."

Rick cut the communication, looked through the electronic help file and found the place where the key had to be activated—the Thermopolis Control Center. All right, now he had to decide what to do with the talisman itself. He still had time to retrieve the second half and come back here to complete the program.

Tommo stood nearby and patiently waited, looking at Rick.

"What?"

The prole pointed at the key, then at himself and waved his hand, as if he was hinting about other rooms. Rick tried to understand, "Are you saying that you will get the second half?"

Tommo nodded.

"Will you be able to find it?"

Another nod.

"What if they catch you? Or if something else will happen, like you getting stuck in an air duct?"

Tommo made a whole series of wild gestures, smacking his fist into his open palm.

"No," Rick shook his head. "That just won't do. We are going to go and get it together."

Rick felt sorry that he did not take the blaster with him. Through force of habit, his hand felt for the handle of the knife on his belt. Rick got up from the chair and looked at Tommo carefully. Tommo pointed at the chair, and made a strange movement as if he wanted to jump. He pointed at the chair again and jumped up high, spreading his arms and flapping them like a bird and pretending to fly. Then he pointed his finger at the ceiling, twisted his hand side to side, lowered his arm, shook his head and pointed at one of the side galleries.

"I don't understand."

Then Tommo set of into the gallery.

"Where are you..." Rick stopped, ordered Ahmed not to leave his post for any reason and hurried after the prole. "Tommo, wait! What do you want to say?"

Rick got worried, having some doubts that the prole was in full working order.

And then he saw the contents of the shelves. There was no mistake. There were cryo chambers full of flasks that contained miniature human embryos. Rick read the label on one of the flasks—it showed their DNA code, probable gender, race and information about the parents of the child. Shelves full of human embryos stretched out into infinity.

"*He* even made provisions for this..."

Tommo led Rick onwards. They made their way through the twisting labyrinth and reached a room that looked like an operating theater There was a glass sarcophagus in the middle. A human lay inside without any gender characteristics or hair, with a smooth face like a doll.

Rick realized that this was a blank slate, a template.

The prole started making gestures again, pointing at himself, then at Rick and then at the body in the glass sarcophagus chamber.

"I am finding it really hard to understand you. What do we need this body for?"

When he said this, Tommo stepped over to a nearby terminal, switched it on, and started to quickly type, bringing the text up on the screen. Rick worked out what Tommo was proposing from the very first lines. The prole continued typing and when he finished, Rick asked, "Do you think we will manage to do this?"

"Believe, because it is absurd," Tommo types in reply.

19

RICK FELT how the space around him filled with a barely audible even hum. The distant growing rumble of generators powering up was almost imperceptible, but the light vibration of the floor could still be felt if you stood still for a long time.

The night was not over yet, so the corridors were empty. The door to Maya Kappa's room was open. Maya herself was not here—she was in a deep sleep in the neighboring room. Aurora was lying on the bed instead of her. Rick wanted to shut the door, but his sister called him by name and he stopped in the doorway.

"Is that you?" Aurora propped herself up on the bed. "Why aren't you sleeping?"

"And why aren't you?"

"I had a bad dream. Sit with me."

Rick slid into the room, stepped over to the bed and perched himself on the edge, looking at his sister. Following their old habit, they did not turn on the light to save power. Aurora gave Rick a hug, pressing her cheek to his chest. Rick smoothed her messy hair—Aurora's forehead seemed too cold and slick with sweat, even though it was obviously hot.

"What did you dream of, little one?"

"That the black people came and took you and uncle Kyoto away and put me into a pit."

"It was only a dream. Don't be afraid."

"They had no eyes. Or noses. Only mouths."

Rick put his sister to bed and covered her with a blanket.

"I will stay with you for a while."

"Please don't go anywhere."

"All right. Do you want me to tell you a fairy tale?"

There was a pause—Aurora was obviously fighting back temptation. Then she firmly declared, "No. I remember them all. I thought I would never see you again. I was very sad when you left. Uncle Kyoto kept saying that you would be back soon, but I did not believe him." She sighed. "Uncle Kyoto made me learn some words about dad. Before the strange people came and took me here."

"Which words?"

"Wait." She was quiet for a moment, as she gathered her thoughts. "Here. Rick, your father is alive and he is down below, there where Omega and Aqua end and even lower. The password is "infinity".

Now it was Rick's turn to get his thoughts together. After a short pause to think, he asked, "Was that it?"

"Yes. Is dad alive? Or was that a joke?"

"I don't know Aurora. Go to sleep."

His sister started to fidget in the darkness of the room. He sat by her side for around half an hour and then sneaked towards the exit. He close the door in complete silence, feeling vigilant eyes on his back...

It was no problem to get the other half of the key that he had left in his room. Maya was fast asleep and did not hear him enter. At least he got lucky here and did not have to explain himself.

His second journey along the narrow ledge turned out to be easier. And this was not because Rick was looking at the wall and there was almost no wind. His perception of it had changed. It seemed to him that he was not standing, but lying flat on a huge flat surface and that he must get into a deep burrow. When he clambered into the niche before the entrance to the corridor, he looked down into a chasm.

The darkness was receding. A pale yellow light was spreading below, painting the gray walls of the lower sectors in copper. The gap had also become narrower in some places. Closed shutters appeared between the segments—the gates which had been open for many years had closed at their appointed hour. And Rick knew the reason for that very well.

The chasm had visibly come to life. He could hear the distant rumble of moving mechanisms and the hum of the generators sending energy along the lines like blood flowing through the veins of a gigantic organism.

Without wasting any more time, Rick ran along the corridor to the Stellar Hall and then to the east wing to get to the genetic engineering room. The body in the sarcophagus had almost completed its transformation and he already recognized its familiar features. Tommo had connected himself to the computer and lay on a table that was pushed by the side of the sarcophagus. Half of the mask had been cut away from his head, revealing the open upper part of his plastic skull and the wires snaking out of it.

Rick came back in time to glance at the screens. The modeling of a clone using Rick's DNA was almost complete. Once the process reached its end, he looked at the prole. He was lying completely still. Rick came right up to the table—the red lights no longer shone in the dark ocular lenses. The prole's body was now only an empty shell.

He heard a quiet hissing. Rick turned around and saw the glass lid of the sarcophagus open, as the nutrient feeding pipes disconnected from the clone's body. The clone suddenly sat up and waved his hands, almost falling to the floor. Rick caught him by the arm right on time and helped him get to his feet.

The old clothing that he had thoughtfully fetched from the room turned out to be a perfect fit for the new Tommo. He dressed himself into the clean uniform of the Omicron Commune Patrol and looked at himself in the mirror on the door of a cabinet. He turned towards Rick.

"Not bad," Rick said.

"Not bad for now," Tommo suddenly answered and started to stretch his arms and legs as he got used to his new body. "The operational lifetime is not too long, but that doesn't matter. The main thing is to complete the mission."

"Would you want to come back into your previous shell?" Rick was not particularly surprised that Tommo could speak as the cloning program and the new body had that sort of function.

Tommo looked at his former body, which lay there in its own jumpsuit, and said, "I lack desires. I complete what is mandated by the program they loaded into me, completing tasks in order of priority. I do not need my old body at the moment."

They left the room and entered the Stellar Hall.

"Did you pick up the second half of the key?" Tommo asked on the way.

Rick showed him the fragments of the cross. Tommo took both halves from him and skilfully joined them together. They made a dull metal cross with barely perceptible carved patterns on the sides.

"The launch of the program is synchronized," Tommo stated. "Those are the conditions of the security protocol. One input device is located in the Control Center above and the other is below on level zero, which is underground."

"But there is only one key."

"Yes. One in two terminals. Alpha and Omega, that form infinity."

Tommo pointed at the symbol engraved on the cross. Then, he pressed a notch on the key and the cross divided in half. Tommo gave one of the halves to Rick and continued.

"Now we need to decide who goes where."

"How do I get down below?"

"Using the main elevator. But the elevators are blocked. The system is put into hibernation before switching to a new level of self sufficiency. Thermopolis adapts itself before the launch of the program. The residential and storage sectors move to the top and the technical sectors move to the bottom."

"The aeons are not isolated yet."

"It is risky and time consuming to descend through the sectors, without even mentioning the segments between the aeons. This is why there is one and only option. It is quick and simple."

They said it at the same time.

"There is outside space."

"That's right," Tommo confirmed. "There are flying machine hangars in sector Alpha. One of them must be taken and flown down to the bottom of the Thermopolis. A perimeter was built there, with shafts leading to underground bunkers. One of them is connected by corridors to sector zero. The door is blocked and it opens using a genetic code and a password. There is a control hall inside. I will do this myself."

"No." Rick shook his head. "I will do this. You must obey my orders."

"This is a high risk decision," Tommo noted. "The probability of your success is approximately fifty-fifty. I would have a better chance. We have no right to make a mistake."

"The Architect said that I was not the first. This means I won't be the last. You can test your luck with someone else again."

"I do not understand why you insist." Tommo blinked indifferently, without expressing any emotion on his face.

"I have my reasons. I will manage— remember that I went through an accelerated learning course and my new knowledge should be enough. Take care of my sister and Maya. Be careful with Paris. It is no easy task to get into the Control Center, but I am sure you will do it. While we still have an advantage. However, they will understand what is going on in about an hour and raise the alarm."

"I concur. There is a shaft nearby. Let's use it to go up."

He led Rick to a grille over a wide ventilation shaft, easily opened it and they climbed upwards together.

The rumble of the generators soon became noticeably louder. Rick had to constantly swallow to unblock his ears. They were climbing for around half an hour, stopping for quick rests, until they saw light appear in a side branch above.

"We must go further," Tommo said in his even tone of voice, and they continued moving.

A strong and dry wind was blowing through the shaft. The temperature rose with every level, as if they were approaching a red hot oven.

"Can you feel that?" Rick asked as he wiped away sweat.

"That is the cooling system of the Main Computer," Tommo replied. "Endure it."

They climbed upwards, level after level. His mouth had gone dry and the muscles of his arms and legs ached with the strain. But Tommo kept moving in front of him and fatigue did not seem to affect him. After thirty floors, Rick could not resist asking, "So what's going on? Is there long left?"

"Thirty floors. Don't interrupt your breathing patterns."

Rick clenched his teeth and decided to listen to Tommo's advice. It really did make things a little easier. However, after some time fatigue did take its toll. Rick started to breath heavily as the sweat poured into his eyes and his hands slipped from the bars built into the walls.

All he needed was to fall at the very end of his journey.

"We're almost there," Tommo reported from above, as if he a mind reader.

Rick was so happy that he missed a bar with his hand and nearly fell. Tommo saved him yet again by grabbing him by the collar and dragging him into a side opening, letting him get his breath back and helping him to get up.

Rick saw colorful circles grow and melt in his vision. Rick closed his eyes for a while, opened them and understood that they were on a... he would call it a hangar deck. The walls and ceiling were covered with a thin layer of hoarfrost. Rick finally felt how cold it was there and regretted leaving his warm jacket in his room.

This was a serious problem—how could he go outside now? It was deadly cold out there and he would freeze immediately!

Tommo had already opened up a wide panel and started digging around inside the closest machine—a silvery, flattened vehicle with smooth, arrow shaped wing and a cabin with a clear cockpit at the front.

"What are you doing?" asked Rick, shivering.

"I am checking the charge. Look for the blue battery cylinders in boxes marked with a yellow diamond."

Rick walked over to the boxes and opened one of them—the batteries Tommo needed lay inside, but all of their cylindrical shells had been breached with something sharp, probably an axe, and were obviously broken. Someone had done some housekeeping here before them. The shell of one of the batteries looked untouched. Rick carefully took it out and shouted, "There's one, but the rest are broken!"

Tommo nodded and slammed the panel on the fuselage shut, running over to another vehicle standing nearby. Rick dragged the battery over and watched Tommo run from vehicle to vehicle on the deck, digging around in their instrument panel.

"Things are bad," the prole concluded. "Important parts have been torn out. Someone deliberately ruined the vehicles. The battery is useless."

"Aren't you cold?" Rick rubbed his frozen palms and waved his arms energetically.

"My nerve receptors are switched off."

"I envy you."

Rick approached the closed cargo elevator and pressed the call button. He did not expect it to work, but the doors smoothly opened and a light came on in the cabin.

"Let's have a look at what's higher up," Rick offered. "Isn't this a multi-level hangar?"

Tommo nodded. They started rising up, but the elevator's gears suddenly squealed and it came to a halt. Rick tried to unsuccessfully press all the buttons, but the cabin remained in place. They were stuck. He tried to slide the doors open with his hands, but he could not do it. Then, Tommo jumped up and broke the maintenance hatch in the roof open with his fist. They clambered out onto the roof of the cabin and stared at a wide shaft which was lit with emergency lighting and the elevator cabins stuck at different levels nearby. There was a rumble and the howl of an activated alarm coming from below.

"You must go back there," Rick said. "I can take care of myself."

"I feel a sense of worry about you. Are you sure you can do it?"

"I have no choice."

Tommo looked at him for a couple of seconds. Rick knew that the prole was now analyzing the situation and his program was rearranging priorities and calculating different solution algorithms. Tommo finally declared, "All right, we shall split up. I will go to the Thermopolis Control Center and you will look for a way to reach level zero. Examine the vehicles on the other decks. Remember, the entrance to the bunker is in segment "O". You need the command post."

He pointed at a wide opening that led to a hangar deck above their heads, grabbed the cable of an adjacent elevator and stepped into the shaft. He swiftly slid down a floor, opened a maintenance hatch on the roof of a cabin and disappeared.

Rick wasted no more time and climbed a cable to the deck of the second hangar. The vehicles here had long blades over their fuselages—they were helicopters and the name had come into his head by itself. But even a quick examination was enough to understand that the vehicles were damaged. Rick climbed further up, investigating the third and fourth hangars. A piercing, cold wind swept the decks. He managed to find a hooded workman's raincoat among the junk in a cold closet covered with hoarfrost.

Each level contained a particular type of flying vehicle, but he still could not find one in working order. Rick was pushing his alarming thoughts away. Once he reached the very top, he stopped, looking up through the transparent dome at the blue of the sky amongst the clouds above.

Outside space. A world which was still mysterious and terrifying, a world where humans had lived before. A world that he already knew so much about, but never visited.

Rick was unable to resist temptation and walked towards the pillar of light that pierced the clouds and the transparent dome. This was the light of a star called the Sun. A star—wasn't that amazing? He entered the light and shut his eyes, as he was not used to it and they burned. Rick knew that he could not look at the Sun as it would make him go blind, but the space far below was visible and he saw a snow covered plain stretch out as far as the eye could see. Once he determined the directions of the compass, he figured out that there were mountains towering far to the east and that there were man-made structures over to the west. It was unknown whether they were inhabited and there was no time to look for allies in outside space anyway.

Chuckling at his own thoughts, as he would have been guessing at what it was that surrounded him without the accelerated learning course, Rick quickly returned to the vehicles and stopped to think things over.

He heard a rumbling growing louder outside and the vibration of the floor started to be a lot more noticeable. Thermopolis was preparing for the launch of the Uranus program. He could not afford to waste a single minute, as Tommo may have already reached his goal and could be waiting for a signal, but there was not much point in checking the vehicles again. He had to find a way to descend to the foot of Thermopolis no matter what.

But how?

Rick looked around. The Architect was right when he called Thermopolis an Ark that collected every achievement and all that had ever been studied, grown and created by the hands of man. His gaze stopped on a dark, far corner, where he could see a container with corrugated sides. Rick had already walked past the container, but paid no attention to what was written on it. He changed from a walk into a run when he made out the letters on the doors and read "Glider model No.21-2..." He never worked out the serial number of that particular model as the numbers had been erased by time, but he now had a chance to descend to the bottom. He just needed to make sure he could roll the flying vehicle out of the container and take off.

Once he opened the doors he looked at the fuselage first—the wings were stored here as well, but in separate boxes. It was no problem to roll the glider onto the deck. The vehicle turned out to be surprisingly light. Rick managed to take the wings out of the boxes and slide them into the slots on the fuselage by himself.

Now he could fly. But how and where could he open the hangar deck?

Tommo's words about the hibernation of the Thermopolis system came into his head. It was doubtful that any mechanisms that would open the gates worked right now—so there was no way to open the deck using electronic control panels. Where would he find them, anyway?

Rick spun around on his heels and stared at a helicopter painted in a combat camouflage pattern—a long, rapid fire cannon which was controlled from the cabin was fixed below the fuselage and rockets were still attached to its stub-wings.

This was a solution! All he needed to do was to supply power to the weapon system of the vehicle and... Rick rushed to the lower deck to get the battery. All of this took him around a quarter of an hour. He even forgot about the cold when he got into the combat pilot's chair and switched on the power.

The dull glow of the instruments and screens reported on the readiness and faults in the systems. Rick did not wait for the reports, activated the weapons system, flipped the safety catches on the controls, breathed out and pressed all the buttons he could find.

A deafening hammering noise came from

below the fuselage and the helicopter shuddered when the rockets flew out from the stub wings, leaving smoke trails behind. A blindingly bright fireball exploded on the glass wall in front.

Rick closed his eyes, and instinctively covered up his face with his hand, turning away. The sound of the explosion had deafened him and he felt the smell of smoke and cordite. In a second, the cloud of smoke was sucked outside through the breach.

Yes!

Rick got out of the cabin and rushed forward to push the glider towards the new aperture. Only one thought kept running through his head—he was hoping against hope that the hole would be wide enough.

Please let it be wide enough!

When there were ten paces left to the edge of the deck, he jumped into the pilot's seat, slammed the cockpit shut and grabbed the glider control joystick.

The flying machine silently rolled out of the breach and fell downwards, nose first.

Rick's heart skipped a beat.

His eyes went wide when he noticed how quickly the glider was falling as it slid along the sheer surface of Thermopolis. For a moment, it seemed to him that the glider was about to catch the wall with its belly, and he instinctively pressed his hand into the instrument panel in front of him, sinking back into the seat. He pulled the joystick towards himself and the nose of the glider tilted upwards...

He was gaining height! Rick shouted in ecstasy, craning his neck to stare at the plain floating by below him, so endless and grand.

He did it. He managed to get out and he was flying! And he had completely lost his fear of heights!

Rick smiled. He would launch the program for his sister, for Maya and Ahmed, for Cornelius and Tommo and for the future of the humans that were left in the freezing aeons.

He soon noticed that he had flown some far away from the tower. He carefully moved the joystick to the side, changing the angle of the ailerons so that the glider smoothly leaned to one side, banking into a turn.

Thermopolis lay before him—a titanic tower that propped up the sky. Rick almost centered and moved the joystick forward, so that the glider started to circle as it smoothly descended. The sunny side of the tower came around and the glass of the cabin dimmed to compensate for the unbearably bright light. Wave upon wave of snowfalls came down the side of Thermopolis, as whole sections and their shell layers moved into gaps which appeared between the segments and arrow shaped fins extended outwards, as elevator platforms filled with cargo containers rapidly moved up and down. Thermopolis was adapting itself for the launch of the Uranus program. Rick craned his neck again—a structure which was far out from the base of the tower could be seen below, with jagged rays leading from it to the barrier ring which circled the territory around the tower.

Rick did not immediately understand that he was descending faster than he had supposed. Only when the structures below started to swiftly come towards him and he started to make out the details of the squat buildings and the little houses with antennae spearing out from their roofs did he pull the joystick sharply towards him. However, the glider maintained its previous course. Something had jammed the ailerons—it could have been ice forming on the wings or it could have been a technical fault. Rick stopped trying to guess at the cause and prepared for a collision with the ground, carefully looking ahead.

He soon saw that the jagged rays were actually high walls that divided the square around the tower in to four segments. There were pyramids towering over the centers of these segments, with easily readable glyphs on their sides.

Rick considered the size of the walls and concluded that if he crashed into one as he swooped down he could easily be killed and that it all depended on the speed of the collision and the distance to the ground.

A moment later, the glider flew over the pyramid with a Delta glyph, then one with the "O" glyph, then the one with the eight lying on its side and finally one marked with a circle that had arrows going outwards from it. The glider passed over the wall that separated the sectors, and yet another pyramid appeared below, although it was much closer now. He would land in a minute or two, and he had to somehow even out and slow down his flight beforehand.

The remains of a flying machine flashed below him, strewn around a crater which was covered in a layer of snow. Rick gathered himself together and pulled on the joystick with all his strength, but the glider continued descending. He took it over another wall and found himself over the "O" segment. Considering the direction of the flight, a collision with another wall was unavoidable now. The only thought that was pulsing through his head was that he had to slow down and even out the glider. He had to change the angle of the ailerons!

Rick looked up—there was the hood of the cockpit! It would do fine as an aileron. He sighed, clicked open the locking mechanisms on the sides and pushed the hood back.

The cold wind stormed into the cabin, burning his lungs. The nose of the glider pulled sharply upwards, the level of the flight evened out for a while, coupled with a decrease in speed, but then the glider shuddered, made a sharp turn and got thrown into a side turn, quickly and relentlessly. Rick only had the time to brace himself when he heard a rasping sound and then a loud impact.

His body was thrown forward, and if it wasn't for the open cockpit, he would have broken his neck on the control panel. However, the inertia carried him forwards and he flew out of the cabin, crashing into a snowdrift a moment later and feeling the scalding cold of the snow that had got under his clothes.

But he was alive! Mother Darkness, he survived!

As he tried to get up, Rick grunted and fell on one knee. It seemed to have been dislocated. But this was nothing, he had managed to land in the correct sector and all he needed to do was get inside the bunker and find the terminal to put his key into.

Once he limped to the nearest gate at the base of the structure, he stopped and raised his head for a moment. Thermopolis was emitting a loud hum as it majestically towered over him, its walls stretching upwards and its summit lost in the clouds.

Without waiting for another second, Rick brushed the snow from the control panel by the gates and pressed his palm onto it. There was a moment when nothing happened, but then the panel beeped and a line ran down the screen. His palm got burned, but Rick did not take his hand away, letting the scanner complete the operation. Another beep and the "Enter Password" prompt appeared on the screen.

He entered just one symbol—the symbol of infinity.

He heard the grinding of gears inside the walls, and the iron gates creaked and slid open in front of him. The dark opening let out a dry breath of dust.

Rick stepped into the darkness.

20

THE DARKNESS PALED and unwillingly gave way to a gray twilight. Rick was at the edge of a huge shaft going under the ground. He came up to a panel and turned the dial. Lamps switched on to light up the space around him—corrugated walls covered with various signs, utility lines, pipes and doors which had been locked for hundreds of years. Rick took one of the signs from the wall and brushed the dust from it. Just what he needed—a plan of the building. And there was the way to the control post. An elevator came when he called it. It was not as fast as the ones in the tower, but it looked robust and reliable.

Rick stood on the platform and observed the floors that sped sway above. Tonnes of steel, plastic, concrete and glass. Kilometers of wires. And all of it was assembled together and created for a single purpose.

He exited on the last floor at the bottom. Signs of destruction could be seen everywhere here. The wall plates were bulging, as if they had suffered a series of heavy impacts and earth had fallen through the cracks. Such tears had appeared all over the walls and Rick noticed two places where there were terrible breaches that a glider could easily fly through. He carefully stepped across the filthy floor, listening to the silence. He could feel someone's presence here.

Rick walked to the end of a short corridor and stopped by a door that had sign saying "Command Post" and which stood slightly ajar, with a dim light shining through the gap. He tried to push the door and enter, but it was stuck. Then, he took a pry bar from a fire rack and pried the door open, with a creak of rusted hinges, finding himself in a low-ceiling hall a moment later. The floor inclined towards the opposite wall, which was dominated by a wide screen with a long table that had a built-in control panel below. It was obvious that the post was designed for a team of trained specialists. Rick slowly approached the table, looking at the empty seats equipped with personal terminals.

Another weak, tangy smell that made Rick's nostrils tingle snaked its way among the smell of dust and plastic. A familiar smell, which could have come from a creature that had once been alive. Rick tightened his grip on the pry bar—anything could happen and he could never know what sort of creature might have made its nest here. He walked around the command post and found the body of a man in the far corner.

It was mummified. A desiccated face with sunken cheeks and sunken pits instead of eyes. A blackened tongue lolled out of an open mouth with yellowed teeth, framed with clumped patches of beard. The fingers of the dead man curled inwards. Rick did not see anything familiar in the rags that had served as the man's clothing. He stood still, looking at the remains and trying to listen to his inner voice. No, he did not feel anything deep down in his soul. This was just a skeleton in a shell of dried flesh. This was obviously not his father.

And then, Rick noticed the writing on the wall. Several words were crudely scrawled in black: "Alea iacta est"[1].

Rick returned to the control panel and activated it. The screens came alive and lights started to blink. He took off his raincoat and started to wait for the local computer to establish communication with the Thermopolis system. The machinery worked perfectly—no one could equal the ancient masters in this regard. Before Rick could enter the system and connect to the Control Center, a notice appeared on the screen: "Video Message".

Rick played the message.

A man with a ratty beard, thinning hair and a sickly looking face appeared on the screen—he had dark circles under his eyes, a thin neck and narrow shoulders. The stranger started to speak.

"Infinity Sector Head Controller Jean Molyneaux speaking. They have all gone insane. All of them. I have barricaded myself here in the command post and they have left three days ago. I know that they will return and I hope that I will leave this world by that time. This is why you must listen to me. The epidemic engulfed us half a year ago. At first, we thought that it was rabies,

---

[1]   The die is cast (*Lat.*).

but the vaccine had no effect and there were more and more people getting infected. No one could understand what was going on. The Government introduced a quarantine, but even that did not help. We were injected with a series of newly developed antiviral serums, but even they were powerless. The infected appeared everywhere. The symptoms of the disease are as follows: it begins with slight dizziness and nausea that last for a couple of days and then sleep disturbances set in, as well as a strong headache and memory loss. The infected person starts to forget names, mixes up times and dates, becomes unable to read or count and the pain in their head get stronger..."

Jean licked his dry lips and got his heavy breathing under control.

"This is a punishment from god. Humanity is being punished for daring to desecrate His glory. Please, God, forgive our sinful ways... Pain. It tortures the infected all the time, sometimes less, sometimes more, but it never recedes. This last for a week or two. And then, the infected goes insane. The diseased man mixes dreams up with reality, their speech becomes incoherent, the infected does not understand what is going on around them and loses control of his mind, because his brains turn to mush! The infected is unable to think and becomes an animal that

416

want to consume everything all the time. Oh god... Oh my god!"

Jean sobbed, and tears streamed from his bright eyes. He still managed to find the strength to continue.

"The disease has struck us all. It is just a question of time now—some will go first, some later. The upper sectors have already isolated themselves and they are refusing to accept refugees. People are jumping down the central shaft in a frenzy. The cleaning robots scrub away all that is left of the bodies from the floor every day. The bottom of the shaft is swimming in blood. One of my subordinates attacked me a week ago. Some citizens are trying to get outside, but the doors are blocked. They go insane and attack the healthy. They scream. They scream without stopping and there are even children among them. We are suffering from water shortages and our stores of food are running out. There's nowhere to run. The workers from the perimeter demanded that we let them out, but we told them that we couldn't. Then, they attacked is. They beat two of my employees to death. We barely managed to fight back and blocked the doors. The last days were especially terrible. My employees sad on the floor with glassy eyes and I did not know whether they were still human or whether sanity had abandoned them. The food ran out four days ago. Then they tried to grab me. I barely got away and locked myself in here."

Jean wiped his face with his sleeve. He stayed silent for a moment, and then concluded, "Those that watch this message should know. We did our duty until the very end."

The recording came to a stop. Rick now understood whose body it was lying in the corner. The computer beeped as it connected to the system. Rick entered several commands and connected to the Control Center. He sent the image to the wide screen and saw the same rows of seats and people sitting in them behind a long table. Bodies could be seen strewn around on the floor by the entrance—several of the operators, lay prone on the floor. Croesus was sitting behind the main control panel, his legs resting on the table. When he saw Rick, he sat up straight, and an expression of fear passed over his face.

Croesus got himself together and asked, "Rick?"

Rick needed no explanations to understand what happened. The dead bodies spoke for themselves. Croesus quickly glanced to the side and back at Rick.

"Is it you, or not?"

"It's me."

"Hah! Oh my! Then who is this?"

Tommo was brought next to Croesus.

"My double, created by machines."

"Oh, I see..." Croesus drawled, visibly impressed. "Fascinating."

Rick waited.

"Why are you so quiet? How are you doing?"

"Well, thank you."

"Great!" Croesus cheered up and nodded at him. "And we decided to impose some order here. Remember when I told you about the expedition beyond the barrier? Well, we did it and we were rather successful. I actually wanted to tell you the whole truth, but things turned out differently. You ran off with these barbarians."

Rick stared at the screen tensely.

"I even thought that I had caught you, but then I saw that there was something wrong about you. This guy doesn't want to talk, no matter how much we ask him." Croesus nodded in the direction of Tommo, whose face was covered in bruises and grazes. "Maybe you'll explain what's going on?"

"Maybe," Rick slowly replied.

Croesus showed him half of the key.

"What's this?"

"The key for the Uranus program."

"What's the Uranus program?"

"Our salvation."

"Don't lie to me."

"I have no reason to lie to you, Warden."

Croesus was looking at the screen, trying to work out if he was being lied to, and this helplessness amused Rick.

"What're you grinning at?" Croesus exclaimed.

"Listen," Rick leaned forward, and Croesus could not help flinching, "I have no idea what you did to Paris and I am not even interested, but can you tell me, what's the point of those deaths?"

Croesus smirked, and went into a pompous speech about freeing the Commune from the cold and resettling it up above. This was a task of primary importance, he assured. The next stage would be to take control of Thermopolis and impose order on all inhabited space, from top to bottom, to destroy the mutants and other degenerates, turn on the heat generators, clean out the levels and live like humans, governed by unified and open principles. The parasitism of Epsilon had come to an end. Croesus had long planned his grand revolution and ordered the attack when the Chorda came to life. They killed the priest advisers and used the occasion of Paris' meeting to take the Chairman of the Council hostage together with Arcadius, forcing him to switch off the security protecting the aeon.

While the Warden described the details of his daring coup, Rick surreptitiously entered several commands on the keyboard and brought up a separate dialog window with the Uranus program activation system.

A message saying "Use key to start" blinked on the screen.

"What is this?" Croesus had also noticed the window open up on the screen where he was sitting.

"This is the key to the future," Rick calmly replied.

"What do you want to do?"

"Haven't you worked it out yet?"

Croesus clicked his fingers and the brought Maya to him. He unceremoniously pulled her down by her arm, making her bend down and putting a hand blaster to her head.

"Don't you dare, you whelp. Otherwise, I'll blow her brains out! And then I will shoot your sister!"

Rick froze in front of the controls, his hands hovering above the keyboard.

"You will do what I say," Croesus emitted a twisted chuckle. "Got it?"

"Yes."

"What's going to happen once the program is launched?"

"The generators get turned on," Rick lied. "Thermopolis will warm up from the energy it receives."

Croesus eyes darted around the room—their

421

conversation could be heard by those surrounding him.

"No. There will be no launch. All we need is the energy in the first aeon and we will leave the keys as a backup option. Come back to the Commune before it's too late. We will forgive all of your misdemeanors. Rick, I will make you my deputy. The second in command. The Commune will spread throughout Thermopolis! We can rule it however we like. We have it all, do you understand?"

"Not entirely..."

"We will impose our own order! Everything will be done fairly and according to the law."

As Croesus said these words, Tommo tore the key out of his hand and stuck it into the slot on the panel.

A scuffle began. There was a deafening gunshot. Rick put his half of the key into the slot. A loud signal sounded and a metallic voice announced, "Attention. The Uranus program has been launched. All crew members and passengers are requested to take their places in their sections and fasten their seat belts The launch will take place in thirty minutes. The countdown has begun."

A timer appeared on every working screen and began the countdown.

"What is this?" Croesus screamed, as he

reappeared in front of the screen. "What have you done?"

Rick did not yet comprehend what he had done. He only felt the foundation of Thermopolis shudder and the loud rumbling sound became even louder, as if a dormant volcano had suddenly awoken below the tower.

"Stop this!" Croesus shook the blaster at the screen. "Stop this at once!"

"I can't." Rick calmly replied and smiled.

Croesus was finally transfixed by his realization His face stretched out in surprise, as if he was a child that had suddenly been given the toy he dreamed of.

"It wasn't the generators that you launched," Croesus breathed out in a whisper.

"They were launched before that," Rick replied. "Turning on the generators is the first stage of the Uranus program, which I had already completed when I was in the Sigma and Tau sectors."

"What is this program? What's the program! Speak!" Croesus shouted, spittle flying everywhere.

"I don't know," Rick replied and laughed uproariously.

"What? You filthy puppy! I should have killed your mother back then? Why did you..."

But the Warden did not get to finish his

sentence. Maya smashed him over the head with a chair. Croesus fell as if struck by lightning. Maya spat in his direction and turned towards the screen.

"Rick! By the Great Axis! What have you done? I thought you were here!"

"Maya, everything is fine! It's Tommo who's with you up there. We managed to... transfer his soul into the body of my double to fool Paris."

"If that's the case, then Tommo is no more," Maya replied sadly. "Croesus shot him."

Suddenly a "Command Center Evacuation" message appeared in a pop-up dialog window. An evacuation plan was displayed with arrows showing the way, as well as a message saying that the plan was also displayed in every room and corridor as a notice on the walls and arrows pointing in the direction of evacuation.

"Rick! Where are you?"

"I am below, under Thermopolis on level zero. I launched the Uranus program. Wait for me, I will be with you soon!"

"Rick," Maya stretched her hands out towards him. Tears streamed down her face. "Oh, Rick... I have a bad feeling about this, hurry up!"

"I'm coming back!"

"I wanted to say something to you... Forgive me!"

But rick never heard her, as he had already

424

left the command post. Once he got out into the corridor, he froze, pushing himself against the wall—there were people moving towards the post.

"Halt!" one of them barked and came into the light of the lamp.

It was Yeshua.

"What are you doing here?" asked Rick with surprise.

"Didn't expect me?" Yeshua seemed happy. "We've been watching you ever since you left Omicron."

Rick was confused.

"What a face," Yeshua said mockingly as he pointed his blaster. "All right, hands up, face to the wall and don't do anything stupid."

"You're too late," Rick replied, showing him his empty hands. "The program has been launched."

"You're going to stop it the same way as you started it. Face the wall!" Yeshua commanded.

"You don't understand..."

Yeshua struck Rick in the chest with the stock of his weapon. Rick yelped with pain and fell to one knee, considering his chances. Four against one, there was no way he could deal with them all. They grabbed him by the shoulder, dragged him up and turned him towards the wall, went through his pockets and took his knife out of the scabbard.

While this was going on, Yeshua kept muttering obscenities about the filthy hole they had ended up in.

"How did you get into Epsilon?" Rick asked when he was turned back to face Yeshua.

"None of your business," he growled, and then added, "You bastard! If I wasn't ordered to deliver you alive, I would smash you into a fine paste on this wall."

Rick carefully watched all four of his opponents, as well as what was happening behind them.

"You don't have the guts for it," he replied.

"Whaat?" Yeshua's face twisted from this insolence.

"You heard. You're just a typical coward!"

Yeshua shook in a fit of rage.

"Just you wait, you vermin! I'm going to light you up so well, that your own mother won't recognize you..."

A piercing scream rang out behind his back. Everyone turned around. The warrior at the rear of the unit was quickly disappearing into the corridor feet first, trying to grab onto the walls and screaming loudly. Two of the others ran to help him, but they were too late—the unfortunate man was sucked into the blackness of the corridor and only his receding, desperate cries could be heard.

426

"Machine God, save us!" one of the warriors whispered, making a ritual gesture of protection.

"What was that?" Yeshua whispered.

They did not even have time to get a grip on themselves when another scream sounded in the corridor. A slimy, snake-like body whipped itself around another victim, dragging him into the opening of the air duct in the ceiling.

"Help!" the condemned man shouted and immediately fell silent as he disappeared through the opening.

No one had the time to say a word when the wide, fanged maw of the worm-like monster bit into the body of the third warrior. Yeshua jumped in the direction of the command post with a terrified squeal. Rick used the opportunity to punch him hard in the stomach. As Yeshua doubled over, Rick knocked the blaster from his hands, but did not bother to keep going and sprinted towards the safety of the exit from the corridor.

He spent some time meandering through the bunker, following the direction of the arrows on the notices until he reached a hall that was the start of a railway that stretched out into a dark tunnel. There was a small carriage in the tunnel, with open entrances on the side. It looked like this was the carriage that would deliver those evacuating from the command post back up above.

Rick jumped inside and approached the controls at the front of the cabin. He pressed his palm against the scanner, bringing up a system message offering to power up the engine. Rick confirmed the instruction—the automatic systems worked perfectly and the carriage smoothly started to roll along, gathering speed.

Rick grabbed onto a railing and stuck his head outside, looking back. Yeshua ran into the hall and raised his blaster. However, he had no time to shoot, as the worm-like monster appeared behind him and opened its maw, biting into him from the top and swallowing his head whole.

The carriage noticeably picked up speed. Rick was expected the rails to turn upwards in a moment and for the tunnel to lead to the surface, and even started to think about the way he would protect his loved ones from Croesus should he wake up and take over the situation again.

However, the carriage continued on its way and kept building up speed. The walls of the tunnel rushed on buy, sometimes lit up with the light of the forebodingly blinking lamps. Rick gripped the railing, tensely looking ahead. According to every calculation, he should have been up in Thermopolis long ago. Maya and Aurora needed him!

But the tunnel seemed to be never-ending.

Rick entered the cabin and pressed his palm to the screen on the controls.

System failure.

What?

He tried to take over the controls again, but the automatic systems did not let him.

"Mother Darkness!" Rick shouted inside his mind through force of habit. Where did this tunnel actually lead?

After a few minutes, the carriage began to gradually decrease. The carriage was moving noticeably slower. Rick was staring ahead, trying to understand which sector he ended up in. Finally, the carriage reached a platform and the brakes squealed as it came to a stop.

Rick rushed outside and looked around the vaulted ceiling of the cave he found himself in and the wide spiral stairway that led upwards. A few dimly glowing lamps hung down from the ceiling on long wires. Without waiting for something unexpected to happen, Rick ran headlong up the stairs.

The steps coiled like a spring through the masses of rock. Rick had no idea of the exact distance he had traveled, but he finally entered a stone hall, feeling completely out of breath. There were lamps here too, but there was not enough light—a lot of them were not in working order. The floor of the hall vibrated slightly and tiny chips of stone fell from the ceiling. Rick stopped for a moment, listening to the distant rumble coming from above.

A flickering white light suddenly added itself to the lamps. Rick turned around—a terminal with a shining screen and flashing diodes stood against the opposite wall, which was incredibly smooth. Without a thought, Rick threw himself towards the keyboard, but all the system offered him was several commands that had nothing to do with Thermopolis. In the end, he selected one and stood still, looking at the steel panels sliding open in front of him.

By this time, the rumble had turned into a thunderous road. Rick instinctively grabbed onto the edge of the control terminal and stole a fearful glance at the ceiling. He hoped that the roof would not crack and bury him in stone...

The soft, reddish light of the setting Sun entered the hall through thick crystal glass. The metallic panels had finally slid completely open and he could see the plain from the mountainside where the observation post was located.

Thermopolis towered opposite, still as massive as a mountain, but it was far, too far away to return to it in time.

The tower had changed a lot from the outside. Its upper section looked different now, like a thin rod with oblong growths in several places.

Tommo's words about the way that Thermopolis adapted itself immediately came into his mind. Rick was struck dumb by a realization

His impotence made him scream.

Clouds of steam billowed beneath the base of the rod, as the sun glinted off its external shell, the roar grew louder with every second and the floor shook beneath Rick's feet. He stumbled, almost losing his balance—he was saved by his tight grip on the control terminal.

The timer on the monitor was counting down the last seconds before the initiation of the Uranus program. Once the numbers became a sting of zeroes, the message "Adaptation Complete" flashed on the screen, followed by the word "LAUNCH".

Thermopolis shuddered. Rick stumbled again as a second sun lit beneath the base of the rod. The glass immediately dimmed, saving his eyes from the incandescent light and letting him see the details.

Rick stood still, without daring to breathe. The light grew so bright that even the artificially darkened glass offered little protection, but Rick kept watching as the rod breathed fire and separated itself from a gigantic conical platform, rising above the plain.

The world shook all around him. It seemed

that the skies were about to be rent asunder. But the inevitable happened—Thermopolis rose ever higher, gathering speed and striking the plain with a stream of fire, annihilating the structures below.

The clouds of smoke and steam soon reached the observation post. Rick stretched out his neck, rising up on his toes, trying to watch the direction of the flight to the last, but the view behind the window got inexorably obscured by an impenetrable fog, and the upward flight of the rod disappeared from sight.

It took a long time until all the dust had settled and Rick Omicron managed to find his way outside and look at the distant star that appeared among the others in the evening sky.

He looked up at the sky until night fell and the unbearable cold forced him to return to his shelter.

"I will find you," he whispered, standing before the window. "No matter how gigantic the Expanse may be."

End of Book One

Want to be the first to know about our latest LitRPG, sci fi and fantasy titles from your favorite authors?

Subscribe to our NEW RELEASES newsletter:
http://eepurl.com/b7niIL

Thank you for reading *The URANUS Code!*
If you like what you've read, check out other LitRPG
novels published by Magic Dome Books:

Dark Paladin LitRPG series by Vasily Mahanenko:
The Beginning
The Quest

**The Dark Herbalist LitRPG series
by Michael Atamanov:**
Video Game Plotline Tester
Stay on the Wing

The Neuro LitRPG series by Andrei Livadny:
The Crystal Sphere
The Curse of Rion Castle
The Reapers

**The Way of the Shaman LitRPG series
by Vasily Mahanenko:**
Survival Quest
The Kartoss Gambit
The Secret of the Dark Forest
The Phantom Castle
The Karmadont Chess Sct
Phaman's Revenge
The Hour of Pain (a bonus short story)

Galactogon LitRPG series by Vasily Mahanenko:
Start the Game!

Phantom Server LitRPG series by Andrei Livadny:
Edge of Reality
The Outlaw
Black Sun

**The Game Master series
by A. Bobl and A. Levitsky:**
The Lag

**Perimeter Defense LitRPG series by Michael
Atamanov:**
*Sector Eight
Beyond Death
New Contract
A Game with No Rules*

Mirror World LitRPG series by Alexey Osadchuk:
*Project Daily Grind
The Citadel
The Way of the Outcast
The Twilight Obelisk*

AlterGame LitRPG series by Andrew Novak:
*The First Player
On the Lost Continent*

**The Expansion (The History of the Galaxy) series
by A. Livadny:**
Blind Punch

**Citadel World series
by Kir Lukovkin:**
The URANUS Code

The Sublime Electricity series by Pavel Kornev
*The Illustrious
The Heartless
The Fallen
Leopold Orso and the Case of the Bloody Tree*
(a short story)

Moskau *(a dystopian thriller)*
by **G. Zotov**

Memoria. A Corporation of Lies
(an action-packed dystopian technothriller)
by Alex Bobl

Point Apocalypse
(a near-future action thriller)
by Alex Bobl
You're in Game!
(LitRPG Stories from Bestselling Authors)

The Naked Demon (a paranormal romance)
by Sherrie L.

More books and series are coming out soon!

In order to have new books of the series translated faster, we need your help and support! Please consider leaving a review or spread the word by recommending *The URANUS Code* to your friends and posting the link on social media. The more people buy the book, the sooner we'll be able to make new translations available.

Thank you!

Till next time!

www.ingramcontent.com/pod-product-compliance
Lightning Source LLC
Chambersburg PA
CBHW071636260626
47170CB00001B/123